I Would Never…But If I Did

Maria Ann Green

I WOULD NEVER…BUT IF I DID
Copyright © 2020 Maria Ann Green

Cover art by Tory McNidder
Cover design by Maria Ann Green

Formatting by Maria Ann Green

Editing by Jackie Hritz
and Carly Green

ISBN: 9781661336912

All works by Maria Ann Green

I Would Never Series:
I Would Never… But If I Did (Book One), contemporary romance

Betting Series:
Betting on Love (Book One), steamy romance

Darkness Series:
Nothing but Darkness (Book One), thriller
Deeper into Darkness (Book Two), thriller
Edge of Darkness (Book Three), thriller
Darkness Series Omnibus (Books One, Two, and Three), thrillers

Short works:
It Only Hurts When I Breathe
The Masque of Annabel

Young Adult:
In the Rearview, young adult poetry and prose

This one's dedicated to the strong-willed and sometimes "unlikable" characters out there, the anti-heroes and villains that I love so fucking much. That is to say, this one's for all the Taryns. You're my very favorite—to write, to read, to be, to have in my life.

And especially for Tory, the Maicy to my Taryn, love you, babes.

Taryn
Now

"I would never cheat on her, but if I did, it would only be with you."

His stupid, insensitive words, from who-the-fuck-knows how long ago, a lifetime—from a couple girlfriends ago—feel more and more like I imagined them. And still, I can't let go; they rattle and clank but just won't leave. So I tip the bottle of booze back, taking another long pull. And I shouldn't be surprised when I have to bite back both the gag and mouthful of saliva that follow way too quickly. At this point, it's almost instant. But I am. Though, after some quick swallowing and a violent shudder, I'm pretty sure it's not coming back up.

Yet.

I don't even know why I'm thinking about him, about *that*, I forget what brought it up this time. But something always does, and, every time, those memories lead to nights like this.

Whatever.

Looking between the bottle in my hand and Maicy eyeing me like I'm a glass on the edge of a shelf, too close to falling, to shattering, I can't take it. I just can't. *No thank you.*

So I take another drink, intending to get drunk. Real fucking drunk. Sloppy even.

"Slow down, Taryn Hope Sams, I'm not cleaning up your puke tonight." Maicy flips her strawberry blonde hair out of her eyes as she tells me what to do. Her feet, bare and dainty, dangle over the arm of our overstuffed chair as she leans back, comfortable in our living room. But, giving me orders is so not a good idea. She should know by now, after decades of friendship, telling me not to do something is the best, and fastest, way to push me right into doing it.

Always.

"You say that every time, *Maicy Abigail Davis*, and then every time I blow chunks, you *still* take care of me." I point my finger at my best friend, trying to focus on her light green eyes with some trouble. Both of her heads finally converge into one after I squint just a little, and she's less blurry too. But sharpened, her hipster glasses and scarf raise my blood pressure along with the color to my cheeks. I grind my teeth, clenching until my jaw hurts, just so I don't say anything. She's so above the phony vibe they're giving off. Granted, she does technically *need* glasses, but she used to have unique ones—they were expressive, artsy with sparkles and neon flecks. Now they look just like everyone else's, melting her into the crowd. I hate when she isn't herself, her true self. I look away, shaking my head, eyes closed.

I guess she can clean up my mess, if I make one, with her scarf, at least. A snort escapes me, followed by her narrowed eyes turning in my direction.

"Nope, fuck that. I'm putting my foot down this time," she assures me.

I deadpan, eyelids drooping and cheeks scrunching to accommodate wide flat lips, then lift the bottle to my numbing lips. Pausing, I move my eyes around our living room, waiting for her say something, to stop me. I'll regret this more than her, but a girl's got to stick to her guns. Maicy rolls her eyes at me, only pushing me the rest of the way.

"What are best friends for then?" I ask.

Another swig down, and I'm positive it was a bad choice. Bad, bad. *Terrible.* This time when I shiver in disgust, my chocolate hair flies in my face, concealing some of my tremor. But only some. I close my eyes, fighting the urges racking my body, willing my stomach to calm.

Don't prove her right. Don't puke. Please, don't puke.

And still, I want to drown out the annoying voice inside my head. The one still whispering about *what-ifs* and *back-thens.*

Maicy shrugs, changing the channel, looking for something more entertaining than a fine-tuned mastery of my gag reflex. Either she's resigned to her near future of pointing me toward the toilet in time or she's just done arguing. Pretending not to care, I put my feet on the coffee table and lean back with my bottle, cradling it like it's a gemstone, precious and worth keeping safe.

Maicy continues ignoring me as she flips through options on TV, flipping past screams and hokey music, past infomercials for mops and previews for new prime-time dramas we'll never watch. She's looking for something to swoon over, some shitty romantic storyline, I know it. When she lands on one, I sneer.

Fuck romance.

It's not real.

I'll argue about it all damn day too, because I've never seen it, not genuine love anyway. There's apathy and comfort and giving up. Or, I guess, there's also lying to yourself and the other person. But that's it. The ones who think they feel honest love are deluding themselves, or they're the ones being lied to. And I'd rather not live in fantasyland, choosing to face reality like a mature adult.

Maicy laughs at some stupid, awkward-romantic moment, and all I do is grunt, annoyed. Apparently it's another night of drinking at home in our cozy—as in "charming but a little worn in"—Minneapolis three-bedroom Craftsman. Just the two of us. A movie and drinking, with nothing better to do and no one else to do it with.

Wow.

This isn't where I wanted to be in my late twenties. I had big plans. Big, still unfulfilled plans. But in line with that unfulfilled potential, instead of being productive, instead of being a grown up, instead of getting up to do *anything* else, I reach under the recliner and pull out the bowl, the weed, and my lighter.

His words from the past weren't drowned out, so maybe I can chase them away with smoke.

"Really?" Mace says, scowling. "That's a stupid idea."

I glare at her, eyes so narrowed, I mostly just see shadows of my eyelashes, already determined. Heels dug in.

"You're gonna fuck yourself up with the spins," she adds, snapping her head back to the TV. Her eyes copy mine, her shoulders sneaking up closer and closer to her ears, but she doesn't add anything else. I almost wish she would.

I'm in the mood to fight.

"Why not? I'm already a mess. *Bring it on*," I cheer, almost feeling bad about my mood, wishing the drinks and the good company would turn me around. But somehow that doesn't keep the animosity out of my voice. Maicy shakes her head, huffing, her pretty hair fluttering all around her shoulders.

And then the guilt hits me. I don't want to ruin her night, but I'm in one of those moods, one of those foggy, numb, so-bleak-everything-is-sepia moods. "What-the-fuck-ever," I say, even though what I meant to say was something much nicer.

She snorts.

I pack the bowl with sticky green leaves, the smell of it circling my head and pulling me into the anticipation. Already feeling calmer, I bring the glass into my mouth. It's like muscle memory, what my fingers itch to do. Lighting the bud, I suck in a breath—a huge gulp, my lungs just shy of bursting, and then I hold it in. My lungs burn, my chest tight, and I can feel the pressure in my head build—but it's a good burn, a good building—the feeling filling me up until I can't hold it any more.

And then I keep holding it just a little longer, getting everything I can from the moment, doing everything to get away from the memory. The memory of him. I don't mean to be an annoying shit; I swear I don't. And I *do* feel bad about it. But when haunted by the ghost of us, of him, desperation takes over.

"I'm sorry," I mouth, still holding everything inside.

Maicy watches me, tugging on that stupid mustache-patterned scarf, and I turn away just as she starts to shrug. I can't stand her eying me with disappointment or whatever sad emotion is etched into her face. Even if she tries to hide it, even if she has no idea that's what she's feeling, I see it. Sometimes…sometimes I think she loves me too much. She cares more about me than, well than most anyone. More than I do.

And sometimes, on nights like this when nothing goes right and I spin farther and farther inside myself, that's too much pressure.

When I do let the breath out, smoke fills the air in front of me, swirling and hanging in front of my eyes. I watch the shades of gray mixing and fading in patterns until all of it has disappeared into the rest of the air. I tingle, all over, right away. My head's full and heavy, and still, I can't forget even as the room shifts.

Shit.

"Okay, you're right. One was enough," I admit, and I set everything down next to my discarded bottle of booze. The room tips to the side as I lean forward, and then it rights itself way too fast. It's disorienting, and my brain rattles from the whiplash, my ears ringing and my eyes stinging.

Fuck. Definitely a bad decision.

But that about sums up my life. I'd say it's just these days, recent mistakes, but there are bad decisions, one after another, as far back as my memory goes. From my bad taste in men, losers and users and all the ones who leave, to taking things for granted on the rare occasion something is real. Being left, betrayed, lied to, you'd think I'd have learned faster about what's real and worth protecting compared to what's bullshit.

Though it doesn't help that I've never been good at thinking things through or resisting the temptations right in front of me. And both have bitten me in the ass when I'm left with less than I started—whether that's happiness or trust or, once, half my bank account.

I'm sick of being disappointed. Disappointed in myself, in my partners, in those who were supposed to take care of me. So at some point, it became easier to start picking the fights myself, turn away from others before they can leave me.

I don't want to do that tonight though; Maicy's one person I'll *never* push away. I just can't. So I guess I'm glad she's happy. Glad she's content, at least. And really, that's great. But I'm *so* not. I don't think I've been happy since…well, for a long while.

Since *him*.

And what a bitch that makes me, to only feel neutral about her good mood, to be resigned to it. Good friends rejoice in each other's happiness, fuel it. I do try; *I think I try anyway.* But lately, right now even more so, I can only fake it, pretend because I should. And even knowing that, knowing what an asshole and terrible best friend that makes me, I can't muster anything more than apathy.

Sighing, I pick up my phone. Then shake my head, trying to clear it just a little. Not too much, though. I try to focus on the screen. It's only eleven at night and already I'm feeling the pull of temptation. I do this every time I drink or smoke. I let myself get upset, and I do what I know will make me feel better.

It *shouldn't* make me feel better, but somehow, it always does.

Trying to shove it back, resist, knowing it's a crutch—a stupid thing to do, I have to swallow back the desire. But it starts to gnaw at me anyway. The want, the need of it, picks at the back of my brain until I feel pushed into making the same mistake for the hundredth time. Millionth maybe. I can't ignore what keeps screaming inside my head. *Do it, do it, DO IT.*

I flip the phone around in my hand a few times, trying to focus on the screen of the TV in front of me, trying to forget. In the movie that's still entertaining one of us, one main character falls for the other, and music chimes in the background as they suck face for the final scene. I laugh, Maicy shushing me.

I've tried to tell her a thousand times, but she doesn't get it. Music doesn't play when real people kiss. That's a lie we try to tell ourselves, making damn fucking sure we'll never be happy with one normal person. How could we be, when all we hear are our own critical thoughts about what should be.

Yeah, yeah, I know it's bleak. But at least I'm realistic.

Maicy sneezes, startling me out of my own head and back into the real world. My phone feels heavy in my hands all of a sudden or like it's taken on a new shape. I feel myself giving into it, into him.

I don't want to be this girl. I've been her too many times.

But I'm not sure I know how to be anyone else, anything else, anymore.

So I open our message thread and type out a few words to him. My fingers shake, touching the wrong letters; it's slow, annoying, and takes several tries with my blurry vision. But then, once it's done, I hit send without thinking. I don't reread for mistakes; I don't check for anything embarrassing, knowing it's all true, even if it's humiliating.

He's always on the other side of my brutal honesty.

He's used to it by now.

Austin

Now

My phone beeps, and I know who the message is from before I even pick it up. It's a Friday night, it's late, and we've done this dance for years. It's been going on so long, it's easy to pick up at any point, to just fall into.

It's Taryn; I know it, and I try so hard not to smile.

Resisting her lure, ignoring it—that's fucking impossible. I do try. I try and I fail. Because after a couple seconds, I pick up my phone anyway. I've never been strong enough. Yet somehow, this doesn't make me feel like a failure.

My smile widens, even as I bite the inside of my cheek, hard.

After snatching my phone from the coffee table, I lean back onto the couch and just hold it in my hand. I saw the name on the lock screen, and of course, I was right. Looking up to the ceiling, I imagine her, the outline of her pretty lips, the seriousness in her eyes; it's so easy to see her poker-face expression. Almost like she's here.

Sighing, I drum my fingers on my thigh.

The room feels warmer now, or maybe it's just the heat rising inside me. That, that right there, makes me feel guilty. I look to Skyler, painting her nails on the floor, and I let the grin fade away. A cringe moves in as replacement. Her long, curly, blonde hair shines like silk, and, feeling my stare, she looks to me with her blue eyes, so big, and an unknowing smile. She's too sweet.

Fuck.

"Who is it?" Of course she asks.

I know what I'm going to say before she even asked, and I'm a horrible person.

"Just Theo," I lie.

Skyler's trusting, kind, and has a body like a model. She might be a little unobservant, but she's built for looks, not as much for the rest. She's also a little *too* nice; she never calls me on any of my shit, and she's kind of boring. Sometimes it feels like she's a puppy following me around, doing whatever I tell her to. That gets old.

Damn it.

Picking out her flaws to justify my shitty behavior is low. I know that. Skyler's great. She's so much better than my last few girlfriends. She's genuine, with a good heart. And still…knowing I'm shitty, and that she's the opposite, doesn't exactly stop me from what I'm going to do next. My hand twitches, the phone still gripped tight, ready to open the text.

"Does he want to hang out?" she asks, her voice high and enthusiastic. She'd never suspect I'm anything but honest. She'd let him come over, no matter the time, whatever the reason.

"Tell him to come over," she says, echoing my thoughts.

Again with the wide eyes, with the blind agreement.

"Nah, he's drunk. Talking 'bout nothing," I say.

I still haven't looked at the message, but touching the screen, thinking her, all I can see are the hazel eyes I used to have memorized. Who am I kidding? I still do. I see her intoxicating and perfect lips, so plump. I've never found lips as good as hers. Not Skyler's. No one's before Taryn or since. And I can picture her dark hair, her curves, her gritty aura like a window into her personality—all of it so vivid. I'd almost swear I could conjure her up, right into my living room. Everything about her is so different from the girl in front of me now.

"Tell him 'hey' for me."

Skyler smiles and turns back to the (revolting) reality TV show she has on and her hot-pink nail polish.

I let myself open the message, and fuck if it doesn't bring the inappropriate smile right back. Taryn's drinking for sure—it's the only time she calls me by my last name.

Theo T: Invite me over, Wright.

Oh yeah, that's how I know how shitty I am. "Theo T" is Taryn. It's a constant reminder that I'm a fuck up but one who still gets to talk to Taryn.

I mean…it's bullshit. I don't have more than one friend named Theo to need it. (Who the hell knows two Theos?) But in my contacts there *are* two saved. It's something I learned a few girlfriends ago.

First, I tried to make up a name of a guy friend who doesn't exist in my circle. I had her saved under Tristan. But that backfired when Caroline, my girlfriend at the time, started asking to meet Tristan. She kept asking how he was doing and when she'd finally get to hang out with one of my closest friends. When it never happened, she caught on that something was up, and then she guessed right.

So I learned, when lying, stick as close to the truth as possible.

No one knows about the trick. Not even my best friend, who happens to be the other Theo—Theo Evans. No one but Taryn knows. She hated it at first too. But then I reminded her it was this or she could find someone else to text when she's drunk. She could find someone else to learn everything about her, inside and out, in order to understand why she pushes people the way she does; find someone who would stick around and stay friends with her after all the shit we've been through, the shit we've put each other through.

Eventually she decided Theo was an okay name after all.

I'm glad she did. I needed her to. Because Taryn and I will never stop talking. *Ever.* We'll always be…friends. I struggle with the label, never knowing how to think of our relationship, friendship, whatever we should be called. Anyway, we'll always be in each other's lives. I'm not cutting her out of the picture, but most people, girlfriends or otherwise, can't understand that. No one's been able to. Theo, the real one, wouldn't; Caroline definitely didn't. So they all stay in the dark. Including Skyler.

"Ohmygod," she says the words in less than a breath, "did you hear that?"

"Mmmm."

She giggles at something on the show as I finally answer Taryn's message. When I send it, I feel just a little bad. This pattern of behavior has been too pervasive for far too long to be unlearned now. Usually it goes away the longer I've been with someone. Maybe that's because they've had longer to show me their shortcomings, or maybe it's just because I've let myself be okay with needing more than one someone.

After all, I'm not doing anything wrong. Well, other than the lying part. I'm just talking to my closest friend. The fact that she's a she— and she's also an ex-girlfriend—doesn't matter. I'm not cheating with her.

We're friends.

Just friends.

Best friends.

Taryn
Now

I can't keep the grin off my face when my phone vibrates in my hand. I knew he'd answer. I hate saying it like this, but he's definitely the one who got away. That's such a stupid saying, but the truth is, he did. He got away, or maybe I did, I'm not sure. But either way he's not here now, and he took a few pieces of me with him when he left.

As dumb as I look, I keep smiling until I open the message. It's the little things.

Austin: Skye is here. Besides, you're drunk.
Me: I'd find a way there if you wanted me.
Austin: You've always been resourceful.

I look to my finger as I tap out another reply and see the tattoo Austin and I share. We got them together on my nineteenth birthday. He was friends with the artist, so mine was free. It's by far, and will always be, my favorite tattoo. None of the dozen others since can compare. Sure, I love them too. Each one always seems to mark me in ways I never expect. They're all special, somehow. But that one, it's the most important.

The ink is faded but still marks me. Every time I look at it, it just takes a few seconds for me to time travel back to happier times. It's heartbreaking but somehow also comforting in a messed-up kind of way.

Distracted, picturing that younger, happier self, I don't send another reply yet.

I doubt stupid *Skyler* knows the permanent ink he wears on his arm matches mine. There's no way she knows that every time he sees it, he thinks of me, of us. I know he does. He's told me. Just like I do.

Thinking of his girlfriend's blonde hair and perky face makes me want to retch. Every time I say her name, or even think it, there's a sneer attached—it's become a curse word, italicized to show off its inadequacy. Thinking about her, picturing her, also makes me feel suffocated, like the air in my body is evaporating or being replaced by a noxious gas. I need to get out of here so I can breathe, so I can think, so my skin feels like it fits over me the right way again instead of like it's a size too small.

I need to be alone.

"Going to bed." I say it, louder than I meant to, before standing, super unsteadily; then I almost fall over. Maicy jumps to catch me, but I right myself with flat palms on the arm of the couch before she has the chance. I should be embarrassed, and I do feel some warmth creeping up my milky chest onto my neck, but I can't quite connect that with the normal feeling of shame. In fact, everything is a little disconnected.

"Take a bucket with you," Maicy says, and it sounds like a jab.

"Just for that I'm taking *your* garbage can," I say.

Before walking more than a step or two toward my room, I reconsider and stoop to grab the packed bowl and lighter. I don't care if it's stupid; they're coming with me to my bedroom. I am thankful, though, when Maicy misses the movement. I'd survive another lecture, another angry side-eye, but it's just easier to be ignored.

Unsteady but quick, I make it to my room. And I light up, taking one more long toke as soon as I close my door, and then flop onto the bed. This time it's different, and I feel weightless, like I'm filled with helium and floating to the ceiling on a wave of overactive nerve endings. I smile with my eyes closed at the peaceful feeling rippling through my cheek and down into my fingers. One more was okay.

As I lie back against the pillow, I pull my phone out of my pocket, no longer able to wait.

**Me: More like determined. And only when it comes to you.
Austin: Go to sleep. I know you're tired.**

Fuck, he's right. I hate when he's right.

And I hate being told what to do, by him or anyone, even more when it's right. I can picture his dumb expression while saying it too. I can just see his scruffy face, with dark hair like mine only short. I love to imagine his deep, dark eyes, his lips begging to be kissed, and his hard muscles. He's smart and edgy and never lets me get away with anything.

Shit, I miss him.

Even though it's been way too long since I've seen him in person, since he's been close enough to touch, the longing never goes away. I've heard his voice a couple times over the phone in all the time we've been apart. I know, it's so pathetic, but I remember the last time we hung out, the last time we talked, all of it. In all that time since then, I've only seen him on social media. Looked at him through a screen. And it hurts; looking at him through the filter of a screen hurts. I'll always remember that it hurts.

So I can't think about it much, or I sink down into this hole. I want to be nearer, more important. I want to be in her place. But it never works that way. He's had his arm around three different girls' shoulders in profile pictures during that time too. They've come and gone while I sit on the sidelines.

Why not me?

It's never me.

This last one feels like a direct punch in my gut, though. She's blonde and simple and happy. She's everything I'm not. He's never been with anyone like her before. And not knowing if that's what makes him happy, having no idea if it was his intention or a coincidence, it kills me a little inside.

Okay, it hurts either way.

So what's the cure-all while I wallow as he gets his dick sucked? Light up once more. Get further under the influence. It's always the simplest answer, the quickest. Forget everything about tonight and blissfully wave goodbye to the dying brain cells. When they go, if enough of them do, maybe I'll lose my grip on the memories of feeling so lonely. Maybe I'll wake up a happier, healthier person. Or maybe I'll just feel less. That's fine too.

I don't like feelings; they're so messy. Numb does me better, so…

I take another huge breath in. And after sucking in the herbal, strong, skunky taste for a third time tonight, I send another text I might regret in the morning, but right now it's the only thing that will make me, and my heart, feel less broken.

It may be temporary, but it works, fills in the cracks from years of breaking. It's effective coping but just for a day or two.

When I look to my phone next, there's already an answer waiting. He said he'll "be right over." So I unlock my window and push it open. The summer breeze washes over my skin and lights the already tingling parts of me on fire. I close my eyes, letting the waves run through me. Waves of nausea and a few of anticipation.

Taryn
Before

A few questions keep making their way around and around my brain since the bad night, the night that reminded me love is a bunch of bullshit. They weigh down on me with their barbed question marks, sinking deeper and deeper until I can't ignore the hurt.

People call me jaded, bitter, but they just have a film over their eyes they refuse to take off in order to see clearly. I know better now, again. I tried to believe, tried to ignore the panic of being happy, but the devastation, the reality, was thrown back in my face again. That's why I can't let go of these thoughts in my head, why I fixate and stew.

Why am I never good enough?

Why did I ever let him in in the first place?

What am I going to do without him? Could we try to be fucked-up friends? Would that be better than nothing at all?

I don't know.

I don't know the answers; I feel like I don't know anything. All I'm sure of is just how much it hurts.

Taryn
Now

When I open my eyes there are warm hands sliding over my wind-cooled skin. It's an intoxicating feeling, and I suck in a breath that's at least half moan. I'm shocked I missed the squeaks of my screen popping out and then back in, but the surprise is a good one.

When my lids pop open, I try not to look at his face. It's awful, I know, but not anything new. I want to picture someone else; I want to think about Austin on top of me instead. I catch the curls of his light brown hair though, before squeezing away the image.

And he knows not to talk anymore.

He used to say things he thought would turn me on or things that turned him on, I'm sure. But I threatened to cut him off, stop the friends-with-benefits deal we'd struck up, if he kept ruining the fantasy with his words and his pressure. I'm sure he knows he's being used—how could he not—but he doesn't seem to care. And that's okay. For now. I think he likes me a little too much. But I choose not to think about it.

Thinking about it would bring up too many messy feelings. And sometimes ignorance is goddamn bliss. Plus, he's a big boy, able to decide what he can handle. Apparently, that includes me.

I'm not mad about it.

And this way, without thought, I can I feel instead. Feel everything he does.

I feel his expert hands taking off my clothes, grazing parts of me desperate for attention, dragging his bare skin against mine as each layer is peeled off. I feel the ripple of his ab muscles as he squirms, one way and then the other, trying to evade my too-light touch. But I pull him to me so I can feel both of our hearts speeding up. I feel his hot breath against my neck as he kisses and nibbles where he knows I like it, turning up my heat until all of me is red, on fire. I feel every inch of well-worn fabric as I tear his clothes from his searing skin. I feel his breath, his heartbeat, his need for me. I feel the room shrinking until there's nothing left but our skin, our fire, our bodies pressing together.

I feel, I feel, I feel him.

I think as little as I can, sinking into every feeling.

Because when I do allow a thought to pass through, it's always of Austin. With my eyes still closed, I pretend I'm arching my back up to meet his skin. When I run my fingers through sweet smelling hair, I imagine it dark. And when his mouth finds mine, I breathe a sigh, trying so hard not to say a name that isn't right.

I've done it before, groaned out the wrong name. And it killed me for days, to the point where I almost called the whole thing off.

He never said anything, though. Not once. He never made me feel guilty, not on purpose. His silence hurt a shit-ton as it was. But I learned, that mistake taught me to bite my lip, keep in the pretend, the fantasy, and only let out my moans and sighs.

But…tonight it's difficult.

The booze and the weed sit heavy in my head and make it hard to remember who's pulling my panties down with his teeth. I shiver from my spine outward, all the way down to my toes.

He's learned well what my body needs.

"Oh, fuck," I groan. He's learned so fucking well.

I let my eyes open this time—I'm not sure why—and look into the clear, ice blue of his. So different from Austin's brown ones. But tonight, somehow, I don't seem to care enough. I keep looking, keep allowing my lashes to part for a quick view. Then a little longer. His smile is so sweet, it breaks my heart a little. And he stares into me, not just into my eyes but into all of me. I hold my breath.

He must take the change in my habit as an invitation.

"Mmm, Pigeon," he moans in my ear, tickling me and sending another warm shudder down my back. He must like my hand where it is, so I keep it there, for once enjoying the look on the face I'm not supposed to be seeing. It pushes me forward, and I smile.

I'm starting to fuzz out a little, as the room grows black spots around the edges. It makes me braver, and stupider too, but I embrace it.

"Make me feel good," I say, almost a whisper.

"Always," he answers.

"Make me forget," I add. He lifts me up into his arms and smothers my mouth with his own. He searches me and fills me with all the feelings he has, pouring it into me. Holding me tight to him, whispering nonsense that falls on deaf ears, he keeps reaching, keeps moving.

I'm close, my eyes closed again, and I dig my nails into his back. I don't think he's ever been buried this deep inside me, and it feels so good. *Fuck*, it feels about as perfect as anything has felt since...maybe ever.

And I let go. I spin out of control into a release as he finds his right after.

He calls my name as he gives in. "Taryn. Oh, Pidge," he mumbles, unable to bite it back.

As the ripples still run through me, I move my fingers through his curly hair, so different than what I'd tried to picture. He collapses on me, and I give him what I know he's wanted for months. It feels right, and I don't hesitate.

"Theo." I'm saying it for him. Whispered into his ear so I can barely hear it, so I can forget I said it. It's not enough, I know that, but it's something. It's what I can give right now.

Then it all drains, the feelings and the excitement, every bit. And in the aftermath of my orgasm, I feel empty again. Still drunk and high, but empty.

Austin
Now

I look to the spot just above my elbow on the inside of my arm. The tattoo sitting there, unobtrusive but perfect, is one of my oldest. It's so loved. I've gotten plenty since; hell, most of that arm's covered in them, three quarters of a sleeve. But that one, that's one of my favorites. *It's special.*

I've never told my girlfriends what it means, that it's for her. And it's not too suspicious, so none have ever asked. Surrounded by other things, other ink, it's easy to miss if you're not looking for it. And honestly, if Skyler did ask, I'd lie.

It's simple, the tattoo, like we were back then. Easy and happy. Starting with the roman numerals of the year we got them, MMVIII, followed by a heart and "K" for king of that suit. The King of Hearts. Hers, Taryn's, is the same but a "Q" replaces my "K." She was my Queen of Hearts for so long too. It's just one little string of solid black letters that somehow packs so much meaning inside the small space.

And it feels huge tonight, blown up by memories.

Lying in bed, next to Skyler, who started breathing evenly hours ago, I remember Taryn's stubborn face when she talked me out of getting the reverse. I wanted the Q so badly, but she always got her way, and there was no room to budge on it. She had me wrapped around her finger, and she never even knew it.

That night she'd convinced me when she said she needed me to remember I was the king of her universe. She kissed me and told me I would always reign over her heart. Her motivation had been so unselfish. She could have said she wanted me to remember to treat her like a queen or something along those lines. But she didn't. And that made it all the more powerful. She didn't have to add anything else.

So now, every time I see the crook above my elbow, every time I touch that sensitive skin, I remember when we ruled our kingdom together. Sometimes my breath catches when I'm thinking about it, about her. Like now. It's stupid, but it's never gone away. When we were dating and she walked into a room, for a second, I couldn't breathe. *Every time.* It was like the air was sucked from the whole space, from my lungs, as it rushed to be nearer to her and her perfection. Every damn time, I had to readjust and catch my breath. She was that special, my queen.

But then it ended.

Skyler rolls over, and her delicate hand lands on my chest. Most other nights I'd find it sweet, but right now it's suffocating, jarring. I gently push her away, but I hear the soft murmur and then seen her eyes flutter open.

Shit.

She moves her hand lower and slips those delicate fingers past the elastic of my boxers. I freeze. Her skin feels too hot, and it tickles instead of feeling good. The guilt bubbles up a little more than earlier, and I react on instinct. I slip my fingers around her wrist and pull it away from my lower half. I don't go so far as to shove her away, but I can feel the rejection building as tension all over her, so I hold her hand to the skin over my pounding heart.

Hopefully she assumes it's pounding from something other than regret.

"But, baby…?" And all I hear is the nasal tone in her whining.

"I don't feel very good," I say, another lie bursting from me. So easy.

Skyler moves her hand to my stomach and rubs it a few times before answering. When she does, she sounds normal again, and I wonder how biased my reactions can get.

"I'm sorry," she murmurs.

Before she can do anything else that'll piss me off for no reason, I turn on my side, away from her, and count the seconds until she's asleep again. Then I wait several more minutes, still counting, before pulling my phone under the covers with me.

Don't let the light of the screen wake her.

I leave it on the home screen waiting for the moment when Skyler jostles awake. It doesn't happen. So I push the carefully laid, and sometimes ignored, boundaries away. Right now it doesn't matter how I've tried to hold them up and enforce a distance.

Me: The Queen of Hearts keeps a tight grip on those still beating under her reign.

I know it sounds a little weird from me, a little spacy, but it's something she whispered into my ear once while she was sitting in my lap. And it stuck with me. Then I turn my phone off after hitting send, afraid I'll do something even more stupid if I get an answer before falling asleep. Tomorrow I'll be stronger; tomorrow I'll be better, and my moment of weakness will be forgotten.

Austin
Now

I open my eyes to see a face that feels like home.

The wind whips her dark hair around in the seat across from mine, and she looks so tempting. It's as if she should have a halo glimmering above her. I can see her lips moving, but I don't hear any words. It doesn't matter, though. Those lips are hypnotizing enough, even without sound. The way they move, the supple invitation they whisper. They beg to be smothered by my mouth.

So I oblige.

But she doesn't linger like I want. She doesn't lean into me and moan with pleasure. Instead she's off, quick as hell and running. Only after she's a few hundred feet away do I realize we've moved from the car to the beach.

I watch her every step, savoring it as the sand flies behind her and the sun lights her up.

My mind wanders, watching her get smaller, loving how she moves. Why did we try to be friends for so long, through the dysfunction and longing? Why didn't we just wake the fuck up and see what we've always been meant to be? Why did I have to screw everything up so bad that night? The questions keep pounding into me like nails smashed by an accusatory hammer. Each one hurts worse than the last.

Then sound is back, waves crashing to my left and her enchanting laugher fading ahead as she gets still farther away. Just before she disappears over a hill of sand and rock, I start after her. I run until my legs feel tight, long past wanting to stop. I can't let her get away. It would destroy me. So I run, gaining ground.

When I catch her, we crash into the sun-soaked earth together, going down as one.

The moment changes from carefree to crackling with untapped passion in a second as I land on top of her. It just takes that one second to untie the bow of her red bikini top with one tug. It holds in place since we're horizontal, and the anticipation builds until it's oppressive. But I extend it, let it writhe.

I kiss her jaw, her neck, her collarbone, trying to watch her reaction with each.

She surprises me with her response when she moves her hands to our sides and tugs the two bows holding her bikini bottoms together, and lets the strings fall aside. My eyes go wide, and hers look away.

I've never seen anything sexier in my fucking life.

Ready to take her right here on the beach, I look around once to make sure we're alone.

But when I look back down, ready to devour her and let my heart be claimed again, she's gone. My stomach touches rough sand. It's nothing like the velvet skin that was just there. Suddenly I feel lost, empty, all alone.

She's gone.

She's been gone.

A quiet "no" escapes my lips.

Austin
Now

"No. Taryn, don't go." The words leave my mouth before I can stop them, waking me up in a heartbeat.

Fuck. I never thought I needed duct tape to cover some of my sins, at least the ones while I sleep, but I guess I might.

Skyler stirs, but she doesn't look completely conscious yet.

"Hmm?" she murmurs.

I sigh, flooded with relief. I'm one lucky son of a bitch.

"Just bad dreams. Don't worry about it," I answer.

She snuggles closer, draping her leg between mine. This time I don't push her away. I let her stake her claim, trying to relax. I want to sink into the warmth, hoping it'll send me back to sleep. It's still dark outside; I should sleep a lot more before dawn.

But it's hard with hazel eyes, dark hair, and full lips burned in my mind. Even with my eyes closed, I can't see anything else. So I stop fighting it and pull Skyler closer, imagining straight hair caressing my cheek instead of curls.

With my eyes squeezed shut like this, I can almost believe it.

But even with that fantasy, even in the comfort of this bed, this room, even under the weight of limbs other than my own, I still can't fucking sleep. The harder I try, the worse it gets. My eyes pop open, and I stare at the ceiling. My brain starts racing, and once it's going, I don't know how to turn it off.

With Skye hanging all over me, I start to sweat where our skin touches. Soon I'm slick and overheating. I try not to get annoyed. I fail, but at least I try. So after a moment I roll away from her, giving Skye my back. She snores but doesn't move, still close but at least not draped all over me.

That's when my breathing, and my thoughts, finally slow down. It's almost as if, without her on top of me, I can relax.

And soon I'm just on the precipice, so close to getting back to sleep, when her arm snakes around my chest. It's hard, but I keep from tensing, from letting a breath catch in my throat. There's no outward evidence that she's woken me. But then she starts stroking my chest in long, slow movements. Each time her fingers get lower and lower, and my body reacts to her touch. When she grabs me, I sigh and turn to face her.

Neither of us say anything, but it's not quiet.

It's an inevitable feeling that washes over me, more so than lust or anything else. But then my brain stops fighting the battle, and I accept.

Taryn
Now

I'm pulled from a vivid dream. Reluctant, I resist waking, desperately trying to hold on to the fantasy. But I feel the tug back to reality somewhere in my chest. Lingering effects bathe me, though, even in the beginnings of morning light. I can almost taste Austin's kiss, and I can still feel the aftermath of a special kind of explosion between my legs, the tingles haunting me.

When I finally open my eyes, I blink at the arm across my torso ending with the hand groping my sensitive chest. Next to his where his thumb hits, there's a dark hickey.

I'm naked. We both are.

I'm still wet.

And Theo's still in my bed.

He's not supposed to stay over. He knows he's supposed to be gone by the time I wake up. Little patches of light break into the corner of the room, and I stare at them, trying not to get pissed. I asked him here, and it was late. I must have passed out, and so did he. But...regardless of intent, if this happens again I'll be putting my foot down. This is his one freebie, and I won't even say anything about it now.

Making the decision to let it go helps a little.

So I reach for my phone, trying to move as little as possible. There are notifications, and I wonder what embarrassing rejection I have from Austin. My stomach clenches uncomfortably. I don't remember everything I sent him last night. Some of it could have been fine, but I know it's never flattering the next day. Inevitably, something I said will make me cringe and not want to talk to him for a few days, maybe longer.

I suck in a breath at what's in my inbox—and not from humiliation. But I don't have much time to overanalyze the words when Theo starts massaging the tender spot where his hand cups. My eyes flutter closed, the smell of him wafting over me for the first time, and it's surprising, somehow perfect.

He's gentle, and it feels fucking fantastic as I melt into him, into his soft and worshipful touch. I forget both my anger at him for staying and my unanswered questions for Austin for a moment. Maybe it's for a lifetime, I'm not sure. My phone clatters to the floor, as I get lost in Theo's slow touch. A need deep in my stomach starts to uncurl, and I let my head tip back. My eyes are closed so tight, I see spots, as his other strong hand, warmer than my already heating skin, parts my knees.

"Once more, then you go." I say.

It almost ruins the moment for me, my own harshness. But I know, for my own protection, I need to hold my ground. If that means being horrible or bitchy, so be it.

It ruins nothing for Theo, though. He laughs against my thigh, the rumble of it sending electricity all over my skin. Then he starts crawling, kissing my stomach, my chest, my neck on the way up. "You'll have me over again," he says, once he's up to my hair, then nibbles my earlobe.

"Probably. But that doesn't change the rules."

"Understood, boss." He moves his face right over mine, so our noses are touching, and he winks. Then, on the cusp of a smile, he dips his tongue into my mouth, his agreement to be a good boy.

This time I keep my eyes closed throughout. Sober, I don't let so many mistakes sneak through the walls I've built up. I debate it, though that isn't normal, but in the end, I keep the walls inside of me standing.

I keep words from forming in my mouth, and I only see the back of my eyelids.

Taryn
Before

"Do you think you'll see your mom this weekend?" Theo asks me, kicking at the dirt while I aimlessly pull up strands of grass.

"I don't know," I answer into my lap. "I don't care."

"Yes you do."

"I know," I say. I do. I hate that he knows that, but I do. "What about you?" I ask.

"I think my aunt is working to move here. For me." His words are almost a whisper. Too quiet.

"Wow." And I mean it. *Wow.* That's amazing, to have someone working so hard to be a part of your life, instead of screwing up so badly that you're taken away and moved to a different school, to a different everything. Throwing my head back, I look to the clouds floating, slow and lazy, through the sky.

"Do you miss her, your mom?" Theo scoots closer to me until our legs touch at the knees, and I squint back at the grass, my neck already getting sore. Neither of us look at each other, neither of us get up. But it's nice.

The other foster kids, our "brothers and sisters"—yeah, right—run all over the park's equipment, shrieking and laughing like it's a week day at recess. I kind of want to join in, but at the same time I don't. On outings like this, I can never make up my mind.

"Sometimes," I say. "Do you miss your parents?"

I don't want to get too attached to any of these kids, to any of my foster parents. I know I'm still going to go back home eventually, unlike some of the lifers. I have to keep believing that.

He doesn't respond. And that's okay, I get it. I don't always have an answer either. Sometimes there isn't one at all.

"I wish I could fly away," I say without context.

"Like the pigeons." Theo looks to one hopping near our feet, still not at me, when he says it. I hadn't cared enough to notice it before, but now that I do there's no hesitation—I kick in its direction. The little thing startles, terrified, eyes bulging and head swiveling in confusion. And then it's off, up into the air, to somewhere safer, to somewhere better.

"Like the pigeons," I say.

"Hey, Turdo," a deep voice interrupts us before I get an answer, casting a shadow across both our legs. My shoulders creep up, and my mouth hardens right away.

"It's Theo," I say. "And knock it off, Paul." I stand, Theo grabbing my hand after I do, grounding me and holding me back with his fingers circling mine.

"Or what?" Paul asks, a sneer on his thin lips and nothing behind his beady eyes.

I *hate* him.

Theo's presence isn't enough, and I shake his hand off as I narrow my eyes. He stands next to me immediately, staying silent but standing ground with me.

"Or I'll kick your ass," I say, sounding braver than I feel.

Paul laughs. It's throaty and loud—obnoxious—making my skin crawl.

"You're a piece of shit, you know that," I add with a smile, taking a step forward until our noses are almost touching, not backing down. "You're a scared little baby, and that's why you pick on Theo. On everyone. You're afraid you're nothing, so you try to show everyone how big your talk is, trying to be something. Anything. But we all know; we all see it. You're less than nothing, and you'll be nothing *forever*," I say.

And it feels so good to say it. This time I laugh, breathing the hilarity all over Paul's reddening face.

"Pidge, he's not worth it," Theo says from behind me, touching my shoulder blade.

"Of course he's not," I say, my eyes still challenging Paul's.

It's fast and fierce—Paul's retaliation. The world explodes in white fireworks from one eye, while the other snaps shut, both watering without my approval. My skin burns, but I won't cry. I won't give him that satisfaction. *I won't.*

He underestimated me though. I move on him before I'm even able to open my eyes back up. And I play dirty. Theo has to pull me off of Paul as I'm scratching his chest, pulling his hair, and screaming in his face about the waste of space he is.

"Don't you *ever* talk to Theo again. You got it? You're the dog shit on the bottom of his shoe, he's so far above you. Never," I say as Theo drags me away, kicking and yelling at Paul the whole time. "Again."

"You're going to have a black eye, you idiot," Theo says to me once we're far enough away to be safe, well for Paul to be safe.

With the good eye, I can see both of our foster moms rushing over.

"Worth it," I say, not looking at him.

"Guess the play date's over," Theo answers as both foster moms shout for everyone to gather up to go.

"Sorry," I say, turning toward the forming groups.

"Don't be." Theo kisses my cheek before running over to his current foster mom, and the skin burns where he touched it after he's gone.

Taryn
Now

I can't get my dreams from last night or the uncertainty from this morning out of my head. After Theo left, I tried distracting myself. I went to open-studio time at the art house to work on pottery, but I kept screwing everything up when I tried creating new. So in the end, all I did was glaze old pieces and get them ready to fire—all while overthinking.

Then when I got home, I even locked my phone in Maicy's car so I couldn't text either of the men clouding my head. But I guess she heard the chirping and brought it in after she got back from the store.

"You have dried clay in your hair," she says as she walks in the house. Then, dropping my phone in my lap, she adds, "Your admirers are waiting."

I'm not too proud to admit that my jaw drops a little at her words. She laughs.

She knows about Theo, despite my best efforts to hide it, and she hates the dysfunction I have with Austin. In actuality…Maicy doesn't approve of many, if any, of my decisions. But even if I wanted to keep them from her, forever a secret, I've known her forever. I just can't. She knows everyone in my life, and she has her opinions on all of them. So I deal, and I sit through the lectures.

I, on the other hand, choose not to tell her how much she changes with every guy she dates or even likes. How she goes through phases, mirroring whoever she's with. It's why her wardrobe evolves every few months and why she sometimes picks up new hobbies. This new phase will morph into another in a while, and the too-cool-hipster stuff will fall away, just like the tweaks she made last time are already gone. But do I say anything? *No.* As long as she keeps the core of herself, the bits that make her, her—I let it go. And yet still, she has no problem calling me on *my* relationship shit.

"How was shopping," I ask, ignoring her goading.

"Theo's in love with you," she says from the bathroom as I flip through the channels on TV, still aiming for a diversion that works. Case in point, by the way. She just needs to comment on everything.

"Don't you *ever* say that again, or you'll wake up on the floor," I say.

"Shut up. Don't be pissy just because I'm telling you the truth."

"Your version of it." I grumble it, mumbling under my breath. So I jump when her hands curl around my shoulders from over the back of the couch. Sneaky little fucker.

"You're cute," I say. "But you know, you're kind of scary."

"You should let go of the hold Austin has over you. Theo's a good guy. A *really* good guy. He'd do anything for you," she says, hovering above me. I try to shake her grip off with a jerk, but she keeps her arms glued. "I've heard you say the wrong name, chicky. And he still comes back."

She lets go then, seeing my blood boil, evident in the red of my ears, angry heat meeting skin. Walking around to sit next to me, she chooses the other side of the couch, out of arm's length. She knows I'll hit her. I've done it before. She adds, "Just think about it."

Not that she always chooses the good guy, but I guess advice is easier to give than to receive. Not that I'm sharing my thoughts, like I said.

I glare at her, letting a slow breath out.

What she's saying isn't wrong, but that doesn't mean I have to like it.

Finally, I nod. That's all she's going to get, but it's more than I'd give any other time.

There's just one thing that *could* help distract me. I look to Maicy again, and there's no way she doesn't read it all over my face. My smirk is wicked, enticing her to join the dark side with me for once.

"You know you want to," I say.

"Fiiiiiiine." She draws it out, like she's whining.

But her lips curl up too, and I have the urge to kiss her dimpled cheek. I love when she gives in. I can count on her for it. That's the deep-down Mace, the one I'll always love, the one I wait for and try to pull out, always. We've been making mistakes together since we were little, and that better never change.

"But eventually you'll have to grow up," Maicy says. "*Eventually.*"

"Doubtful."

I glare too, but not for long since I don't want to give her time to reconsider. I hop up and run to my room for the bowl and lighter. The textured walls of our hall blur as I run past them, excited. But in my room, I hesitate. After swiveling back and forth, I end up leaving my phone on the bed. This tactic could either work or backfire like it did last night when I reached out to both of my temptations while in bed. We'll see.

When I jump back onto the couch, I practically sit on top of Maicy and her inviting-looking lap, feeling much friendlier. The sun's dipping down outside the living room's bay window, and the evening feels so much better now. I can feel myself letting go of earlier, of my problems.

When I bounce on the couch cushions, she laughs and takes the paraphernalia from my hand to light up first.

"I know why you still do this, you know." She peers at me from the corner of her eyes, sparkling green and so light sometimes I think I can see into her mind. Then she inhales and passes the items back, holding her breath as she hands me everything.

I love how she says that right before she's got a chest full of smoke swirling inside her.

"Because it's fucking awesome," I say, choking it out as I let go of my own lung-full after a few moments.

"Nope." She pokes my shoulder and starts laughing, her pale hair falling in waves all round her as her grin just widens. She's always a fun high, sweet and happy. I've missed this, and I almost tell her that, but I worry it'll ruin her good mood.

"Then why, genius?" I ask instead.

"Because it lets you keep living in the past. When it was cool to smoke and be edgy."

Whoa.

Way too deep.

"With your thick, black eyeliner, and trigger-happy middle fingers, your tight leggings and better-than-everyone attitude," Maicy says through laughter. "You're still just the same. You've always been cooler than everyone. And you love that feeling."

Maicy stops laughing as she watches my jaw fall, knowing I may blow up over the idea. Lashing out, especially when my feelings are hurt, isn't out of the realm of possibilities. She used to be edgy *with me*; we were in it, in everything, together. But then again, just as with her sentiment from earlier, it's hard to ignore the little nugget of truth in her words.

The past is comfortable. I understand it.

She cringes, then stumbles over herself to fix the blunt words still hanging in the air. "I mean…I just know you were happier then…fuck…nevermind. Forget it. I'm high. I have no idea what I'm talking about." The words jumble together as she rushes.

I don't answer. I let the ideas swirl around my head along with the fog filling the room.

She stares at me as the silence lengthens.

And I know the contrasting emotions all zip across my face.

But I land on acceptance. "You're probably right." This time it's her turn to drop her mouth open. "But it's also fun," I say, lighting up again.

It really is.

****

Several bowls and some major munchies later, Maicy's in her own bed. She started losing steam too soon, but I didn't argue as she shuffled down the hall. I did offer to let her sleep next to me, but she didn't want to stay up talking. She left me sitting cross-legged on the couch with too many thoughts to keep me company.

Of course she left a mushy TV show playing when she went. And at some point, my phone made its way back to my lap. I swear it grew legs and walked from my bedroom though. I don't remember going to get it. At all.

Regardless of how it happened, it's here now, and sitting alone in the dark presents temptations that have my heart thudding against my ribs. There's a drumbeat inside me, making my breath deeper and faster; making me so antsy, I can't sit still. Thump, thump, thump—do it, do it, do it—my heart eggs me on, telling me to do what I know, somewhere inside, I shouldn't.

I take in one more breath of hazy bravery, tingling in the aftereffects of my green courage. And I hold it as long as I can, getting every single bit of help possible.

When I let it go, I dial the ten numbers I still have memorized.

Austin
Now

When my phone vibrates in my pocket, I almost let it go without checking. Theo's here, and so is Skyler. We're at the bar, surrounded by music and booze. It's loud and crowded; I probably couldn't hear anything anyway. But at the last second I change my mind, thinking it may be a friend wanting to join us and needing to know where we are.

As "Theo T" blinks on my screen, my stomach drops to the floor. I can feel the bang of it between my feet, silent but reverberating.

I shouldn't answer. I *seriously* fucking shouldn't.

But with yet another beer in my left hand, my right has a mind of its own. My thumb brushes the answer button, as I lift the whole phone to my ear. It's surreal, and I feel like maybe someone else is doing all of this for me, like I'm watching it happen. The anticipation builds as my feet start moving toward the coatroom to get away from the noise; my body still taking over while my brain is on vacation or in shock. Somehow, I don't mind though; instinct is fine. It'll be fine. I don't say a word until I know I'll be able to hear the response.

"Hey," I say, once I'm away from the noise.

Wow, how fucking brilliant. Forever and a day since we last spoke, and all I can come up with is "hey." *Smooth, moron.*

The lighting is still dim here. There are lots of red bulbs, but somehow that seems appropriate. And it's a lot brighter than near the bar or the stage. My legs feel like they're made of jelly, and my stomach might be turning inside out.

"Austin," she breathes the two syllables instead of just saying them, and I sink into the chair near me. It may have been someone else's seat, but that doesn't matter anymore. Nothing matters more than the one word I just heard…Well, maybe the voice that said it. But still.

Somehow as Taryn says my name, years of feelings, thousands of memories, all come rushing to the front of my mind. In one word, she packed a punch so hard I don't know if I'll recover from it. She sounds sweet and tempting. Each letter so full of promise, it's easy to ignore the potential for heartbreak.

"I can't talk long. Skyler isn't far." As soon as I say another name, I regret it. She may be in the next room, but there are tons of people and countless steps between us. I never intended to let reality crash into the excitement I was feeling. Now I worry it'll burst Taryn's bubble too.

Shit.

"I miss you," she says, surprising and electrifying me all over again. The raw emotion in her voice sends my head spinning. It's scratchy and familiar, hoarse and needy. It yanks on my heart—and other parts of me.

I'm so glad my misstep didn't faze her that I blurt out the first thing that comes to mind. "I've been thinking about you a lot lately." And once it's out there, I'm shocked I don't want to take it back.

It's the truth anyway.

I was surprised, and a little disappointed, when she didn't answer my late-night text. But now hearing her voice and feeling the weakness in my limbs, in my chest, being honest is the only thing to do right now. I can feel it, like she's actually said, *just be real with me.*

"It's kind of hard to talk right now," I say.

Looking around, I see nothing. My eyes can't focus any better than my racing mind. Everything seems to tingle until my fingers are throbbing. I didn't realize I was gripping the phone so tight until my knuckles groan in protest. They're almost as tense as my jaw. When I loosen my hold, I have to wipe the sweat off my palms. I know what I want to say, but I hesitate. Is it worth giving everything up? But the booze pushes me to be brave, and as I open my mouth to add more, I could swear my heart is trying to crawl into my throat.

"Can I come over later?" I ask. "Just to talk."

I won't cheat.

Not again. Not with her.

I won't make her that girl.

I'm terrified to put my heart back in such a dangerous place, but I'm just as terrified not to.

We'll just talk.

Besides, we're friends.

We can reconnect as *best friends*. It's been too long since we saw each other anyway.

"I'll be up. Waiting," she says. Then she breathes deep, and I picture her eyes closing as she exhales. It's a sweet sound, and I wish I could feel the air on my face, my chest, as she adds, "You know where it is. The door'll be unlocked."

I hold the seat of the chair with my free hand, tensed again.

"I'll be there later…" I hesitate, having no idea how she'll take what I'm about to say next. *Fuck it.* "Angel." I whisper the nickname I used to use for her. She has bits of both devil and angel in her, and I used to love calling her Angel in bed.

She doesn't answer. All I hear is the line go dead as my phone lights up again.

I think she still wants me there.

But what if she doesn't? What if my last word was too much and she changed her mind?

Someone behind me clears his throat, deep and loud, scaring the shit out of me, making me jump. It drives all questions from my mind. As I turn around, I'm glad, at least, that the sound came from a guy.

But my relief turns tail and runs the fuck away when my eyes meet Theo's.

"Tell me I heard you wrong," he says.

It's harsh and rough, sounding like he's yelling at me despite his lowered volume. Maybe because of it. His face is hard. His jaw is clenched tighter than his fists. It's better than Skyler hearing the conversation, but only barely.

"Tell me that wasn't who I think it was." His face is getting a little red, and there's a vein popping out of his neck, pulsating. "Tell me you didn't just say you'd go over there. To her. Tell me I'm wrong."

He breathes heavily, like he can't get air, as I stand so we're eye to eye.

Theo's my best friend, other than her, and he's seen every fucked-up emotion I've had over her. He's stuck with me through all of it, all my shit. He helped me piece myself back together after she and I destroyed each other. He helped, and he stayed.

But he never got mad like this. Not once.

I drop my phone back into my pocket, trying to think up a response.

Nothing good comes, though. So I shrug my shoulders. "You're wrong—" I try to lie.

But he shakes his head, stopping me. "Fine, you're right. But you're not stopping me." He groans, the sound, a clear beginning to an argument, coming from deep in his chest. It's my turn to interrupt him, though. "I'm going over to *talk* to her. Only talk. I'm not gonna do anything wrong. We're still friends."

"Bullshit," he says.

"Fuck off. You have no idea."

The words tumble out, tripping over each other as I start to walk away. There's a fire in my chest that threatens to burn the whole bar down. Theo, Skyler, no one can tell me what to do. As I slam a foot down on the floor, pushing past him, he grabs my arm. And I resist the urge to shake it off, knowing he's just being a friend, if an annoying one, right now.

"How are you getting there? You can't drive. Not like this." He points to my beer. He's right. We've been here less than two hours, and I downed every drink until this. I had a shot somewhere in there too. I can't exactly walk straight.

"I guess I'll get a car," I say, the only thought that comes to mind. It'll have to do.

"And what about Skyler?" Theo asks, ever the responsible one, thinking ahead.

It's annoying.

"Fuck."

I don't have an answer. He knows it.

"I'll drive you there. Go tell your girl you're staying at my place tonight," Theo says. It's through gritted teeth, and, though he's dropped my arm, his hands aren't any less tense. At least they're at his sides now.

I smile at him with the dumbest grin I've worn since we were kids. His words may be ground out through clenched teeth, but he's still helping me, still saying what I need to hear.

"But *this* happens," he accentuates the word and pauses before continuing, "just once. It'll never happen again. And I'm only doing it now because you're about to promise me that nothing more than talking is going to happen."

He looks me hard in the eyes, still working his jaw, and I know how serious he is.

"And you're going to promise me that during this *platonic* conversation, you're going to tell her that you can't see her again after tonight."

I think again; I've never seen him this pissed off.

So I nod, but he doesn't move yet, doesn't relax.

"I promise, fucker," I say.

I hate making promises.

****

Theo revs the engine of his truck in Taryn's and Maicy's driveway.

Asshole.

It's almost three in the morning, and he all but lays on his horn. I'll be lucky if the door is still unlocked. As he backs up from the driveway into the end of the cul-de-sac, I watch. He glares back at me as he peels out, down the silent street, as loud as fucking possible.

When I turn to reach for the doorknob, annoyed but determined, I swear I see a flicker of fabric in Taryn's window.

Austin
Before

"So," Taryn says into the quiet room, introducing a creeping apprehension. This could either be really bad or freaking fantastic. "I've been looking up scholarships and grants, and I think you could make this work, if you really want to start your own business."

Out of nowhere, my heart starts beating faster and faster until it's a little uncomfortable.

Her eyes are still on the book propped in her lap, even when she continues. "You're talented. You can do absolutely anything you set your mind to. I mean you convinced me to go out with you, right?" She looks up to make a kissing face at me, then back down to complicated poetry I'd never quite understand. "I can help too. I mean, I've learned a lot from Cooper."

Then she trails off, letting the thought dangle in the air, hovering above us.

"Oh, be quiet," I say, trying to bite down on my lips that want to curl up.

"I mean it, babe. You're brilliant. And you're charismatic. Everything you do is gold. And you could change the world if you decided to. You just have to make up your mind," she says. I make a disbelieving little grunt. She gets wild ideas in her head sometimes and just starts running with them. "Or, if you hate that idea, I can help you think of something else that would fulfill you, make you happy. That's all I want, you know," she adds.

I don't know how to respond.

She goes back to reading, and I let my mind drift lazily, trying to land on the right words. Nothing feels good enough, and I want to say this right. So chewing on the inside of my cheek, I watch her. Taryn's hair is down to the middle of her back now, so silky I can't keep my hands out of it most of the time. And she sees everything, her eyes sharper than anyone else I know. Her bite is a harsh as her bark, and she uses both often; but behind that, behind the walls, she's the kindest, most supportive person I've ever met. She's perfect.

I just…

"You're my best friend, you know," I say as she tucks some of that perfect, dark hair behind her ear.

"Don't tell Theo," she says without looking up.

"Hey." I put just my pointer under her chin so I can tilt it up until our eyes meet. "I mean it," I add.

Her eyes don't show appreciation or affection; she's just confused.

"Why?" she asks, and that little word makes me feel terrible.

There are so, so many things I could say right now. But I sift through them all for what will hit home most to her.

"I've never had someone support me like you do," I start.

"But…"

"Let me finish, Angel," I interrupt her interruption, and she snaps her lips closed, eying me. "Theo is great, amazing. And he's always there for me. Probably always will be. But that's different than support. *This* kind of support. You lift me up. You push me to be better than I ever knew I could be. You don't take my shit, and that's kind of a big deal. I've never had someone push as hard back against me as I push everyone else. You really see me, and you still stick around, giving me new ideas and motivation, helping me to be my best. I just wanted you to know that I see that. And I'm trying to live up to it, to give you the same," I say. It's all in a rush, and I've been looking down since the first sentence in that whole rambling mess.

Her eyes cloud over when I look back to them, and for a moment, I wonder if I've gone too far, said too much.

My brain whirls, trying to backpedal, and I know I shouldn't say more.

Though, of course I do. "You're not just supportive. You're addictive too. Maybe that's because you're supportive, and the *best* person I've ever known. Or maybe it's because you blow my fucking mind in bed," I say with a wink. She rolls her eyes, but I can see she's hanging on my every syllable. "But whatever the reason, and it will always be the case, you're my addiction."

Then she smiles, the fog turning to glass, and she wraps me in a hug so tight I can't quite breathe until she lets go.

I know, I've always had a feeling she loves the devotion an addiction provides, the constancy of it. But behind all of that, I'm even more sure that inside that addiction—the love fueling it—is more important to her, even if she pretends it isn't.

"I am a pretty amazing girlfriend, aren't I," she whispers in my ear. And that's the first time she's said it. *Girlfriend.*

Taryn

Now

Theo.

And Austin.

I try to breathe as I watch Theo drive away after dropping Austin off at my house in the middle of the night. The air catches in my throat. I let the curtain drop along with my confidence, and also my stomach. Maybe I should run to lock the door. Maybe I should climb out my window and get away.

But it's too late, as I hear the front door creak open.

I start to panic, anxiety creeping into the deepest parts of me.

I don't know why, but the thought of my standing here in the middle of my room when Austin finds me is scarier than being face-to-face with him again somewhere else. Oh, my fucking shit. Why did I let him come over? Why did I call him? This was all a mistake. Then I hear his footsteps padding down the hall, and there are new knots in my stomach. Knots on top of knots. I can almost picture his stance as he moves slowly toward where he guesses I might be.

And then I can't breathe. My heart is going too fast, and my breath is shallow, quick. I might pass out if I don't calm down.

Without thinking any more I whisper-yell, "Wait." Then after taking a few slow breaths I add, "I just need a second."

I know he's still in the hall, he didn't make it as far as my room. So with my eyes closed, I go out there and turn toward the living room before opening them again. If I can't see him, then maybe I can keep my cool just long enough. Then I speed to the couch and breathe deeply once more. "Okay."

I hear Austin's warm chuckle and some of my nerves disappear.

Theo knew what he was getting into. He's always known the rules. He's known about, and how to navigate, the walls built around me. He knows to respect them, and if he's smart he won't mention this. *Ever.* So knowing all of that, I tell myself this will be okay. It doesn't matter who dropped Austin off.

I sit with my feet tucked underneath me on the couch and with my bowl in hand. I absolutely brought that with me, out of my room. And I clutch it like a security blanket, ready to use it for courage, as necessary. Austin starts moving again, coming toward me. Each sound of boot to tile brings back more of the anxiety I'd let go with his laughter. Then his footsteps stop somewhere behind me.

I start to turn around when his hands land on my shoulders, and I stop.

I almost burst out with laughter, remembering that Maicy was doing the exact same thing a couple hours before. But then he starts rubbing them for a moment, and it's nothing like how Maicy's hands felt. I let out a quiet little noise, making me freeze as soon as it's past my lips.

This is *just* talking.

He's not coming on to me. He's taken. His touch isn't sexual. My damn sounds shouldn't be either.

He doesn't stop, though. He goes for a few more moments. And when I tip my head to the side he cups my cheek in his hand. The roughness, the calluses, feel familiar. Despite my better judgment, I rub my skin into his palm for a second.

It feels like home.

Then, finally, I think smarter and sit up straight. But I also pull the glass to my lips and light the pre-packed green, sucking in deeper than

I have all night, than I have in a while. He walks around the couch as I hold in the smoke.

I exhale as he comes into view and sits down across from me.

It's surreal, like I'm dreaming, as the smoke clears from my eyes and his face materializes, I see hope and a curious depth to his eyes. After the burning fades from my throat, my chest, and I catch my breath, he grins. That's what does it. I'm lifted up into happiness and inebriation. They combine into something I haven't felt in a really long fucking time. His face, his smell, his body. It's all here, right in front of me.

It's been too long. I want to hug him, to wrap myself in his arms, his warmth.

But I still don't say anything, don't move. I think I've forgotten how to interact with him.

So I pull the bowl back to my lips with one hand, the lighter still in the other, poised. But he reaches out before I can light it, and he puts his hand on top of mine, surprising me. "You don't need that," he says.

Oh.

Shit.

Even his voice is coated with memories. It sounds like…but I stop myself before finishing the thought. Instead, I drop my hands to my lap, listening to him for once.

"I don't know why I'm so fucking nervous," I say. So awkward. Then I laugh after finishing, and I sound like a fucking moron. Cringing, I keep my eyes down in my lap. It's easier, less terrifying, if I'm not looking into his eyes.

"I am too," he says. And, even if it's a lie to make me feel better, it works.

"Still friends with Theo?" I ask.

"Still friends with Maicy?" he counters.

"Fair enough. Guess nothing changes," I say. I let it go, not wanting to think about Theo in this moment anyway. "Still with Skyler?" I hate myself right after adding it, but I don't try to undo it or stop an answer.

"Right now I'm sitting here with you. Can't that be enough, Angel?"

And he uses the name again. I melt inside, heating up and closing my eyes. I had no idea how much I missed it until he uttered it over the phone earlier. I never really liked it back then, but now, now it feels different.

"It's enough," I say, meaning it.

This time when I lift my hands for another toke he doesn't disagree. I need it. So I suck it in, hoping that some semblance of maturity, of clarity, comes with it. I'm not sure if anything changes, but after I finish, I offer it to him. And when he takes it, I smile. *Finally.* I don't know the last time he smoked, but it must have been a while judging by the amount of coughing during his exhale.

Maybe Maicy was right about my living in the past with these habits. But I push the thought aside and focus on the more pressing situation sitting in front of me. "So..." I say, having no idea where to go from here.

He catches his breath before echoing me, "So..."

When we both start laughing, it feels normal, for the first time tonight.

And then something unravels, like he flipped a switch and I remembered how to talk. Neither of us seem nervous, and the conversation starts to flow. It feels like we haven't spent a day apart. It feels good. We try to keep it quiet with Maicy just a few walls away from us, but as we start talking about old memories, and new updates, it gets a little harder. We keep smoking, falling back into old habits, and the conversation flows better than I ever expected. I keep reminding him to shush, and he keeps making excuses to touch my leg, my side, my hands.

At least I think he's making excuses.

Or maybe I'm reading too much into him. Who the fuck knows.

Eventually, we run out of things to talk about. We already texted about his parking ticket last week and how the cop refused to let it go, even though he was only one minute over the limit. And I messaged not long after about my issues with my mother—not that that's anything new—for a few hours while he gave me pointers on dealing with her. We talk every damn day, but suddenly I wish we'd left some things to catch up on.

So I turn reruns on. And we sit side-by-side, just watching TV together. Laugh tracks fade in and out; no mentions of a live audience. Dramatic music plays as dark colors and high contrast fill the screen. It's one show after another that I've seen before, and still, somehow, it feels nice.

My head starts to feel heavy, and I fight against droopy eyelids. Despite internal screaming, they keep falling. I have no idea when we might have a night like this again. And…we may never hang out after this. I don't know. So I need to make the most of it. Awake.

But when my head drops to Austin's shoulder, I let myself breathe him in. Snaking my arm through his, I hold on to him tight as I listen to the quiet humming from the TV. Or maybe those sounds are dialogue and intro music. Either way, it's soothing.

Austin

Now

It's so fucking hard not to touch her, not to grab her. I don't think I've ever resisted anything so actively in my entire life. I rub little circles with my thumb on her knee as she breathes in and out. I watch her chest rise and fall, each time wanting to put my hand where her heart beats. Everything about her seems perfect.

This whole moment is perfect, this whole night.

But after an entire episode starts and ends while she sleeps in my arms, I can't take it anymore. I can't resist any longer.

I let my arm untangle from hers, and I move it behind her back to rest on her hip. I let my itching fingers squeeze there, just a little. It feels so good to have her skin beneath my hand again. It feels right.

She stirs then.

The sweet sound of her breath pushes me onward. I grab her chin with my other hand and turn it toward me, tipping it up. Her eyes flutter open, and her fucking perfect lips part to say something. I don't let her get anything out before pressing my mouth to hers though. The passion, reckless and raw, bursts out as she grants my tongue access. It's an invitation I could never pass up. It's all I need. I feel the soft warmth of her, and she tastes just like I remember. She turns in my arms, toward me so we're tucked into each other. I worry she'll try to pull back, so I crush her to my chest.

One of my hands, I'm not sure which anymore and I fucking don't care, finds a home in the satiny strands of her hair. I wrap my fingers in it.

I use the position to bring her in deeper.

Even though it's hard to breathe through the kiss and the nonexistence of space, I want her closer. Nothing feels like enough. I need her skin. Her lips, her tongue, her breath, they're amazing, better than I remember, but they aren't enough.

I slip my hand beneath the loose shirt she's wearing and find the overheated skin of her stomach. My touch is light, and a groan escapes from my mouth into hers.

I should be embarrassed by my reactions. They're so intense, so quick. I mean, we're just kissing, and I've only grazed her stomach. This shouldn't have me like this. But it does. It really does. I've done everything with her, but not in a long time.

And I'm not sure it ever felt like this.

I never felt so vulnerable, so needy.

When I bite her lip, I get the breathy moan I wanted. She's out of her head and as in the moment as I am. So I push her back until I'm on top of her, never opening my eyes. And I hope hers are closed as tightly as mine. One of my hands is still in her hair, the other goes from her stomach to her ribcage. I let my fingers move across her skin upward, so slow. My temperature rises as both of our heartbeats speed up. She flushes beneath me too; I feel it. Her hands go under my shirt on my back, then they're gripping my arms. Her hips tilt up as her back arches, and her knees part so I fall between her legs.

It's magic.

I drop my hand from her hair to wrap around her hip. I pull her closer still; our bodies flush against each other. The only way we could be closer is if I was buried inside her. I moan at the thought as I kiss her neck. It also pushes my other hand the rest of the way, until I'm cupping her amazing tits.

Fuck, I missed her body.

As I move to cover her mouth with mine again, it isn't just desire or lust, growing in me—it's need. It burns, almost to the point of pain. So without thinking I pull back enough to utter what I know I shouldn't.

"I need you," I whisper with my lips still against hers.

I regret the sound a moment later, wondering if it will break the spell we've been under.

I could fucking kick myself when she pauses.

She pulls back a little more, just enough to look into my eyes. I can see the searching in hers. She's looking for something, maybe the truth. She blinks those longs lashes a few times, and I start to wonder if she's going to say anything at all. So I move to close the distance again, but she stops me, holds me up with firm hands.

Never looking away from me, she takes a shaky breath and starts. "You're my one-who-got-away."

I've always labeled her the same. But it's different to hear it reciprocated, out loud.

A sigh escapes.

I consider sitting up for the rest, but she doesn't give me time. She pushes on while I'm hovering over her, our faces so close together in this dark room.

"I've thought about you every day since we ended. I keep you close, as one of my best friends, because I can't let you go. If you ran away, I'd find you or die trying," She says. Then something catches at the end, like she's hurting. It all sends me reeling.

She's never been so honest with me, with herself, in the whole time I've known her.

But she isn't done.

"Every guy I've been with since you, every single relationship has crashed and burned because I compare *everyone* to you. No one can measure up next to your memory." She bites her lip and sucks in another jagged breath. "Do you know whose face I see every time I close my eyes when I have someone inside me?" she says.

Fuck.

I shake my head no, too scared to make a sound.

"You," she whispers.

Her words start to speed up then, like if she doesn't get it all out right now then she won't say it at all. And I want her to say it so fucking bad.

"Every time we talk, I wonder what we could have done differently, back then, to have saved or fixed us. So don't tell me *you* need *me*, because you don't know what need is. I know what need is. I feel it every day."

She finally pauses for air, and my heart breaks a little when she looks away to add the part I know is hardest for her to say, "I need you." Until then, her eyes were locked on mine the entire time, and now they're across the room, trying to protect herself. It hurts so fucking bad to know that the protection she thinks she needs is *from me*.

I have no idea what to say.

How can she tell me I don't know what need is? I feel it creeping into my chest and leaking through my veins. I feel the cord starting to form again, connecting her heart to mine, like they were strung together before.

I drop her hip to move and grab her chin. I lift it, like before, until she's looking at me again.

But then she closes her lids, like she can't look at me and hear my words at the same time. That hurts worse than before, but I push through it. I have to be honest. I have to let it all out.

"Ever since I fucked it all up, I've known I was your biggest mistake. I was the problem. I'm the black mark smudged in the pages of your past. But I don't want to be a mistake any more. I know what I lost, and losing it showed how important it was, you were, to me all along." She opens her eyes just when I start to lose hope that my words could be enough. And the movement, the eye contact, has me continuing when I might have stopped otherwise. "I may have been your mistake, but you were *never* mine. Not ever. I'd do anything to correct that mistake, to make sure you couldn't live without me. Because, the truth is, I don't want to live without you anymore."

She blinks. And as her eyes flutter several times, her mouth falls open. But I don't give her time to answer. I keep going.

"You're fucking crazy if you think I don't know need. Need is the ache right here," I let go of her chin to touch my chest with my fist. "I wasn't kidding. I've needed you. I need you now. I'll always need you, even if I didn't let myself feel it before. It was always there."

Can't get any more truthful than that. But as she considers, killing me with anticipation with every second ticking by, I'm not sure it's enough for her. And can I blame her after so many years?

Finally she narrows her eyes, and I prepare myself for the worst.

Whatever she has to say could be horrible; it could break my soul right here. And then Theo would be right. I think I'm ready, even for something awful, but I hold my breath as she opens her mouth to answer.

Then she shocks me when she smirks and says, "Prove it."

Taryn
Now

I have no fucking clue how I expect him to prove it, but after that embarrassing outpouring of hopeful shit I just let out, he'd better make it good. I was just trying to convince myself the other day that love doesn't exist. So how could I let those private thoughts out?

This is why I hate feelings.

Starting to squirm, wanting to get away from this whole situation, I regret it a little. I don't know why I said everything I did. Maybe it's the nostalgia, maybe it's the weed; I don't know. But feeling like this, so exposed, is starting to make me edgy. I almost feel like jumping up and going for a run or maybe breaking a bunch of glass. So I start moving, trying to get out from under him, but Austin stops me.

His face is soft as he raises his eyebrow.

"How do you want me to prove it? Name it. I'll call Skyler right now and tell her it's over."

"Don't," almost squeaking I say it so fast, so panicked.

It was her name that did it, reality crashing in with a side of anxiety. We've been broken up for years. There's a reason way back there why we split up before. Plus he has a girlfriend. He's had lots of girlfriends. We've both fucked other people since we had each other. And he's never once begged for me back, but he's had plenty of time. One phone call, one conversation, one kiss isn't going to erase years of mistakes and pain.

And...and after all this time. After all of the back and forth. After all of the longing and dysfunction, after all of it for so many years—now that it's finally happening, I'm not convinced I'm ready. I want to be. I think I could be. But in this moment, I'm terrified of being ready. Or maybe I'm scared of finally giving myself over, only to have it fail again.

So I need proof. I need more than words.

He sits up then, and when his body heat leaves mine, I feel icy. He looks crushed with a heavy disappointment. The pain in his eyes pierces me; it's so clear. And then it's everywhere, expanding throughout his whole frame, as he coils with fresh tension. I feel even colder, watching him retreat inside himself and move a few inches away from me as I sit up too. There's nothing hopeful left in the room, nothing warm at all.

Maybe I am frozen, starting with my heart. Maybe I'm just a cold bitch.

Or maybe I'm just not explaining this right.

"I don't mean don't. Or, I mean I do. Ugh, I'm not saying any of this right." I talk into my lap again, looking at my fingers as they strain and twist around each other. "Maybe I just need time to trust again," I add. It's soft, tentative.

"Tell me how to get that back. I'll do anything," Austin says. He sounds deflated, and I look up at him. The pain is erased from his face, and on instinct I reach out to cup his scruffy cheek, wanting to keep seeing hope in his eyes.

He deserves a chance. And maybe so do I.

He's not going to like my offer, though. I know him.

"Stay with Skyler. Sleep in her bed at night, if you have to, but prove to me I'm *more* important still, even then. Come to me when you need. Be honest with just me. Then, only when I've become the most important part of your world, despite all the other distractions and options, then I'll trust my heart in your hands again. Then we can be together, completely and the right way."

His face shows total confusion. I don't know how to explain it right, how to make him understand. But I need to try.

When I look at him again he opens his mouth to question or protest.

"Wait," I say, pleading, and I move my fingers to his lips to stop him so I can finish.

"Start me as your dirty secret. Come to me only when you feel overwrought with that need you think you feel, and let us grow until I'm *all* you need."

He still doesn't get it as his eyes dart between mine, so I try one last time.

"Nurture something ugly, something almost beyond repair, until it's something beautiful and special." I hold both sides of his face willing him to get inside my head and pull out what I mean in a way that he understands. He smiles, but I don't allow myself to yet. "Bring us from this, messed-up and ugly as usual…to something special again, something beautiful. Because if we can make it through this, through all the bad, then there's something worth fighting for here. Make me believe in *that*, in our going from plan B to the only plan there ever was."

"Done," he says.

His one word is a promise.

A promise I hope he can keep.

****

Austin leaves before Maicy wakes up, just before the sun comes up.

And I hold firm to another decision made, letting it sink in as I lie in bed after he gets a ride home. We can't just be fucked up on one end. We both brought problems into the mess we had before. We've been a shit-show for so long, true, but not just because of him. It was always because of me too. So we need to be messy on both sides now, both of us having an alternate we could turn to in order to see if we really do chose each other in the end. I have to prove to myself the same thing that I'm asking him to prove to me.

I need to see us change from as bad as it gets to as good as it can be.

Plus, I don't think I'm ready to let go of the other yet.

So I texted Theo as he sat in my driveway, watching Austin walk from my house toward him.

Me: Come over after you drop him off. Don't say anything about us to him. Just come back to my bed.
Me: Through the front door.
Theo: You sure?

He sends the message as Austin opens his passenger side door.

Me: Yes.
Me: Will you?

I watch his face from my bedroom window, not knowing if it'll be enough, knowing I'm asking too much. His eyes hold me, and, though it's too far to tell, I imagine there are a hundred emotions flashing inside those eyes. He looks down as he shifts the truck into reverse without answering.

I close my eyes, so disappointed. I pushed too far, too hard.

I used him without giving enough back.

But then he looks up again, right at me, and he nods. Just two chaste dips of his chin while he stares at me. No text. No smile. But it's still a yes. So I get what I want in the end. Again.

It hasn't been long, but my brain's been on overdrive since they left. So I almost miss the front door creaking open again. But when I do hear it, I breathe easier, which is weird. It opens then closes as I sit perfectly still. I didn't smoke after Austin left, and I'm surprised my anxiety isn't spiking worse right now. I don't think I've ever been sober with Theo.

God, that's shitty.

I keep still on top of the covers, eyes open, as he walks though the hall toward me. I won't close them this time. He isn't stepping lightly like Austin did; there's no sneaking now, and I like it.

His footsteps sound proud.

Theo walks to my doorway and stops, leaning sideways against the frame. His face isn't as sure as his steps, but that's okay. His light brown hair looks rumpled, almost as if he's been tugging it in frustration while trying and failing to sleep. And maybe he has. His icy eyes look hopeful, but he stands there, unmoving, with his hands shoved into his pockets. I notice the scruff on his face and smile.

"Are you going to come here and fuck me or what?" I hope for a grin, but he keeps his lip between his teeth as he signs. "Well?"

With my head tilted back, examining as I wait, I realize for the first time he's taller than Austin.

"You're not going to like my answer," he says. His voice is so strong, and the depth of it surprises me, making my eyes widen. I pat the bed, and he finally walks over. After sitting, a heaviness to his hesitation, he turns to face me.

His hands go to my hair, and I flash to hours before. Blinking, I shake it off as he puts his forehead to mine before continuing.

"I'll keep it quiet. You know, for you I'll do anything. But I'm not screwing you right now." My shoulders slump. "I'm making love to you."

I jerk back to look at his face. He's serious. *But I don't make love;* I haven't in a really long time, and he knows that. I start to protest, but his fingers find my lips. Fuck, it's like he can read my mind, reach inside me with psychic feelers to repeat little pieces of what happened not so many minutes earlier. I mean, I know he isn't, but the repetition hits a nerve inside me, helping me soften more than I might otherwise.

"I know, you don't do that. But *I* do. And if you want me right now, if you want us to continue, then that's what you're getting," he says.

I want to be close to someone, to him actually. *I do.*

It might be because I have no idea if Austin will grasp what I asked of him, understand enough to be able to give it to me. If he doesn't, I'll lose him completely, as my hope and as my friend. If that happens, I need this to fall back on. Or it could be something else.

So I nod, still watching him. And the light in Theo's eyes appears then.

I frown in response, knowing I'm going to stomp his heart to shards. Either way, I can't be what he deserves. If Austin does break down my walls and claims me, then Theo won't stand a chance. But on the other hand, if Austin fails, I'll be worse off than I am now, so I'll surely push Theo away too. He loses here no matter what.

But he does want me now. He's always seen who I am, the real me on the inside, and somehow he accepts it, always coming back for more. So I'll let him get close, for whatever time we have anyway.

I know it'll screw up my heart, and my head, even more but fuck it.

My eyes fix on Theo's lips as an invitation. That's all he needs. He leans forward, slow but steady. His hands touch the corners of my mouth, smoothing out the frown still there. Then he closes the rest of the gap.

His kiss is so different from Austin's.

This one is deliberate and supple, and though it deepens with passion, it never speeds up. I try to keep my eyes open as much as I can, and I don't stop the sounds from escaping. I let go. I fall into the moment.

It's better than anything we've had yet.

One freak tear falls from my eyes, and I scramble to swipe it away before he can notice. It would crush him to know that it's because I'm focused on how screwed up and confused I am. I worry I'll be like this forever; even with a good man here against me, inside me, I can't focus or be a good person.

It's hard to let go completely again after that, but I do my best. I run my fingers over his skin as he touches and moves with me, our hearts in sync. His rhythm, his desire to prove himself to me, helps me to give in—to him, to the moment—altogether.

When he's inside me, with his hands holding my face and his lips to mine, I say the right name, "Theo."

And afterward, after it's all over and we're both gasping for air, he tucks me into him. Theo's wrapped around me, holding me, and still I think of the web, the tangled mess I've started weaving.

Austin
Now

I don't even remember most of the ride home with Theo. He didn't say a word the whole time, I don't think. Though I do remember seeing his knuckles white as bone on the steering wheel, but that's about it. He's still pissed off, but whatever.

And then I got home; stood in the parking lot as Theo sped out of there as fast as he could. I must have walked inside the building and up to my apartment, unlocked the door, and gotten into bed. But I don't recall any of it. I don't know if it was the booze, the green, or my elation over having Taryn back in my life. Or some heady combination of all three.

Now I'm laying here, on top of the comforter.

I keep staring at the ceiling, blinking sometimes, but unable to sleep. I haven't at all yet, and I don't think I will. Skyler is up and moving around the living room. Lazy Sundays for her start at nine. To be honest, I was just glad when she got up and left me alone in here. I didn't want to be near anyone, really, but most of all her. It seemed better after she left at first, but then she annoyed me with each sound she made out there. I guess she could tell. She closed the door for me a while ago.

Then I almost felt bad.

When I got home and into bed next to her, she didn't ask what I'd done all night with Theo; she didn't badger or pressure me. She just moved over, snuggling into me. Her blind trust was a hard pill to swallow. Harder than I guessed it would be. But even with that guilt, I wanted to push her away again, until Taryn's words echoed in my head. *Stay with Skyler. Sleep in her bed at night, but prove to me I'm more important.* Letting go of Skyler right away, right now, isn't what she wanted. It would be too easy. I have to get her trust in her way. So I let Skyler lie on my chest as my heart pinches a little more with each beat.

I'd like to be able to say that my heart hurt for her, for what I was doing to her. But that would be a lie. It was wounded for me. I was with the wrong girl; I was tangled up in the wrong limbs. And it still hurts to hear Taryn's voice in my head saying, *Start me as your dirty secret.* So many emotions flooded through me with those words. It had been hard not to get up and leave or collapse in on myself. Why can't she just do things easy? Ever.

I wanted to tell the world she's mine again, hold on to her forever without letting go.

But Taryn's wants are first now. They should have always been. That's is why I'm on board. Everything her way, for her, always. And fuck if it isn't going to get messy and confusing before it will have the chance to get good.

But fine.

Now with Skyler out of bed, a different problem still lingers. I can't sleep. I should be crashing hard. I've been up for something like twenty-four hours, but my brain won't shut off long enough. Every time I close my eyes, I see Taryn. I keep thinking about what just happened, and what could happen if I don't fuck up. I try to stop myself, but I play out, fantasize about, the possible future.

I get stuck on old memories. Memories I kept hidden in a locked and almost forgotten box in a dark corner of my mind. There were so many other boxes piled on top, it may as well have been in the trash. But now they're back, pulled to the front and lying open, playing like movies on the big screen in my head, looped on repeat, and so fucking vivid.

She, and this, may be the undoing of me.

Maybe my resistance is what's keeping me awake. Maybe I just need to allow myself to be engulfed by thoughts of Taryn before I can fall asleep.

Austin

Before

Taryn sits on my lap with her hand in my hair. She strokes it, on autopilot, and I could fall asleep, it feels so fucking good. She's reading a book of poetry by someone I've never heard of. I'm watching TV. And even though we aren't exactly interacting, it's as intimate as if we were naked.

When I think she's particularly engrossed in her prose, I try to just watch her without her noticing. Her emotions play out on her face, and it's so beautiful. Taryn's always worn everything about her on her sleeve—her feelings, her thoughts, she's so expressive—and well, on her face. Every muscle in her body is connected to her feelings. It's one of the things I love about her.

There's the word again.

I've known for a few weeks that I'm in love with her, but I still haven't said it out loud.

I'm such a chickenshit.

But she's always been so anti-love and anti-romance, I've been terrified she'll laugh at me, or worse yet, she'll run screaming from what we have if I say the big bad "L" word. It was hard enough just getting her to date me, and that came without promises, without forevers. Love is different. Love is longer, and it scares the shit out of her. I know it, even if she's never said that. She has so many walls built up, I'm lucky I've gotten this close. I've knocked some down, but I have so many more to go.

For the millionth time, I think about what made her so hard, so scared to share her heart. I wish she'd tell me more, open up.

And for the four millionth time, I hope I never make it worse.

Because I could. And I have. I've done it to others before. I've been the thing that builds walls up too many times before.

I tuck her hair behind her ear and kiss the base of her neck, and I'm rewarded with a little sound, sending my nerves, my heart, my breath sprinting. Her skin is so gorgeous, and the curves of her shoulder and neck are impossible to ignore. Taryn drops her book behind the chair we're sharing and leans into my lips.

She tastes like a rain shower.

"How am I supposed to stay brilliant if you keep distracting me from reading?" She laughs after finishing, and I'm amazed, again, by how addicting the sound is. Pretty much everything about her amazes me.

I don't want to, but I let my lips leave her sweet skin to answer. "You'll never lose your brilliance." I snake my hand inside her shirt and draw the lightest touch across her side, bringing out the laughter I love.

Love.

Damn it.

"Make me happy," she begs. It's her way of asking to make love. The first time she said it, she followed it with, "I'm happiest when I'm with you. *You* make me happy." It was the closest she's ever come to that love word. And even if she wouldn't say it, I felt it.

I don't say anything. I just stand and carry her to the bedroom. Too much talking can scare Taryn, so I do as she asks without explanation. Her weight in my arms feels like a promise, one that should last forever.

I drop to my knees on the bed and lay her down, slow and gentle. But then we undress each other in a frenzy, like there's a time limit and we're racing. In no time, we're naked, and time slows down again as we enjoy each other. We couldn't get any closer, but I always want more. We fit perfectly. Sometimes I wonder if we were made for each other.

Again with the sweet, mushy shit she hates. But I can't help it, I can't get these thoughts out of my head, and the more I try, the more they multiply, pushing harder, trying to get out of my mouth.

Too soon I'm close to finishing. Taryn lets out a little squeal, and she clenches everywhere. It's my undoing. My eyes screw shut and incoherent words flow from my mouth. I'm not sure what all I say, but I know once my brain starts working again something really, really fucking stupid slips out.

"Taryn, I love you."

And then I freeze, petrified.

Austin
Now

After I let myself fall into the memory, I sink into sleep fast. Taryn *was* the answer. I should have known.

And I sleep for a long time.

I hear Skyler come in and out of the room, checking on me, a few times. I don't invite her to stay, and I don't even acknowledge her presence. I just try to get back into dreamland where I'm with Taryn.

Eventually, though, I force myself to get up and face the reality I'm in right now.

It's dinner when I drag my ass down the hall. Skyler looks pretty in her pink top and cheerful smile. But suddenly pretty is miles short of stunning. She used to be so much, and now it's just not enough.

Skye hops up to plant a kiss on my cheek.

"You hungry, sleepyhead?" she asks, and it sounds too high-pitched. I try to swallow down my misplaced anger. This isn't how I'm supposed to be doing this. But I never did multitask well.

"Sure, babe," I say. Then I sigh.

She doesn't seem to notice anything different. Either she's a little slow or she can tell and she's just hiding it well. I hope it's the former.

We have a quiet meal and watch TV together. That's it. It's plain, boring, but I don't mind. We don't touch much, but we don't argue, and I don't intentionally move away from her. So there's that, at least.

We just coexist in the same space for a few hours. But those few hours are all I can take. After too long my skin starts to feel tight and scratchy.

I know what's begging to be itched, and I can't wait any longer.

I pull out my phone.

Me: I need you.

Taryn

Now

I slept for a few hours in Theo's arms. I can't remember the last time I've done that, with anyone. But I did this morning. And it felt good. So good. But when I woke up, everything came flooding back in, and I did something horrible, something unthinkable for me.

So stupid.

I started crying while Theo held me. A little pinprick of pain—a tiny, black dot of hollow nothingness—started to pierce my composure. It spread then, and soon I felt covered in darkness, overtaken by it. I was reduced to my every flaw, my every mistake, and it hurt to breathe. I turned to Theo, to his forgiving nature, to his strong and warm arms, and I sobbed. I tried to let my problems fall out through my tears, but with every shaky breath, I felt worse.

I do not cry, as a rule, if I can help it. And never in front of *anyone* but Maicy anymore.

But today I did. And Theo could hear the terror and the pain in my cries. I know he could because he didn't say a word. He didn't try to comfort me or say stupid things like, "It'll be okay."

He wrapped me up in security, void of judgment, and stayed silent.

The sad sounds I made were foreign, and it felt like I was falling apart. Only he wouldn't let the pieces come all of the way unglued. He held my shit together by a string. It may have been thin, but he didn't let it fray.

It was a new experience for me, and being that vulnerable, that raw, was horrifying. I can't take it back now though. Theo will forever know what the worst of me looks like. And he didn't run while I soaked his chest with tears.

In all of that, after coming back to see me, after pushing me to do more than just let him fuck me, and then holding me through my break down…he proved he's a worthy distraction. Better yet, he's the *perfect* complication. A welcome one.

It couldn't get messier. And that's what I wanted.

After I calmed the hell down and Theo left, I spent my day doing the things I've neglected. I finished chores I hate, did errands I like even less, had lunch with my parents; I kept myself busy. It was hard, but I did my best not to think about Austin, Skyler, Theo, love, sex, or the future. Any of them; all of it.

Who am I kidding, it was fucking impossible. But I let the thoughts through as little as possible. My filter got better throughout the day.

Well, until my phone starts buzzing on the counter as my arms are wrist deep in dishwater. I ignore it at first, trying to continue with the work that needs doing if I want to continue eating like a human adult. But then the sound starts along with the vibration, and it's the ringtone I have set for both Austin and Theo—which, actually, could be a problem real soon. I dry off as fast as I can, trying so hard not to wish more for one or the other.

Austin: I need you.
Me: Show me.

Fuck, I'm so back and forth. Plus, maybe I'm a horrible person. But I try to remind myself, that's what this whole test is about, getting past this awfulness into something better, something worth having and showing off. And it's true; I'm honestly testing both of us.

I finish the dishes quick, then speed through a shower. I don't give myself any more time to worry about the inevitable. I've thrown myself into this, and it's time to face whatever will happen.

While I'm still in a towel, there's a knock at the door. The anxiety I didn't let in before now waterfalls down from my brain, in a rush, all the way to my toes. It's quick and forceful, almost enough to knock me over. But instead of falling down or running away, I clutch the top of my towel and move to the entryway, shuffling. I stop a few feet short of the door. Once there, I can't move anymore though.

My throat feels dry, rough, when I call out, "It's open."

I must have been too quiet; I have to say it twice more before he reacts. When he does, he turns the knob so slowly, it makes my whole body ache, twitching from the anticipation. The door creaks open an inch before he pauses.

Then I get some of my normal attitude back. "I said it's open, but if you don't get your ass in here, I'm going to take the offer back."

That gets him to react.

He shoves himself through the door so fast, he runs right into me. With too many limbs tangling, and a rush of excitement, we topple to the floor together. My ass takes the brunt of the impact on the tile.

"Fuck me," I grumble. Definitely *not* how I pictured this night starting.

Austin laughs before looking to me with an emotion I can't quite place. His dark eyes don't tell me what he's feeling. That kills me. I'm supposed to be the hard one to figure out. And without an explanation, he twirls my wet hair around his finger; then he tucks it behind my ear. But I shrug his arm away. I don't want the stereotypical movie bullshit.

"I want real," I say in response to the sudden pain in his eyes. It wasn't a rejection. It was a request for more, for better.

"This has always been real for me." He shoves himself up onto his elbows. "I never faked anything. Not once. Never with you." But with others—I know he finished the thought in his head. And I hear the honesty in his voice. It's too scary to answer, so I just nod as he helps me to my feet.

"I still think you owe me after that tackle." I say, trying to fix the soured mood. I twist my towel between tense fingers, wishing I'd taken one more minute to dress—I feel extra exposed this way, almost worse than if I'd answered the door naked.

"Anything," Austin says.

There's longing in his voice.

"Foot rub," I say then wink. "While we watch whatever I pick." He smirks. There's no trace of annoyance left anywhere on his face. I wanted to get a rise out of him, so I keep pushing. "You might need me, but I need foreplay," I say as he follows me to the couch. Always the couch.

I immediately regret the joke, and my smile drops from my face as soon as I'm not facing him anymore, leading the way to the living room. It was supposed to be funny, but now it feels like I put a whole lot of unnecessary pressure onto the situation, into the room, to sit right on my stupid fucking shoulders.

I still hear his footsteps behind me, though, so he hasn't changed his mind. Yet. He clears his throat right before I sit down. Then he says, *"Anything* you need," and there's an emphasis on the first word that I'm not ready to examine.

"Then get to rubbin', big man," I say, trying to lighten my own mood more than the atmosphere. If I wanted serious, I could just have Theo over for another breakdown. No, this isn't about my vulnerability, it's about Austin and if he's enough, if together we're enough. "Time to put up or shut up," I add.

"I think I'll do both." He winks at me as I throw my feet into his lap and look for something to watch. I don't take special care to keep my towel tight as I lie back and let him comfort me. It's an oddly intimate feeling, but I try not to fight it like instinct wants me to.

I let my head fall back. I'd forgotten how attentive Austin is. It's a giving experience on his part, and at some point, I stop trying to watch

TV. I just feel his hands on my skin. The rough spots are so familiar, and soon I'm breathing deeper, melting into myself. I open my mouth and eyes to say something but stop when I look to his strong arms and notice the tattoo I think about so often.

Taryn

Before

"Y ou assumed wrong, buddy." I cock my eyebrow at Austin, trying so hard not to laugh. I'll never give in, so there's no sense in drawing the debate out with a false sense of flexibility. It's going to be my way or no way.

But he should be used to that by now.

"But, babe…" he whines. He's so fucking cute when he whines, and it's so rare.

Must stay focused, I remind myself.

"Nope. No way." I turn my back, starting to walk toward the door to leave the shop. "I'm serious; it's this or nothing." Okay I feel like a bitch, but he should know by now how damn stubborn I am. I want what I want, and I'm not willing to compromise.

He grabs me at the waist, refusing to let me leave.

"I just want the world to know you're my Queen of Hearts," he says, his voice low. And I hate how it starts to creep its way into my resolve. "You're the queen of my heart," he adds.

Well, shit.

But no. *No.* I couldn't live every day being reminded my king left if we ever split up. Call me pessimistic, call me a realist, I don't give a shit what anyone calls me, but nothing lasts forever. And if he leaves I cannot—abso-fucking-lutely cannot—have the sad truth shoved in my face, by my own skin, that he's the best I'll ever have. These walls are made of unbreakable shit for a reason. I can't have my own ink mocking me when he isn't here to hold me. I won't willingly add to my own baggage.

So fuck his whining.

I need to be honest; it's the one thing that works with him. But I'll just be honest about the unselfish parts. So I keep my voice low and answer.

"I need you to remember you're the king of my universe." I take a breath. That hurts to admit. It fucking stings, a lot.

He grabs my other side and spins me to him. The happiness in his eyes makes the stupid emotional crap worth it. I lean in and tell him the things I can't say out loud, with my lips against his instead. But I let one last argument slip out to seal the deal

"You will always reign over my heart. I don't want you to ever forget that. You get the K." I say it with his hands still in my hair, as his chest rises against me.

"You win." He drops my hips and grabs my hand, twisting his fingers between mine to pull me over to the chair.

"It's gonna hurt, baby, so squeeze as hard as you need," he adds, looking like he'll feel worse than I do, just watching. The worry is written all over him, and it's kind of a turn on.

He's warned me so many times about the pain. Then he always follows it up with how fast it will be over since we picked little designs. It's my first tattoo though, so he's freaking out. The idea of me in pain scares him. That's laughable. By this point I'm pretty much numb to it. The actual pain these needles will cause should be refreshing. They'll remind me I'm still here.

I'm here with Austin.

Austin

Now

"I think it's the stupidest thing you've ever done," Theo says, trying to hide his anger behind a turned head and eyes looking anywhere but at me. "Just saying."

He refuses to listen to anything about Taryn. He's against my seeing her at all, and when I tried to explain that we haven't done anything but kiss yet, he all but punched me to shut me up. He was short through the rest of dinner. It made me regret opening up at all.

Before, he always liked her when no one else did. I never understood that, but it resulted in my cutting friends out of my life. Not Theo, though. He always stood by me, by Taryn, and stood up for her. Even if it was because he knew her first, it mattered more to me than he'll ever know.

So it's fucking annoying that, as the pieces come together now for me to try again, he's changed his mind.

"You haven't given me one reason why though." I trust him, but I trust myself more. I just wish my best friend was willing to see my side. "Can't you at least try to hear it out? Or fucking pretend?"

"No." His jaw muscles flex, and his eyes harden. I've known him too long to try to push anymore. So I give up, leading the way to my car, quiet now. I'll do it anyway, without approval or support.

His feet stomp behind me, letting out a little misplaced aggression, I imagine. He seems fine by the time we get into the car, but as we close our doors he adds, "The past is the past for a reason. When you replay it, it's easy to gloss over the hard parts in the movie that was your relationship, but that doesn't make them exist any less. They still happened. You still ended. *There's a reason.*"

I have no response.

I want to scream at him, hit him, storm out of my own car.

But I know his heart is in the right place, and he isn't *all* wrong. I fucking hate that any of those words could be true, but some are. Taryn and I will never make it if we don't address the shit that broke us up last time. But before I can have that conversation with her, I still need to gain enough trust to talk about it at all.

One step before the other.

"Okay, okay. Last time we talk about it," I say.

Theo nods, his eyes never leaving the windshield. He's allowed to have his own opinion and his own feelings. I'm realizing I may not want to hear about them. It's probably better to skip the heart-to-hearts for a while, until he sees my side or until Taryn and I are a legitimate couple, together again, and he can't say anything.

This was not the afternoon I anticipated having after work. I imagined more beers, more laughing.

We go to the gas station, and Theo gets out of the car while I fill up. He slams the door without a word, his hands deep in his pockets as he walks inside. Leaning against my car, I watch while the cents and dollars increase on the ticker in front of me, and I try hard to let go of his words. It's tough. I don't want to care about what he thinks, what he says. As I walk inside, still ruminating, I remind myself he's never known Taryn like I do, and that helps. He's biased—he's clueless—so I feel better when I get to the counter.

As I get there, I see Theo paying for condoms.

"What the fuck, dude? Who?" I jab him with my elbow and smile as he turns. I haven't seen Theo bring home anyone from the bar in months. I can't remember when he last had a girlfriend…maybe a year or more? I haven't heard a word about any action. "You've been holding out on me."

He shoves the box in his back pocket and shrugs. "You never asked," he says so flatly, it could have been someone else talking.

Now *I* feel like the shitty friend. "You didn't volunteer either. And I'm asking now."

"Always be prepared." He smirks and walks past me, outside.

I pay as fast as I can and jog after him. "That's the worst answer ever," I say, prodding.

"Well, it's the only one you're gonna get," Theo says. And just like that, the conversation's over. Like he ended the last one. He does it again.

Sneaky fucker.

We get into my car, and I rev the engine, grinning at him. He'll spill *at some point.*

****

A few hours later, Skyler, some of her friends, Theo, and I all sit at my kitchen table with drinks in front of us and a deck of cards strewn everywhere. None of us has to work tomorrow, which pretty much never happens. So we took advantage, with lots of booze. We tried playing a drinking game, but I got frustrated when the girls couldn't focus enough to understand or follow the rules. So then we abandoned the idea and just put on a movie, taking a drink every time a name was said.

It worked.

We're all smashed. I don't even know what movie we're watching, but they say first names *a lot.*

And in my lap, my left hand fidgets. I won't let go of two cards from the deck, red ones. I pick at the corners, peeling apart the layers with my thumb.

When the girls get up to blend more fruity drinks, I lean in to Theo. "Whatcha think about Natasha?" I lift my chin toward the general direction of the kitchen. "She's nice. Pretty cute too," I add.

He shakes his head and downs the rest of his beer. "Not interested."

I know he wants me to let it go, but he's shut down way too many conversations already today. I'm not letting shit go this time. "Why not? She's got a great body, she's not a bitch, and you're prepared." I can feel myself getting angry, and I try to suppress it, but it's a little hard with the booze swimming in my system. And fuck me if I don't keep going. "You said yourself earlier you're not *with* anyone." I narrow my eyes, begging him to tell me the truth. But I get nothing back. "So what's the fucking problem? You've never been scared of pussy before, dude. Unless there's more you're not telling me."

The challenge hangs between us as the blender whines and the girls giggle, having no idea what tensions fill the room out here. It starts to get unbearable, suffocating. So I slam my fist onto the table, letting go of my hearts.

"Okay, you win," he says, putting his hands up, breaking our eye contact.

And with his words, it's like he flips a switch, every trace of anger gone. Theo shrugs and cracks open another beer, standing to face the kitchen. His eyes are the only feature to give much away, just a hint about how much he'd like to break my jaw. As he passes me, walking toward Natasha, he leans over a little to say, "Don't *ever* pretend again that I'm the only one with secrets."

I sit a little stunned, enough to stare for a while at the group in the kitchen before getting up, before doing anything. He couldn't have threatened me to leave his personal life alone… Could he? That's so not what friends do. It's not how he's *ever* acted, not towards me. Then Natasha's laugh breaks me from my thoughts. I focus again, and Theo's arm is around her waist as they stand together talking with Skyler and her friends.

I stand, telling myself I'll be a better friend from now on, trying not to wonder how many times I've said that throughout my life. And I head to the kitchen. Sitting by myself will get me nowhere. I'll just want to go see Taryn, and with Theo here, I can't dip out.

Not yet, at least.

"What's so funny, kitten?" I snake my arm around Skyler's back when I get to the group. It feels stiff, but it's the best I'll be able to do. I try to mirror Theo's comfort, his ease and charisma, with someone I'm assuming he has little interest in and with the entire situation. I get close, at least, but he's a good actor. I never knew that before.

I keep my eyes on Natasha. Her blonde hair falls almost to Theo's arm around her. Her eyes are big, but they seem a little empty, like there isn't much going on inside, behind them. Her complex emotions are limited, but her smile is big. I was right; she's nice.

Skyler's nice too. Pretty and nice. But she's not Taryn.

I wonder who Natasha isn't.

Two of Skyler's other friends, blonde Barbie carbon copies of sweet and simple, chime in to the conversation occasionally. But it's mostly Skyler, Natasha, and sometimes Theo participating. I don't care enough to follow along, so I don't interject either. And my hand starts to feel numb holding onto Skyler. Her laughs start to feel obnoxious, and the comments she makes seem more and more annoying.

There isn't much that could bring me out of my sinking mood.

Taryn
Now

Austin: I need you. Can I come over?

Theo: Don't let him come over. He got you yesterday. Pick me instead tonight.

Well, I hit the nail on the head with aiming for messy and confusing. I hit it over and over with a fucking jackhammer until every piece of it, and what it was nailed into, disintegrated. Obliterated. This is how I do things, I guess. I skip right past normal and move all the way to over-the-top, overdone.

I read the messages on my phone again and again, until I start to panic.

It gets a little hard to breathe, and my hands can't stop moving. I work tomorrow, so I know I shouldn't, but I pound two shots and light up. Maybe I'll call in. At least I don't have to be there till later. I stow the booze right away, but I leave out the green for any break-through nerves.

The texts came in almost synchronized, and I have this picture in my head of Theo, obnoxious and leaning over Austin to see what he's texting me, like he's copying answers on a test. The thought helps a little. It's the first thing to make me laugh all day. Work sucked, and then shit like this makes me question my sanity. I don't really know why I thought juggling all of this would lead to any sort of happy possibility. I mean, I do. I do; I know why. But I guess I just thought it would be easier for me, only hard on them, on him.

I still haven't answered either. But that's because I don't know what that the fuck to do. I know I'll say something. I can't leave them wondering. There's a tug coming from somewhere deep inside, and when I'm honest about the feelings—though they don't make total sense to me—that tug is telling me I want to see *both*.

So I take a breath, and then that's how I answer, with the truth.

I let myself fall farther down the rabbit hole, giving in to everything I want.

Me: If you need me, then prove it...with more than a foot rub tonight.
Austin: Heading over now.

Me: You knew what you were getting into. You can walk away any time and I'd understand. Completely. He's coming over. But I want to see you after. If you will, I'd like you to spend the night again.
Theo: Tell me when, and I'll be there.

After I set my phone down, I light up like my life depends on it. Maicy comes out of her room, shaking her head at me, her new brown low-lights apparent, while I puff out smoky clouds, one after another.

I told her the truth about everything earlier today. She said that while she wouldn't put herself in the position I have, she understands. That straight-up blew me away. My brain stopped working for a second, I was so shocked. And even if she lied, it helped. Why she'd understand now but didn't earlier when it was less complicated, I seriously don't get. But I'm not arguing. I crushed her in a hug that surprised us both.

Of course, she couldn't help but say something about Theo being far superior before letting the conversation end. But *that* I expected. I know it won't be the last time she mentions it either. That's okay though.

I only have time to smoke a little more before Austin shows up in a cab. I check the time, thinking I must be wrong; it only took a couple minutes to get here.

"I'm going out, babe," Maicy says on her way to the front door. "Good luck," she adds with a smirk and flick of her bangled wrist.

At the door, looking through the glass, I watch as they pass each other. Both nod, and neither utters a word out loud. It's weird, and I bite my bottom lip. I'm thankful, at least, that Austin didn't have Theo drive him here again.

The final thing going through my head before opening the door is Skyler. I could fucking bash my head into the wall, but I wonder if she wonders where Austin disappears to. I wonder if it would kill her to know that he's coming here to try and prove I should let him back in my heart. I wonder how I could let this happen to another girl, knowing what it feels like. I know her relationship isn't my responsibility, but still.

I wonder how low I'll sink before finding the bottom.

But I don't have time to worry about it anymore when I open the door and his smile gives me butterflies. Real, stupid, fucking butterflies, like idiotic kids get. It wipes every anxiety away, at least, and for that I'm grateful.

"You seem to need me a lot," I say, teasing and adding a flutter of my eyelashes.

Austin steps inside and hangs his head to take off his shoes. It seems like such a normal thing to do, but it makes me feel weird. It's too considerate. When he stands again and looks at me, he's wearing a frown. I take a step back, not prepared for whatever he's about to say.

"I told you, I always need you." His dark eyes convey how much he means it as they search mine. I nod and walk out of the entryway, not knowing how to respond, not in any sort of appropriate way, at least.

My head still feels light, and my body tingles from both the bowls I packed into a few minutes. But they're also pushing me forward. I turn into my bedroom, instead of toward the living room, and close my eyes. Like an idiot, I stand facing my bed with my back to the door, seeing nothing, just listening, unmoving.

My chest tightens; maybe anticipation can cause a heart attack.

"Are you sure?" Austin presses his chest to my back, running his palms down my arms. Then it's hard to stand still, well, to even stay standing at all.

I breathe three times, unhurried, letting my skin crackle where he touches it, before answering. Again, I let my instincts answer for me, saying what I feel deep down. "Tonight, I need you too." He knows it's a yes, despite the word never leaving my drying mouth.

He lets go of my arms, and I open my eyes after a moment, thinking he left. But it's not footsteps I hear behind me. Then his shirt hits the floor, and before I can turn to him, he's in front of me. Austin kneels on the end of my bed, facing me now. He reaches out and curls his fingers around my shoulders. My breath hitches, and I inhale twice, in a stutter, before letting any air back out.

Austin pulls me down on top of him, and we're kissing like it's our first time. There's some hesitation and a little bit of awkwardness, but we get through it. I find myself a little disappointed a few times for a second or two, thinking it should be smoother. We're passionate, and there's a desire there that comes from deep inside us both, but there's also an expectation that's a little too high. We haven't done this in years; I should've realized there would be kinks to work out.

The first time we slept together, the very first time, we fell on the floor. I sprained my wrist, though I didn't realize that until later. So at least this isn't *that* bad. But, in my haze of inebriation, I thought it would be perfect.

I forgot, perfect doesn't exist.

After we get though the weird moments, I am glad we didn't let it stop us.

When he pushes into me, I cry out. I clutch at his back, keeping him pressed against me when he tries to kiss me, not wanting him to see my face. I know I'd give away the mixture of bliss and grief there, and it would crush him. I don't even know the reasoning behind each conflicting emotion, but they're both there, fighting it out to be the only one left.

In the end, I'm satisfied. It isn't the most connected I've felt to him, but I don't feel empty or detached afterward either. But Austin may have felt more. His fingers pulled me closer to him, never seeming satisfied, always trying to get more.

I try not to feel too bad.

Next time will be better.

When we're finished, I try to lie still in his arms. I've never been good at just being there, sitting in my vulnerability, but I try. And after a few minutes, he kisses my temple gently and says, "I can't believe you're staying still so long. We should document this as a personal record." I try not to, but it makes me laugh. He hooks a finger beneath my chin and tips my face up to his. He kisses the tip of my nose, then whispers with eyes closed, "I'll always need you."

"Don't make promises you don't know you can keep," I say, countering.

"You're not the boss of me." He grabs my side and tickles me, so I make a fist, narrowing my eyes, and threaten to blacken one of his. "Okay, okay I give." He lifts palms in surrender with a goofy grin, making me even happier we got past the uncomfortable so we could get here. "Who am I kidding, anyway? You've always had me wrapped around that finger." He pulls my hand to his face and kisses the pad of my ring finger. "You've always been the boss," he finishes.

I can't be serious any longer. I can't let every feeling in at once.

So I answer like the smartass I've always been. "As long as we both agree who wears the pants," I say and grab the pillow underneath my head to hit him.

He doesn't budge, and the smirk stays on his face too. It's obnoxious.

"You gotta go home to her, you know," I say. It's the one thing that can deflate the mood. I know he doesn't want to hear it, but it's what he agreed to.

"What if I don't want to?" he asks. The hope in his eyes makes my heart hurt.

Stay strong.

"Then go stay with a friend. Go to a hotel." I shrug. "But you can't stay here. You agreed to the deal." I reach across him to grab his boxers from the floor, and I push them to his chest, trying to make my point. "You haven't proved enough yet. You have to make me feel the same need."

There. Honesty, and me, at the very worst it can get.

I shrug.

"I'm working on it." He smiles and starts to get dressed. He isn't deflated at all like I'd expected. I can't believe he's still smiling; I don't get it. He orders a ride and grins at me the whole time. It's weird.

I feel like I missed something, but I try burying the worry.

Wrapped in a blanket, I walk him to the door. Austin kisses me goodbye, and this time he's smart enough not to make commitments, not to promise anything, about when he'll be over next, or anything else he can't guarantee.

"I'll see you when I see you," I say.

He kisses me again before walking outside, still without response. But he keeps his good mood all the way out. And back in my room, letting my brain make the shift, I text Theo. I should have time to shower and smoke before he gets here.

Me: Wait five minutes then head over.

Austin

Now

When the car drops me off at home, I sit outside on the front steps for way too long, smoking a bunch of cigarettes, just thinking. I light the next one from the end of last, chain-smoking. Really, I know I'm procrastinating, killing time with tobacco and whisky from my flask, trying to numb the things still bristling just under my skin. It's getting harder and harder to sleep next to Skyler when my heart is elsewhere, in another orbit. I'll go inside soon; I swear I will. I only need a break to let everything sink in, to let everything settle down.

I didn't know I'd fall back in love again with Taryn so fast. So hard.

I think I was deluding myself when I'd forgotten how happy she made me.

And falling in love is fucking terrifying. Falling in love with her is like jumping with eyes closed, having no idea how much room you have between you and the ground. Even when we did it the first time, in more normal circumstances, I was scared. This is way worse with so much up in the air. I stand to lose *so* much now.

She's always been worth it, though.

I text her, trying to plant the seed, one I know I need to get growing before I'll get her to fall with me again.

Me: It's cold without you in my arms.

She doesn't answer right away—probably asleep already.

Standing feels impossible, but I do it anyway, to the tune of protesting knees and a little unease. When I get to my apartment door, after snubbing out another cigarette and downing the last two shots of booze I have with me, a sigh escapes my lips as I unlock the door.

I'm instantly bathed in light.

Fuck.

I didn't think Skyler would still be up.

"Hey, baby," she calls without turning to look, her eyes glued to the cartoon movie she's got on. No fucking joke, she's watching a princess movie.

A few weeks ago, that might've been cute.

"Hey yourself, kitten." I hesitate for a fraction of a second before uttering the pet name I gave her ages ago. I used to tell her she was my sex kitten. But now…now I haven't slept with her since going to *just talk* at Taryn's. And I know that was just a few days ago, but it already feels like forever, so much already changed.

"Watching a movie?" I ask the obvious, not knowing what else to talk about.

"Mmm," she says, patting the spot next to her.

I don't want to watch whatever the hell this is, but I know if I don't put in some face time, a little effort, she's going to get pissed or suspicious too quick. I've already been bordering on pushing it. Truth be told, I wouldn't care if she left. But, I know Taryn would. I have to fake it here to get what I want there.

So I do.

"Popcorn?" I ask. Anything to stall until I can crash in bed.

Skyler squeals, clapping her hands, in response.

"I guess that's a 'yes,'" I say, forcing a chuckle afterward and moving over to the kitchen.

As the kernels pop, I check my phone. Three times. And then a fourth as I dump the popcorn into a bowl. Taryn's definitely gone to sleep. It feels a little hollow knowing I won't hear from her again tonight. I don't want to wait until tomorrow.

So I turn the damn thing off as I walk back to the couch. I will *not* obsess.

"Natasha likes Theo," Skyler says, grabbing the bowl as I sit down. She drops her head to my shoulder without ever looking away from the TV. I wonder if she can smell Taryn's perfume. I wonder, but I don't worry about it.

"Oh yeah?"

I choose to drop my hand to her knee instead of wind it around her waist or over her shoulder. This should be enough, still connected for her, but without too much intimacy for me. Even though it's a bunch of analyzing, it feels important somehow.

I might be cheating on Skyler; okay I *know* I am, no might. But I won't cheat on Taryn. *Not again.* It was the biggest mistake of my entire life. And even if I get Taryn back now, I'll never forgive myself for that stupid situation I let myself get into. I'll never forget it, and I'll spend the rest of my life trying to make up for it, now that I have that chance.

And I'm only cheating on Skye now because it's the way to win Taryn back. I cheated a lot before Taryn, a lot. And I did what I thought was my best with her. But it wasn't good enough, not by a long shot. Since then I've started most of my relationships intending not to cheat…but then it happens. Only Taryn could get me to change my worldview. She did before, and I already want to prove that I'm better than I was last time, that I can be the guy she deserves, that I'll never do it again.

"Yeah, she couldn't stop talking about him after you guys left," Skye says, breaking into my thoughts. "She said she's going to ask him out soon. Wouldn't that just be perfect?" She tips her head enough to kiss my arm. I close my eyes, wishing it felt good.

"Perfect how, kitten?"

The name cuts into me, like a paper cut to my heart. Not fatal, but uncomfortable anyway.

"Duh, for double dates," she answers, like I should've read her mind. My eyes narrow at the TV. "My friend dating your friend. *Perfection.*" She smacks her lips, kissing the air, and it's too much for me.

I feel sick after digging up what I did to Taryn. And Skye's not helping my mood. I need to start working more on making up for it rather than stewing in my own shit, I know. So I stand, not thinking to tell Skyler beforehand, jerking her head up hard enough for her teeth to snap together when I do.

But she doesn't whine.

I should feel bad, should say sorry.

"Baby…" she starts, making eye contact for the first time since I got home. The spark that used to be there, the draw between us, it's so far receded, I'm not sure it could ever come back, even if Taryn walked away now. I just tip my head, using the least amount of effort and hopefully eliciting as little from her as possible. "I thought, maybe, we could…" she stops without finishing, eyes big and waiting.

Maybe something flashes across my face that stops her.

Maybe she thinks it would be more alluring to leave it open-ended.

Maybe it occurs to her if she doesn't say it, my rejection will hurt less.

Maybe she thinks I'll ask her to finish.

"I'm sorry, I'm too tired." Her lip juts out, so I add, "I had too much to drink."

She sucks her lip back in to answer. "Okay," she says, barely audible, nodding and trying to hide her disappointment. "I'll go to bed with you still." She grabs my hand, following after me.

I should be thankful I have someone to take care of me, to keep me busy, while I wait.

Taryn

Then

"Don't ever call me again," I say, though I'm not even sure my words are audible.

"But, I…"

"No. You don't deserve one more word. Not a single extra syllable to spew your worthless shit. If it's not a lie, it's pathetic." I hope that stings. "You promised things you couldn't do. You took away some of the protection I took years to build up, and then you broke me. And now I'm exposed. You hurt me worse than anyone else. And fuck you for that." I take in a shaking breath, no remorse. "It will *never* happen again. Do you understand? Not with anyone else and especially not with you."

My own tears fall again; I thought I'd be out of them by now.

"I've never felt worse before, and that's a serious accomplishment because I was always falling apart. So I guess, bravo to you for reaching new levels. I'll be forever changed." I breathe through the sob. "Because. Of. You."

And I hang up the phone on Austin, choking on the pain.

Taryn
Now

I stare off into space, picking at my chipped black polish without actually looking at my nails, sitting and doing nothing at work. Today feels weird. I can't shake the icky feeling that's been clouding everything, hovering over my head, pulling at my shoulder blades.

"Hey, baby girl." I hear my mom's voice before she even comes into view. It's a sound full of scratches and bruises and rattling gravel after so many years of smoking. As many fights as we've had through most of my teenage years, it's still the sound of comfort, of home. And as her face comes into view, the bad feeling disappears.

"Lunch?" I ask as she and my step-dad appear out of nowhere.

They nod, and I stand as she starts talking about her day. I don't even listen, just follow the promise of free food. She shows up once a week, give or take, and we go out to eat as a family. She insisted we start the tradition a couple years ago so we could all try to be closer. And my working for the step-dad made these meals easy to arrange. I thought I'd hate it, feel weird about it the first time we walked to a diner down the street. But even that first time it was just…nice. Weirdly normal. And now it's one of my favorite things most weeks.

Today I don't add much to the conversation, though. My parents are pretty good people, *now*, and I love them, but my brain is away, elsewhere. We eat, she talks, we hug, and she leaves. It's a normal kind of lunch, and after it's done, I remember exactly nothing about it.

After lunch, the rest of work goes by in a haze. I do the same thing I've always done. Muscle memory, repetitive consistency. Having a similar job since high school does have its perks. And here, I have freedom to think about my juggling act, wondering if there's any way I could possibly screw up more lives at once.

At least Maicy is free from the shitstorm that's bound to roll in.

Toward the end of my day, I text Theo.

Me: Just you tonight.
Theo: Promise?
Me: I don't do promises.
Me: But
Me: How about you come over for dinner and a movie at my place first?

The idea feels really weird, stranger than I thought it would, to have Theo over in the daylight hours. It's too domestic, but he does deserve a little more. He deserves a lot more actually, but this is what little I can give. And even this is a concession for me. So I'm trying.

I think he knows it too.

Because he shows up with one sunflower, a bottle of booze, a new glass bowl, and a book. The most perfect gifts I've ever gotten. "My kind of chocolate and flowers," I say.

I smile as Theo walks in, and I have the urge to kiss the corner of his mouth as he brushes his fingers down my arm, the hairs rising from his gentle touch. But I resist. That would be too confusing...for me. For both of us. Plus, he may fall over from the shock of it.

"So what did you make for me? I assume it's all from scratch, took hours to cook."

The teasing in his voice borders on goofy. I hate that I like it.

"I called for delivery. Chinese. That's the max amount of effort you'll ever get out of me," I say.

"I beg to differ. You put in lots of effort. In bed." He squeezes my shoulder as we move to the kitchen. His significant height makes me feel comforted, and I warm next to him. He could wrap me into his chest and hold me there forever.

Bad thoughts.

Don't think those things.

I shake my head, clearing that away.

"Based on both your loud asses, I agree with Theo." Maicy bounces into the kitchen from the living room, her messy bun swaying above the bangs she's apparently decided to grow out. She smiles, opening a white container, sniffing inside, and digging her fingers in to grab a piece of sauce-covered broccoli.

"Sure, get your nasty hands all over everything." Maicy glares at me and does it again. "Girl, I see paint on your wrist; I know they aren't clean. Did you even wash them, Miss O'Keefe?" I shake my head. I shouldn't be criticizing her passion but gross. "Plus, hello, go ahead and just assume I got enough for you too," I say, glaring at her before adding, "Snot."

Maicy tips her heads back and laughs, deep from her belly. That's why I love her. And that's why she'll always be stuck with me, no matter the phase she's in. I'd track her ass down if she ever tried to move on. Some things are unchangeable, no matter what else is going on.

"You love me," Maicy says.

She cocks her eyebrow up, way up, when she realizes Theo's still standing behind me with his hands on my shoulders. I'm all but tipping my head back into the cushion of his body. It feels nice, but I didn't think she'd notice.

I watch her eyes as they assess me, us. Her mascara's thicker than it's been in a while, and the eyeliner's darker; it makes the whole look she's giving me seem menacing. It makes me tense, and I know Theo can feel it as he drops his hands to my lower back, out of sight. But he doesn't take them off me.

"So…are we not talking about how weird all this is?" Maicy asks while drawing a circle in the air with her finger around us. She and I stare at each other for a moment, threats coming from my hazel eyes, and stubbornness screaming back from her green ones. "I mean I'm more than happy to give my opinions." She winks at Theo. "Unless it's the unspoken clown in the room?" she asks.

Cringing, I yell, "Don't say that! Why would you say clown?"

Then we all bust out laughing. She might be too fucking blunt, but at least she cleared the air a little. Neither Theo nor I answer, but we go back to the too-close, too-sweet interaction we'd had before.

"Thank you," I mouth to Maicy.

She winks at me and kisses the air in my direction. *My girl.*

We all grab a carton of our own greasy food and move out to the couch, to the safety of the living room.

"Rock-paper-scissors tourney to pick the entertainment," I suggest.

I don't give a shit if this is living in the past, like Maicy said; it makes me happy.

She and I compete first since Theo, as the guest, should get a fifty-fifty shot. I kick her ass with scissors. But then Theo beats me, and he gets to pick the movie. I don't tell him that I let him win, knowing he'd throw paper. He always threw paper, ever since we were little.

"Gimme the remote," Theo says, wiggling his fingers, demanding.

"Entitled," I reply. I give it over, though. After a few clicks through the cable menu, he lands on the girliest, piece-of-crap chick-flick he can find.

"I hate you." I glare at him, hard.

"Oh shut up, you love me." Theo drops the remote onto the coffee table while he says it, then he freezes. We all freeze. I'm so full of awkward, I feel like I might puke. The apprehension boils inside, ready to pour out and take over the room. When he sits back, he looks like he wants to run.

"No, she loves me most," Maicy says full of confidence, completely nonchalant. Leave it to her to save the day. Again. And as she packs my new bowl with fresh, sticky green, I blow her a kiss of her own. Theo's not a smoker, not much since college, but he sure sucks in a chest-full when Maicy passes it to him after her toke.

I do two hard hits too.

It helps.

After the weed takes effect, the movie isn't half bad. It's actually pretty funny. I forget about Theo's slip up, along with the tension from it, and sink into his side. It was an accident, and I've forgiven far more; we all know that now. It's not even halfway into the movie when I'm tucked under his arm, burrowing into him, and soaking in his smell. The scruff on his chin scratches against the top of my head, while his hand tucks beneath my ass, and my toes under me curl back toward that hand. All of it is more comfortable than I expected.

We each pick at our take out, munchies taking over.

And it's quiet, in a content type of way.

When the movie's over, we start another, and the bowl gets passed around once more. After a few minutes I stand, thinking I'll head to the bathroom and come back, maybe grab the bottle Theo brought on my way. But I quickly I reevaluate. After leaving the warmth of his body, I feel like I've been doused with ice.

So I don't think, letting my body take over. Grabbing his hand with mine, I intertwine our fingers, yanking on his arm.

"Just you," I whisper.

A smirk creeps across his face, excitement in his eyes.

He stands, and we head toward my bedroom with raunchy catcalls from Maicy following us.

Inside my room Theo's arms wrap around my waist and sneak up my shirt. He ducks his chin into the curve where my neck meets shoulder, and I tip my head to give him access to the sensitive skin. After kissing there, he mumbles against my skin, leaving goose bumps, "Only you," he says. "*Always.*"

My hand tugs at his hair, pulling us both to the bed.

****

"Why can't this just be it? Why can't it just be us, like this, always?" Theo asks me in a deep whisper, and I come back from my drift toward sleep. It's jarring and abrupt.

"Don't," I say.

I can't do this right now.

I don't want to at all, for real, but especially not now.

"I'm serious." He sounds so hurt, I have to squeeze my eyes shut until there's pain in them too. Forcing myself to feel what he does, in some kind of way, seems like it'll help me gather my thoughts, maybe say this right.

"So am I. I don't want to talk about this right now. You know me better than…" and I stop myself before I can say anything else I'll regret.

"That's exactly my point." Theo gets up on an elbow; I can feel it even though my eyes are still closed tight. I don't want to look at the grief in his face, the hollow disappointment that I know I'm the cause of.

"I know it is. And you're not wrong, okay? I get it. But I have nothing else to give," I say.

"You act like you're this piece of trash. Like you're some island not meant to be near other people. It pisses me off. It's so far from the truth. You don't let anyone in. I get it, you know I do. But I'm also sick of it." His words hurt, worse than I thought they could.

He leans over, his scent and his warmth blanketing me, and he kisses my temple. But then there's a shift in the bed as he stands. I let my eyes spring open, as a panicky feeling takes me over.

"Wait," I say, louder than I meant.

"That's the problem, Pigeon. I have been waiting. I've been waiting a long time," he says, with a weight in his words that I haven't heard before. "And I'm getting tired of it. I don't know how much longer I *can* wait." He has his boxers back on, his socks too.

My heart lurches again, not wanting him to leave. But I don't know how to say that right.

I don't know how to say *anything* right, I don't think.

"Are you serious?" I shout it. I don't mean to, but I feel a little better after it anyway.

"You know I am," Theo says as he rips his shirt down over his head, anger in his every movement, every breath around us, and the seconds that skip by on fast-forward.

"Come here," I beg.

But he just shakes his head, his pants already back on, and he walks to my bedroom door.

He doesn't leave, though. Theo just stands there with his hands spread out, each one on the opposite side of the wooden frame. Taking a deep breath, I get up and walk over to him. My skin presses into his shirt, and I try to show him what I can't say.

But he stops me, his hands against mine, stilling them against his chest.

"You can't just show me. I need more," he says, quieter.

"Just you," I say again. "Right now, it's just me and you."

It's not enough, I know that. It's not fair, and he has every right to storm out. I can feel the anger still wriggling inside of him. But he turns anyway, and he grabs my face with both of his strong hands.

"I'll fight for you; I'll fight with you if I have to. I'm not scared of you," he says against my lips. Then he moves to my hair as we back up toward my bed again.

But he probably should be.

****

The rest of the week passes by in a blur of held breath, anticipation, and confusing emotions. Both Austin and Theo come over most days. Austin never stays over because of Skyler, but Theo does sometimes.

I have almost no time alone, which I thought would drive me crazy, but it doesn't. I just get sucked into the whirlwind, letting myself enjoy the ride for once, without overthinking.

The biggest difference is when Theo asks me over to his place. I'd almost forgotten he isn't with anyone else, unlike Austin. He lives alone too, and it's shockingly peaceful there. Maicy isn't around to make awkward jokes, and there isn't another girlfriend to feel bad about. We just coexist in the same space, gentle and quiet, until we fall into each other's arms in bed.

Then night bleeds into day, and I start all over again. It's easy; it's complicated; I try not to love it too much.

Austin
Before

I didn't want to come to this stupid fucking party. Taryn dragged me, along with Maicy and Theo. She said we'd each have someone to keep us company. She's smart; she knew I'd get pissy, get trashed, and need a guy. But I shouldn't have come at all. I was already in a horrible mood from her bullshit all week.

For someone who says she loves me back, she sure hasn't shown it at all recently. She's picked a fight with me every damn day and refused to apologize, not even when I do first. Whatever she's gotten into her head, she won't let it go, and I'm just not in the fucking mood to play along right now.

I don't want my feet to get cold, because I do want forever with her—there's nothing else I've wanted more in my life—but the finality of it…that's starting to hit me, harder than I expected. So maybe some of the arguments are my fault too.

Not that I'd admit it. Not today, at least.

There was a little yelling, plenty of swearing, and regrets all around.

But then she pouted, ran her fingers through my hair, and said we'd have fun. She wanted me to come with so we could spend some time together, let loose, be us again. I kept asking if she had Maicy there, why she'd need me. It wasn't that I didn't want be with her, I do—but not here, not drunk, not with a bunch of other drunk idiots.

Then she kissed me, with her whole body and soul behind it, and I shut up.

But now I can't find her, and I don't know where the fuck Theo went either. Taryn ditched me minutes after we showed up, and Theo went off with some other girl a while ago. I'm about four drinks past too far, and I can barely see through the spots. I don't think my brain is even recording memories anymore.

Baby is gonna be pissed when I puke in her car on the way home.

Too bad.

Her fault.

"Did you get lost, or did you come down here looking for something you haven't found yet?" A voice purrs behind me, and even as shit-faced as I am now, there's a little voice inside of me telling me I'm in trouble. All of my senses go on alert. As best they can anyway. Looking around, there's no one else down here in the basement, and suddenly, I feel trapped. "For me," she adds with seduction.

"Lost and looking for my *girlfriend*."

I try to shove past her, but I trip. She catches me and holds tight to my waist with fire in her eyes. It feels like the tentacles of an octopus, strangling and glued to me, the moment she latches on. Even through the whisky and weed, I can feel her fingers digging into me. I'd be shocked if I don't end up with bruises.

Warning bells are freaking the fuck out inside my head.

Big, red flashing ones with whistles.

"I think you found exactly what you need." This random bitch is too persistent.

"Back off," I growl.

She doesn't say no, but she doesn't let go. Instead she grabs my face and pulls it to hers. She kisses me. My delayed reaction isn't just from the alcohol. I hesitate, holding still. And then…and then I kiss her back. I open my mouth and let her tongue fight with mine. I let her hands go to my hair. Then she pulls us into the bathroom, kicking the door closed.

I let her kiss me for way too long. I let feelings well inside that had no place to land before now.

I don't know why—I mean I know this whole thing is a mistake, even as I do it—but I don't stop.

And I don't *just* let her kiss me, I kiss her back. I kiss hard, rough, unrelenting. Every bottled-up emotion, every problem with Taryn, every fear of what forever is supposed to mean, it's through my lips and tongue into this girl kissing me. I bite her, and she likes it, so I do it harder still.

It's healing somehow.

I let my hand go to her ass and pull her tight against me. The other hand goes up her shirt. I let way too much happen for too many minutes. I feel too much when it should be nothing at all. I should've never got this close, but at the moment, I can't remember why. I shouldn't have my hands on her skin, inside her panties, her tongue down my throat, but I do because it feels so good. It feels meant to be.

It goes on for too long and too much happens.

Soon her skirt is up around her waist, and those panties my hand was in are down around her ankles. She wastes no time pulling my zipper down and working her hand into the opening of my boxers.

I don't think; I don't wait. I just give her what she wants, what I want too, in this one second. Forgetting everything that bothers me, everything that isn't perfect with what I already have, I plunge into something I can never erase. I go where I can never get back from.

It lasts a while, and I have plenty of time to stop, but I don't. I finish with her hands in my hair and her teeth on my ear as grunts start to sink in.

"Give it to me," she moans.

"Shut up," I groan.

But she doesn't. She keeps saying things, things I don't want to hear from her, things it took Taryn years to say to me.

And then, *then* I remember.

I see Taryn's face behind closed eyelids, but not until it's too late. I shove this stranger away, hard. I push her with both my hands on both her shoulders, and she staggers back. It's too late, though. The alcohol, the anger, they encouraged me to this, but I can't undo it.

What the fuck have I done?

"Call me any time, handsome." I watch as blonde hair flies past me, and she grazes her finger across my face. She got her skirt fixed, and her underwear into her pocket, before I could even zip up. She's sober, I notice, not that that matters much.

When she's gone, I fall back against the wall and sink all the way to the floor. I've never fucked up so badly. I didn't think I was this guy anymore. I haven't been this guy since high school, since meeting Taryn. I was supposed to be different for her; I was supposed to show her that someone was good enough to deserve her. And I fucked it all up so fast.

I need to find Taryn; I have to tell her before the lie gets bigger and takes my whole life with it. So I stand, dragging my boots in dread. Probably because I'm so scared, I find her right away. And when I see Taryn, I want to run. I want to lie. I want to take it back. But instead I grab her hand.

"Maicy needs to take us home." She starts to shake her head, but stops when she sees the sadness in my eyes, the seriousness of our situation. "Now," I beg.

"Mace?" she says.

Blonde hair stalks past us on our way outside, a wiggle in her walk, and she has the audacity to bump Taryn's shoulder, laughing the whole time. Taryn looks to her as she saunters away, then to me, and I'm overwhelmed by a falling sensation. My face gives away my guilt, and Taryn starts shaking as she holds onto Maicy.

It's horrible.

And the feeling builds as we walk, as I text Theo to find a different ride home, as Maicy unlocks the car and turns on the radio, as I hold the horrible truth inside, even for only a few moments. I can feel it tearing into my organs, destroying everything I've built, everything I love. The car ride was agonizing, silence the whole time, from everyone.

"Maicy, can we have a minute?" I ask once we're to their house.

She nods, her face granite and her eyes fire.

I tell Taryn. It's the hardest thing I've ever done in my whole life, but I tell her. And Taryn just stands there, silent and stoic. She doesn't scream. She doesn't hit me. She doesn't call me names or ask why. There's so little emotion in her face and body that I wonder if she's even heard. After a heartbreaking, and terrifying, two full minutes of my guts coming out in confessions and pleading, she just looks into my eyes the whole time. Hers are full of tears, and that in itself says something much worse than I expected.

"I knew love wasn't real."

And as she hands me her ring, then walks away; as her sobs start crashing through her, I hit the ground with my knees as my heart splits into hundreds of pieces. I don't feel the pain when I land. Well, I do, but it's in my chest instead.

Because of me, two hearts break. They shatter.

Austin
Now

It's finally Friday, and the first night I'm out with Skyler since the night Taryn called me. Skye hasn't asked for much from me at all lately, so I thought it was fair. In truth, I think she's stayed quiet and appeasing on purpose, but that could be paranoia.

Theo chats with Natasha, but I can see there's no real interest there. He didn't know Skye had invited her, and he wasn't thrilled. But he's such a good friend—he knows how to fake it, not that she can tell. We pay the cover and walk to the bar. It's loud near the bartender, so loud that I can't hear any voices. That's okay, though. I can feel the thick beats of the music roll across my skin, and I relax a little.

The dim lights seem to play into the mood, pinks and purples and blues flashing across skin and tight fabric. Maybe getting out wasn't such a bad idea. I can let go, uncoil my worry just a little.

I get the first round for all four of us, while the other three stand outside of the throng of drunks, and leave the bartender with a tip— paying cash instead of leaving my card. Even if I'm feeling good now, I'm not sure how long we'll stay.

Turning around with four drinks tucked in my arm and balanced precariously, I watch as Theo's smile fades, and then he freezes. I follow his sightline and drop two of our beers from one hand. As they crash to the floor, I let out a mumbled, "Fucking fuck," as I see Taryn and Maicy looking right at me.

Skyler starts laughing at my clumsiness, having no idea what I'm seeing. "Butterfingers only gets half rounds from now on." She takes the drinks for her and Natasha, then kisses my cheek. "We'll get a table while you get new ones."

Theo walks up to me and cracks a shit-eating grin before slapping my shoulder, hard. "Leave it to you."

"Shut the fuck up, and tell me what to do," I say, in a frustrated rush.

"I don't think I can both shut up *and* tell you what to do. Those are mutually exclusive."

He keeps laughing as he orders our replacement beers, side-eying me over and over.

"Seriously, what the fuck am I going to do here? Should we leave?" My eyes dart from Theo to Taryn and to Skyler, then start over again. This has potential for huge disaster written all over it. If we leave, Skyler may put up a stink or ask why. Plus if we leave then I may hurt Taryn's feelings, since she's already seen, and she's the one I care more about.

But if we don't leave...

"*Shit*," I say.

"Here," Theo hands me two shots. I down both, slapping the glasses back onto wood one after another. He hands me a beer after I finish. "Let's just go to the table and ride it out. It'll be fine."

"Are you sure?" I can't think straight right now, so I trust his judgment more than mine.

"Go, idiot," Theo says, shaking his head at me.

I march over to Skyler with tunnel vision, looking nowhere else. I don't even notice that Theo isn't right behind me until I'm sitting and look back. "Where'd he go?" I ask Skye and Natasha. Both shrug their shoulders.

A nervous feeling collects in the back of my throat and starts to scratch at me. I try to clear the feeling away with a grunt, then a cough, but it remains. Nat and Skye keep chatting away, neither worried about me in the least.

Then I find out where the feeling came from. Holy hell.

Fucking Theo.

I see him towering a foot above two beautiful girls, one on each side underneath an arm, like he's king of the goddamn world. And he's smiling broader than I've ever seen. If his smirk were any wider, his face would split in two. The scratching in my throat doubles. Maybe I'm having an allergic reaction; I can't breathe right. Those girls on his arms are Taryn and Maicy.

That fucking motherfucker.

He went to grab the girls, not just to say hello but to torture me. He must actually want to die. Because that's what's about to happen. I'm going to punch him until he blacks out, then I'm going to keep going until that face can never smile again. I see red, and have to blink it away when he stops at the table with his new guests.

"Look who I found," Theo says loud and ecstatic when he reaches the table.

Natasha's face sours, but Skyler smiles, just like she does toward anyone else. My stomach falls.

"I'm going to get shots at the bar. Who wants one?" I stand and start moving without waiting.

"Me," Taryn raises her hand then points to Maicy.

Theo nods.

The sitting ladies shake their heads no.

"Okay, so four. Got it. Be right back."

As I walk away, I hear Theo introduce all four girls while my head keeps spinning.

Taryn
Now

Theo was right; *this is fun.*

When he came over to Mace and I, I never thought he'd be right. I thought he was trying to be a dick and make Austin squirm. Show him up without letting the secret out. Well, okay that part is still true. But he was spot-on about it being fun too.

It was a little *too* fun watching the color drain from Austin's cheeks as we walked up. As his voice shook, and he practically ran away, I struggled to keep my cool. It helped to have Theo's arm over my shoulder. Moving his hand, tucking it into my back pocket now feels even better. I sigh, sinking into the moment.

That Natasha girl doesn't look too happy about Theo's interest in other women though.

Actually, she looks a little crazy in the eyes, narrowed and wide at the same time somehow. "So how do you know these…" Natasha points to Maicy and I, squinting a little and pursing her lips—somehow only at the corners, "two?" She finishes with a quiet little huff.

Well, *bitch,* two can play that game.

"We've known each other *forever.*" I bat my eyelashes and squeeze into his size, looking up with wide eyes and a little smile. "Friends for life."

Ha.

I can feel the laughter rumble through Theo's chest, and I hear Mace snicker too.

Then I feel something shift right before I hear, "We all went to school together, at some point."

I try not to flinch. Austin pauses as he walks around us to hover between the table and my misfit group, still standing, and I wonder if he's going to say it. I hope he doesn't say it.

"Plus, Taryn's my ex-girlfriend."

Well, shit.

He got the one up on Theo, and everyone, with that, I guess.

I hold my breath, knowing Theo and Maicy are too. I'm pretty sure there are ten eyeballs all looking at Skyler. Well, maybe eight; there might be two on me, plus hers. I peek over and, sure enough, Austin's sight is trained on my face instead of his girlfriend's. *Bad form, dude.* But since she's looking at me, she hasn't noticed.

Theo breaks the silence, and I could kiss him for it. "Pidge got me in the custody battle, though."

Another sour face from the table at his nickname for me.

"Only because Austin fought the child support," I say, ignoring the rest.

Maicy laughs and drums her sparkling black nails on the tabletop, leaning toward it like she's ready to sit. I let myself get distracted for one relief-filled moment.

But then my gaze moves, and she still looks shocked. She desperately tries to hide it and move on when she sees me look, blinking away her surprise as fast as she can. I'm baffled about the fact that there's no anger in her face or body language. If I were her, I'd be *pissed.* But she looks like someone who tries to please everyone, and that makes me feel a little cheap and petty, wishing we hadn't done this.

"Well, it was nice to meet you ladies," I nod to both and back the fuck out of the conversation. Literally, I'm moving backwards as my head bobs up and down. I reach for Maicy's hand behind Theo to drag her with me so we can run away.

To my surprise Skyler speaks up after two steps, "You don't have to leave. We're all adults. We can drink together, be civil, and hang for an evening."

Wow.

Wooooooow.

Barbie is a grown-up with a huge heart.

Just twist the knife deeper, why don't ya.

Even though it isn't a challenge, since she has no idea about any of it, it feels like one. So I sit down. Maicy eyes me before following suit. The booth is squished, and it's weird, but I can tough it out. For a little while, at least.

I'm sandwiched between Skyler and Theo, with Maicy across from me and Austin between her and Natasha. It's possibly the weirdest seating arrangement we could have decided on but too late now. Mace keeps looking to Austin like he's going to breathe fire on her, but to me, he just looks scared. Theo hands out the shots, and the four of us down them immediately. It burns my throat until landing, thick and heavy, in my stomach. I hadn't planned on getting wasted tonight...but extenuating circumstances may just allow for it.

After pushing my shot glass toward him, I slip my hand onto Theo's thigh under the table, out of sight, and I squeeze. I need another. Even though I don't want him to leave me alone with the girl I'm fucking over, I so need another.

"I'll get another round. Who's in this time?" Theo asks.

I raise my hand, not wanting to talk unless I have to. And this time everyone goes along with me, even both Barbies.

"Guess it'll be that kind of night." Theo laughs his way to the bar, and I wish I hadn't sat down at all. It would've been better if we'd run away. At the moment, going to a different bar, or home, sounds like a fabulous idea.

I open my mouth to tell Maicy we should get going, but Skyler beats me to it.

"So, Taryn, right?" she asks, and I nod, closing my mouth, inspecting my chipping nail polish and my thumb ring. So then no eye contact. Ever again. That seems smart. "What do you do?"

Okay, an easy one.

Talking to the empty space in the middle of the table, not turning toward her at all because I'm both a coward and a bitch, I answer, "I work for my step-dad. Went to college for English and art, but those don't pay the bills yet." Keep it simple. "You?"

"I'm entry-level, part-time and entry-level, but still, it's a job. I've gotten a few hints that it'll lead to a move up, to something permanent, though." She didn't say where she works to give me a clue about her field, but I don't ask. I don't even know why I asked her what she does in the first place. I don't need to know her as a person.

I don't want to.

I'm realizing real fucking quick that all of this was a bad idea, terrible. Getting to know her is the *worst* idea in the world. *Ever.* My heart starts to beat faster, and I'm pretty sure my breathing follows suit. It's too hot in here, and I hate this. I hate everything. I wish we were nearer the loud music or in more shadow. This sucks, and I didn't want her to have a face, a voice; she was never supposed to be a real person. She was a name before, an easily forgotten picture. Not…

But she's a real person now.

And I'm the goddamn she-devil.

If I leave now, maybe I can forget her face, her voice, and go back to my perfect little chaotic and messed-up world, the one I was living in just an hour ago, the one where I know nothing and love that. But just as I start to move over and get out of the booth, Theo gets back, squeezing me back in. He has an entire wait-staff tray with shots and a few drinks, ready to trap me here.

"Double shots all around!" He passes out the huge glasses with inviting, dark liquid. I tip mine back while the others are still waiting for their glasses. Rude. But too bad. "Cheers," Theo shouts raising his glass, and everyone clinks. Mine's empty, but whatever, I still join the party.

What a weird-ass party.

So with that thought, and a glare directed at no one in particular, I suck down the drink I originally brought over to the table. The ice is melted, and I already forgot what was inside it. But it doesn't matter.

After shots, Theo sets down beers for the boys and passes out fresh drinks to Maicy and me. I should feel bad Skyler and what's-her-name are left out, but they're both still clutching their big fruity cocktails with white knuckles and pink nails.

When Theo slides over my Long Island iced tea, he lets his fingers stay on mine a while. It shouldn't be funny, but somehow it is, and I start snort-laughing. For no reason. Luckily my lunacy encourages Skyler and sour-face-Barbie (shit what's her name again? Natalie, maybe?) to start their own conversation, probably trying to ignore my psycho ass.

Theo balances the empty tray against the booth after waving toward the bartender to send someone. A way-too-chipper girl with a short, blonde angled bob and big blue eyes comes over to take our orders. I want to punch her face because she looks like another Barbie, fake and made up, coming over to compete for the attention of all men, my men.

Blondes are not inherently more fun. *They're boring.* They're horrible. I don't care that I'm being irrational or unfair either. I take issue with blondes, unless they're strawberry and my best friend, like Maicy.

I order another Long Island while I suck this one down, along with another shot.

"I'm so not on hair-holding duty tonight," Maicy says and smirks at me.

"Blah, blah, blah, Mommie Dearest," I shoot back, already feeling the slur in my words. I lost count, but now that I'm on a roll, I don't want to stop.

Theo leans over until his lips are touching my ear. I force my eyes to stay open and not let everything shiver because Austin's wide, pissed-off eyes are watching, intense and intent. Theo's breath is warm, and it tickles as he says, "You should come home with me tonight."

Don't smirk, don't smirk, *don't fucking smirk.*

"I'll do more than hold your hair," he adds.

I shrug, but I let my hand drop beneath the table and rest on his knee.

My phone buzzes. I know who it's from, but I don't know how to read it sitting here, between the two worst possible people to chance reading it. So I nudge Theo to move with an excuse that I'm going to the bathroom.

I sit in the stall reading, then typing out my answer.

Austin: I'd leave with you right now if you asked me to, in front of everyone.

Austin: I wouldn't care what anyone thought. I swear I'll do it.

Me: But I haven't asked yet.

When I get back with another a new drink in hand after getting sidetracked at the bar, Austin looks like he might explode. Both Maicy and I watch his nostrils flair, and I can feel his knee bouncing next to hers even from this side. After watching him too long, Mace shakes her head then interjects to make the situation bearable, "Who here has slept with a carnie? Anyone? No? Well, shit, I feel a game of never-have-I-ever coming on strong." She smiles and takes a big gulp from her drink. "You guys don't know what you're missing."

"What about an exterminator, or how about someone twice your age?" Theo eggs her on, and soon we're all laughing.

The Barbies are giggling too and talking a mile a minute to each other, still in their own bubble, so I let myself relax a little. Maicy and the booze both help.

Austin moves his feet until both go beneath mine. It's the most he can do, and I give him a smile. Then Theo's hand slips into mine, and as his thumb rubs circles across my wrist I realize a lot of things in a matter of seconds. I try so fucking hard not to choke on my Long Island, because I feel like spitting on everyone across the table would be noticeable.

I'm slammed with thoughts so truthful they hurt, one after another in quick succession. First, I see the fire in Austin's eyes. I don't know how long he's going to put up with my plan to grow a lotus in the mud. I have a feeling he'll be putting more pressure on me soon. Second, I never meant for it to happen, but fuck if I'm not falling for both of these boys. Maybe I was already. Like…sick and sticky feelings of gooey, romantic…the bad word comes to mind.

As Theo rubs the spot where I'm marked with the memory of Austin and they both sit close enough to touch, I feel my heart cracking as it pulls two different ways. It can't last forever, and I'm going to have to choose one. Even then, love has tried to kill me before, so making a choice at all may be bad for me.

But lastly, I know deeper than I know much else that I can't walk away from both. There will be an actual decision, one way or the other, that lands my heart in the hands of another. So until then, I guess I'll see how long I can get away with juggling both, until I know who my heart is reaching toward more.

I'm a little terrified as I take another sip.

Austin
Now

Theo's gonna get his ass handed to him. Swear to fucking god.

That was horrible, torture.

And the car ride home is way worse. Theo is up front with the driver since he's getting dropped home first, lucky fucker, so I'm between Natasha and Skyler, who are both in bitchy moods. I'm surrounded by eye-rolls and loud sighs. I might choke on and die from an overload of passive-aggressiveness.

They're both mad for different reasons, though. Skye's pissed about having to meet an ex and interact with her. I suspect Natasha's bubble was burst, leaving disillusionment about her chances with Theo when he spent no time talking with her.

So now I'm stuck between two scorned women.

Fucking great.

I may have my dick protected, my fists in my lap, just in case.

When we were leaving the bar, Skye kept trying to talk to me when all I wanted to do was stew in my own anger. Anger at Theo, at myself, at Skye, at Taryn. Then when she finally got fed up, she pinched my side and turned to stare out the window. That has been my last ten minutes. Pained silence.

I cannot wait to get home. I fully plan to sleep on the couch.

We get to Theo's place, and he seems too excited, pissing me off more. He slams the door after getting out and leans in to pay the driver. "Keep the change," he smiles as I watch a fifty passed over.

Show off.

"Night." Theo waves before jogging toward his house.

No one answers him.

I lean forward to give Nat's address. If she'd thought she was staying over, she's just been corrected. We continue the drive in total silence to her place, and Nat gets out without a word after handing me ten bucks.

I say, "Thanks," and move over to the seat she'd been occupying.

We head to our place, Skye and I both staring out our respective windows. I have no idea what she's thinking about, but I'm pretty sure it's not good. All I can think about is Taryn, and I'm dying to text her. I hold back though, knowing what a stupid idea it would be right now.

But it hurts to wait.

When the car gets to our apartment, I hand the driver the ten Nat gave me plus one of my own. He got paid well for a non-eventful ride, and he smiles before driving off. Skye storms up the stairs after the car is gone, not waiting for me. So I linger on the steps, lighting a cigarette.

What starts as one ends in three butts at my feet, crushed like my spirit. I want to but I know I can't put it off any longer, so I stomp up the stairs. But I walk softer as I get closer to my apartment door. If Skye's asleep, I don't want to wake her up.

No such luck though.

When I start to twist the knob, she yanks the door open for me, pulling me forward.

"You didn't need to tell me, and everyone, that she was your ex-girlfriend. You could have left it as friends from school." Skye keeps her voice at an inside volume, but each word is bitten off, one at a time. Her eyes are slits, and she already has red cheeks.

I let the door fall closed as I walk inside, taking my time. My shoes come off slowly, and I sit on the couch before answering. Drawing it out doesn't gain me much, but at least I'm calmer when I do say something. Looking straight ahead to the wall while she still stands, I remain disengaged.

"So you'd rather I omitted truths?" I say, just wanting to win. "You'd prefer I lie?" There's as much acid in my voice as in hers, and it's burning a hole through her resolve. My eyes flash to her face, begging her to tell me yes.

"You paid more attention to her than me. How do you think that makes me feel?" She gets quieter, hoping for sympathy. Waterworks won't work on me though. Not tonight. Not from her. There's no empathy left inside me. When my face remains cold, she drops to the chair across from me, trying to force eye contact.

"You and Nat were in your own conversation. You weren't asking for my inclusion." I'm sure I have an answer for everything she can shoot at me, and I know it'll drive her crazy.

"Did she know we'd be there tonight? Did you ask her to join us?" she asks, angry again.

"Nope." I leave no room for negotiation. My tolerance left, along with my patience.

"Fine." Skye opens her mouth, closes it, then huffs. But just when I think it's over, she adds, "Don't you even care that you hurt my feelings?"

"No, I don't. You're being immature and selfish. I was alive before I met you, and I wouldn't change my past if I could. I am who I am because of everything I've lived through before. If you can't think about anyone other than yourself, then it's your own fucking fault you're upset. Go pout somewhere else," I say.

Then I stand to take the bedroom. She can have the couch.

I start to walk around Skye as she stands, staring me down. Four eyes narrowed; there's no way to win or lose this one. We just watch each other for a moment. Then, when she moves first, I don't see what's coming until it's too late to stop it. Skyler slaps me across the face with as much strength as she can put into her swing.

It hurts, but not enough to give her the satisfaction of a reaction. I keep still, my eyes locked on hers. After blinking, I step to the side and move around her. I'd never hit her back, *never*, but if things weren't already over in my heart, that slap would've sealed the deal.

"Fucking feel something," she shouts as she counters my step, getting in my path again so we're face-to-face, her anger getting the better of her.

"I feel plenty," I say. I'd love to add that none of those feelings are for her anymore, but that would be too far, even for me.

"Prove it."

She raises her hand to hit me again, but I snatch her wrist, holding her hand above her head.

"Don't. Not ever again," I say, almost growling.

She surprises me with her answer as she slams into me with her lips, her chest, her entire body. She puts everything into the kiss, and I'm shocked. I react without thinking, going off the rage and letting it consume me. I grab her other wrist in my empty hand, twisting so both of her hands are behind her back. We back up until I'm against the wall.

"Feel," she says against my lips.

So I stop thinking. Stop worrying. Stop caring. And I just let the moment wash over me, doing nothing but feeling. In bed, I keep my eyes closed tight. The anger ebbs and flows, fueling the passion.

Sex with Skye has never been like this. She's pissed, and it's better.

It's also the first time we've been together since I left my heart at Taryn's.

Taryn
Now

Maicy puts me in a car outside the bar and gives the driver Theo's address. With a smirk, she makes some comment about right choices, and then I'm off, heading toward him. I have no idea how long the drive lasted, but it seems I'm to his place in a few blinks, a couple of breaths. Knowing this will be our first time together since I realized I might care too much about him gives me anxiety, but I also feel excitement. That surprises me more than anything.

Not that I'll tell him any of that.

Fuck that.

But to me, it'll be special, I think.

Theo's waiting outside when I arrive, and he pays before I can even reach into my pocket for cash. Then he opens my car door. He opens my fucking door. I wink at him in some weird way of showing my thanks as the car drives away.

"Took you long enough to get here," Theo jokes. "I was beginning to think I'd have to come find you." He wraps his arms around me and pulls us through his door, into the house. In just a second his lips are on my neck, and my hands go to his hair.

"Shut up, you love me," I echo the words he said at my house. They just fall out of my mouth. I know I shouldn't have said it. I hate the word; I hate its meaning. And I hate hearing it said anywhere near me, let alone from my own stupid fucking mouth. But I'm wasted. That's my only excuse, even if it's not a good enough one.

His answer is a grunt as he slips an arm around my neck, and the other behind my knees, lifting me into his arms and up in the air. He's carrying me, and I'm so thankful he didn't call me out that I close my eyes and smile, letting him do it.

My entire body is humming with need.

Since when do I need?

So I throw caution to the wind once more. The boundary has already been pushed, so why not go even further? "Theo…" I wait for something. He has to give me just enough, or I'll lose the momentum and let the moment—what I was going to say—slip away forever. Maybe that wouldn't be so bad, though.

I open my eyes and look into his as he lays me onto the bed, never breaking contact with my body or with his stare. He crawls over me, hovering. "Tell me."

And that's enough.

"I need you, Theo." Not Austin, not tonight. Not a nameless person, a faceless replacement. But him. Tonight I need, and I want, no one else.

His eyes close for a moment, and in that brief time, my heart soars.

Taryn
Before

I walk away from Austin, every step a struggle, and hear him fall to the ground a second after the ring does. The metallic sound is my undoing; it's the finality of it. I hate crying. I hate being this way; I can't stand the weakness in this moment. This is exactly why I never should've been exclusive with anyone. This, right here, proves is why love, why needing anyone, is a lie.

I knew better than to get attached, and yet I did it anyway. Serves me right, I guess.

There's always someone out there better than me, waiting to find the one I've fallen for.

I'm not meant to have a happy ending. I've known that from the beginning, for years. My mom taught me long before any romantic relationship. So I knew better than to let Austin trick me into falling for him. I fucking deserve this, but never again will I let myself end up here.

I lock the door behind me once I'm inside, without turning around. I can't look at him; if I do, I'll lose my nerve. Feeling his heart breaking is worse than the breaking of my own. Once the lock clicks, I let myself mirror him, crashing to the floor in a heap. And when I do, the entire world around me comes falling down.

I can't breathe.

I can't do anything but feel. I feel so much that I'm sure I'll tear apart. All of the disappointment, it's shattering, as the realization that this was always meant to be crashes into me. Waves of nausea, of pain, come at me, unrelenting. I can't stand, can't walk, so I crawl to my room. On my hands and knees, I make my way to my bed, where I drink myself to sleep.

That's it. I don't talk to Maicy; I don't watch TV; I don't answer my phone. I just drink and I cry and I try to sleep.

Then the vomiting begins around dawn. And along with the contents of my stomach—nothing but alcohol and soda—comes pieces of my resolve, maybe my soul too. My emotions, my strength, may never be quite the same. Little pieces of my heart are gone forever, flushed down the toilet with the rest of the shit I never should have forced down.

When I'm done, no longer banished to the cold tile of the bathroom floor, I move back to my bed. At least I walk this time, crouching but off all fours. And I wrap myself into a cocoon of green haze, tears, and blankets. I smoke away my problems until I can't feel anymore. The numb becomes my best friend, replacing everyone and everything. For days. I don't count how many. My phone battery died the same night my hope for a future did, and I don't give a shit about charging it.

Maicy's in my room a lot, but I have no idea how long she tries to cheer me up. It doesn't work anyway. She mentions how many times Austin's called her worrying about me. She says he'd do anything to get me back. But he can't turn time backward. He can't undo what happened or erase my memory of it.

He can't do anything to fix this, so there's no point.

After I can't stand the sight of my bed any longer, though it takes a while, I eventually get up. I push myself to move. Showering takes a lot of effort, and I don't chance looking in the mirror after. I know I won't like what I see.

Somehow a month goes by, in a blink almost, but I still can't function without thinking of what I lost, of what I had and then had taken away. In the days that pass, I find myself believing I'm to blame. For all of it. I did something wrong to make Austin betray me. I push everyone to leave me. *Always*. He was just doing what I expected all along. He was just fulfilling the destiny of my broken heart.

And with that realization, I let a sad, stupid little thought in: maybe we could be friends. Maybe I'd feel better still having him in my life, even if it's not in the same way. Maybe that's what we should have done from the beginning.

Taryn
Now

I wake up from bad dreams, hung over as fuck and sweating against Theo's beating heart. I can't remember much after my clothes came off. I do have this memory of floating to the ceiling, but I'm pretty sure that wasn't real. I mean, probably.

After stirring, Theo presses his hot lips to my clammy forehead, and I cringe, trying to back away. He just hugs me tighter. "Don't ruin it, you weirdo." His voice is light, and it rumbles against my naked body.

I wish I'd at least put a t-shirt on before passing out.

I feel too open. Too exposed. The dreams of Austin didn't help either, and I know this is all my issue, not in any way Theo's fault. So I try to shake off the uncomfortable feeling by breathing him in.

"I ruin everything," I whisper.

"Don't you dare," he starts. "I don't have patience for your crap this early in the morning. Not before coffee." He laughs, but I don't. I want to so badly, but I can't. So he tries again. "Don't you know...you *are everything* that matters," he says almost as softly. Then he stops. He doesn't elaborate. He doesn't go far enough to push me into running, even though I'm pretty sure he has more he could add. He just lets it sink in as he holds me as close as I'll allow, stroking my back as his breath slows again.

Tricky boy.

Austin
Now

Saturday's sun is fucking awful. I'm tangled in Skyler and the sheets. I'm sweating out the booze I drank too much of, and my mouth tastes like unwanted sex plus stale ashtray. *Not appealing.*

I shouldn't have fucked her.

I may not know much, but that's for positive.

It was stupid; it was a gut reaction made in anger, and it's too close to the night that ruined my entire life. I was drunk, and I put myself in a terrible situation. I could've asked the driver to take me to a hotel after Skye stormed off. I didn't have to come upstairs. Now that I'm sober, I see it as a perfect solution. *Why the fuck didn't I think of that?*

But it's too late for what ifs.

Besides, this is kind of exactly what Taryn was pushing for. It's what she wanted—complicated as fuck. Well, that's what we've stepped even further into.

I know she's underestimating me and the lengths I'll take to fix the missed years. My Queen of Hearts expects nothing but the worst, and I can't blame her. After all, I take most of the blame. But I can work my ass off to show her different this time.

So I detach myself from the mess of last night and get into the shower. I scrub until my skin is raw, and I brush my teeth twice. Afterward I feel better, cleaner, like a fresh page. When I'm dressed, I grab my phone and keys, slamming the door as I leave Skyler still sleeping in bed.

The phone rings as I hold it to my ear while pulling out of the parking lot.

I hear mumbling as Theo answers the call. There's a "Shhh," and he laughs in response.

Before he can say hello I start in on him. "Whoever that skank is, send her home. I'm on my way over."

Then I hang up before he says a single word to me. And I'm pretty sure I made my point.

When I pull onto Theo's street, a car pulls out of his driveway and heads away from me. Whatever chick he's been hiding must be awful to keep her a secret so long. I imagine an older woman, or maybe he's too scared to admit to his best friend that he's gay. I don't know, but whatever he's hiding, it's stupid. And it's unfair. I've never made an issue of his choices before, and I didn't plan on starting now.

But I don't like the lying, the secrets, not from him.

Theo stands in his driveway, shirtless, as I slam the car into park and crank the engine off. I remember to breathe before getting out.

"What the fuck was that last night? What the *fuck* were you thinking?" I yell.

"If I'd have known you'd take it so seriously, I wouldn't have brought them over. It was just a joke," Theo says, and it makes my temper rise even higher. "It was supposed to be fun. I didn't know you'd blab to everyone about who she really was. No one else was going to do that." He puffs out his chest as he defends his shitty moves.

I plant my feet on his driveway, as hard as the stone beneath, and my hands ball at my sides. Thinking better of it, trying to breathe slowly, I hook each thumb into a pocket. No matter what he did, it's not worth that.

"And why the hell were you flirting with her in front of me? That was a low fucking thing to do. You could've done something else to get a reaction out of me but not that." I see a flash of something I can't pinpoint in his eyes before it's gone.

And a new emotion adds itself to my anger. Fear trickles into my veins, slow and cold.

Theo backs up and sits on his front steps before answering, and when he does, he has the courtesy to look me in the eye finally.

"My opinion of what you're doing hasn't changed. I guess it got the better of me last night, and I shouldn't have taken it so far. I can admit that. But I really was just trying to be funny at first. But then I kept going. I did think it was funny though." He drops his hands to hang by his feet. "Maybe we should hang out a little less for a while."

"Seriously?" The waver in my voice gives away the disappointment. He drops his gaze.

"I'm not going to change my mind." Theo sighs and looks at me again. "I may not deserve to have an opinion, and more importantly I shouldn't act on it, but I can't seem to let it go. I think we should spend a little less time together until you're just with Taryn, or until..." He doesn't finish.

But I know what he's thinking. I can fill in the rest of what wasn't said.

I don't answer. I turn and get into my car. Driving away, as a cab comes around the corner, I wonder what the fuck is going on. How did the best week of my life crumble into this stupid moment?

****

After driving around, I realize I have no destination in mind. I feel lost.

I have no messages from Taryn.

I don't go home to Skyler after leaving Theo's; there's no point. Instead, I use my good idea, if a little late, and check into a hotel. Skye hasn't texted me either. I could guarantee she knows enough to let me have my space right now. She probably figures I still need cooling down, even if she's chilled out about it all already.

It doesn't bother me she's neglected to say anything.

I don't even care that Theo let the conversation stop with my leaving.

Missing Taryn, feeling her absence, is the one thing that bothers me most right now. And I completely wallow in it, sinking deeper with each minute that pass by. I try not to dwell, but it's fucking impossible. And then I start to let questions pass through my head, making me even crazier.

Has she decided this isn't worth it and her silence is my answer?

Did she flirt back with Theo to show me I'm still far from earning her trust back?

Is she going to ruin me for everyone else and still leave me in the end?

Could she be with someone else right now?

Eventually, with room service getting cold in my lap and a boring rerun playing on the TV, I can't take it anymore. My fingers dial her number. Even though I could've just clicked on her contact, I wanted to draw it out more, scared of what will happen once she answers. If she answers. And I hold my breath as it rings.

Taryn's giggle when she answers makes me smile, and I let the air out of my lungs.

"Well, that was weird as fuck last night," she says. I can hear the smile in her voice and almost see the spark in her eyes as she says it. My blunt Taryn.

"Couldn't've put it better myself," I say.

"I don't know why you told her. Was she mad?" The concern for Skyler throws me.

"Does it matter?"

"You're right. I don't want to know," she says. The smile's gone now, and I hesitate.

"Will you come over?" I ask. "I need you."

I could say it a million times, and each one would be true. She'd find a way to rationalize them all away, though I'll never stop trying, never stop saying it.

"Isn't she there? No, thank you," Taryn says.

"I'm in a hotel. I wanted to be alone. But I've changed my mind. I want you more." There's background noise I can't decipher. Maicy may be walking into her room, or maybe she's going somewhere more private. It's hard to tell. "I want you here. I need you," I say again.

"I can't tonight. I'm sorry. Need me again tomorrow. Okay?"

She doesn't sound up for convincing, and then I'm angrier than I've been yet. But I try to hide it from my response. "Angel, I always need you. I'll need you tomorrow, until the day I die. Call me when you need me."

I want to say more. I want to tell her I love her.

But I hit the red button instead. I don't let her answer, and that may be a huge mistake that I can't take back. I switch the channel and turn off my phone. A night to myself might be the best thing I can have.

I know I'll call her tomorrow, even if she doesn't reach out to me.

The thing is, I don't mind begging her.

Austin

Before

My heart squeezes in uncomfortable patterns, picking up speed and then abruptly slowing down again out of nowhere. It actually hurts. Not a lot, but just enough to be annoying as hell. I'm glad she's not a mind reader.

My hands, they've never been so sweaty before; it's like I dunked them in water.

Wiping my palms on my pants another time, I try not to turn and look at Taryn. She's engrossed in the reading, so much so that from the corner of my eye, I can see her huge smile and wide eyes. She watches as her favorite author stands between bookshelves and reads from her work.

I could swear I saw her mouthing the words, but now she's got that bottom lip between her teeth.

When the reading finishes, Taryn claps louder than anyone else, and longer too. She's so happy, it was worth the price tag on this event—not that she knows I paid anything. Then we wait in line for almost an hour to get her book signed, and I'm sure I've never seen her more excited.

Everything is perfect.

"You happy?" I ask her once she's got her message scrawled on the first page, and she's clutching the book to her chest.

"The happiest," she says, letting one hand free from her prize to trail along the spines of other books. "Thank you." She doesn't turn, and it's almost like she's talking to the books. It makes me smile too.

This shop, a bookstore she comes to whenever she needs cheering up, is the perfect backdrop. I knew right away that I wanted to do it here, and I got fucking lucky about the events they had posted this month.

Though I could wait forever for her, to do this right.

I shift, stopping my step-for-step match of Taryn. It takes her a while to notice that I'm no longer next to her, and when she almost crosses into the next aisle of books, my heart picks up more speed.

Feeling like a moron, waiting for her to look at me, I almost stand up.

But then she sees, and I can't help myself as I laugh at her double take. She backs up a few steps, her mouth about as open as it goes, and her eyes even wider. Then her brand new signed book hits the floor, and her breathing gets a little too fast.

"Shit. Are you okay?" I ask, as I get off my knee and rush over to her. With the one hand I have available, I touch her chest, trying to ground her. "Breathe, Angel. Breathe."

Maybe this was a terrible idea.

She nods, sucking in air as slowly as she can manage, but her face is still getting more flushed, and I can feel her hands shaking at her sides. She keeps nodding, tears forming in her gorgeous eyes.

"Oh, fuck," I say, dropping the little black box in my other hand so I can hold both sides of her face. It bounces off her book and lands with a thud on the floor near our feet. "I'm sorry, baby. Forget it. I don't need that; I just need you." I say into her hair, and I crush her against me.

"Do you mean it?" she whispers.

"Of course. You matter so much more to me than any label." My answer is quick, sure.

"That's not what I meant by *it*," Taryn says even quieter.

And I'm pretty sure I didn't hear her right.

I pull back so I can see her, and the liquid sheen is still in her eyes, but her chest isn't heaving so fast, and her fingers are on my arms—strong now. Her cheeks are still red, but there's a ghost of a smile on her lips.

"Don't say those four words," she says, and my heart fucking sinks. "If you don't mean them. Don't give me that thing if you aren't absolute, more than positive, that you're ready, that you mean it when you say forever," she finishes.

And I laugh.

I laugh when she calls a diamond ring a "thing," because of course she would.

"I've never meant anything more in my whole life," I say.

"Prove it," she answers.

I bend down, get back into the position I was in before, and look up to her with the biggest smile I've ever worn in my life as her head starts bobbing up and down in a resounding yes before I can even say the words.

Austin
Now

"Who's in there?" I ask Taryn, looking to Maicy's closed bedroom door where murmurs escape from.

"Honestly?" Taryn says, with a smirk.

"Of course." I reach over and pull her legs into my lap, easing her socks off as I do. Her toe nails are painted black, and I don't know why but it makes me smile.

"I have no idea." She laughs after saying it, throwing her head back into the couch cushions. My heart swells, and her smile is contagious.

"Good for her," I yell.

Taryn covers her mouth with a hand, trying to stifle her sounds. Only it doesn't work that well. Maicy's door snaps open but just a crack. Then she pops her head out, and I join with Taryn in the laughter.

"Will you two go somewhere else? You're so loud," Maicy says with hard eyes. I assume they are supposed to look menacing, but she's the opposite of scary. They contrast with her come-and-fuck-me tousled hair, the smear of lipstick on the side of her mouth, and the lack of clothing. She's topless, no doubt. Maybe more, though all we can see is from her shoulders up.

"Bow-chicka-wow-wow," I shout.

"Get it, girl," Taryn adds.

Maicy slams the door and cranks the sound up on the music playing in her room.

"Your house is crowded," I say, turning to Taryn.

She looks at me, cocking her head to the side, and a little jolt hits me in the chest. I have no idea what I said wrong, but I know it's something based on the way she starts shaking her head and looking to the ceiling.

"Yeah, well, babe. So is yours," she says.

And now I feel like shit.

"Sorry," I mutter.

Taryn answers by pulling her legs from my lap and tucking them beneath her on the couch, so she's sitting cross-legged. She turns on a movie, and I resist the urge to ask her to go to bed now. It's just easier to apologize with my hands rather than my stupid mouth. I fuck up so much more with the latter.

She lets me scoot closer to her, and eventually, my arm's around her shoulders. She does lean into me, but it's not without a little more space than normal. And I wish we could get our own place. If she were ready, I'd break my lease and move in here—or help her sell this place and find Maicy something new. I'd go any route she wanted.

I just wish she wanted it already.

I've been thinking a lot about how to get her to agree to forever. Again. She did it once, and there's nothing I wouldn't do to get her to say it again. *Nothing.* I'd move anywhere, do anything.

But if I asked now, if I brought out that ring that I still have tucked in a bag in a box somewhere in the back of my closet, she'd flip her shit and start running. I could have—maybe should have—pawned the ring after she gave it back. But it never felt right. Then I kept telling myself I'd do it later; I'd do it when I needed money or when I drove past the right place. But that never happened, so it still sits tucked away, waiting on a second chance too. But if I tried to give it to her now, before she's ready? She'd kick me to the curb so fast that I'd end up with a concussion and an empty bed.

I don't mind waiting, not if it means that I don't scare her off.

Because I also get it. I haven't done enough to prove myself worthy of a full, a real, second chance. I'm following every instruction, doing my best. But I know that it's not there, I'm not there, yet.

I just wish I knew the magic answer, the thing that would get her to see that I'm for real this time, that I won't screw up again. I keep trying to think of a big gesture, something that will say in actions what I haven't been able to with words. But nothing's come to me yet. I'll have to keep thinking.

"I'm hungry," Taryn says bringing me back to her, to now.

"Again?" I ask.

"You'd better think long and hard about your next words if you want to keep breathing." When Taryn tries to sound threatening, it only ever comes out as adorable. But I know better than to start laughing now.

She's not so sensitive as a rule though.

Instead of saying anything, I lean over into her, reach my hand back, and pull my car keys from my pocket.

"Anything your heart desires," I say. "I'm driving and paying. So get creative."

Moaning starts breaking through the music in Maicy's room, and I stand. That's not something I want to hear, so the food run is looking even better.

"Cheeseburger with pickles and barbeque sauce and maybe some waffle fries. Can you ask for mustard too?" Taryn turns back to the TV as she rattles off her order. I kiss the top her head as I walk behind the couch and toward the front door.

"Be right back, Angel."

She waves over the top of her head and leans back to watch her movie.

✳✳✳✳

When I get back, Taryn is crying. Real crying, with tears and all. And I almost drop her food as I rush to see what's wrong.

"Baby?"

"Ohmygod," she says all in one breath. "Don't look at me, go away." She gulps some air just before a hiccup escapes her mouth, and my stomach knots up even more.

"What's going on? Are you okay?"

Fear chills me as I wait for her to wipe her tears before she'll answer. Crouching in front of her with my hands on her knees and hers slapping at her face, I can't calm my racing heart. I've only seen Taryn cry two or three times in all the years I've known her. And the last time was the one I try never to think too hard about.

Then, when she's collected—her eyes still red and a little puffy though—she smiles big but glassy-eyed.

"It's so stupid. It was just the movie. That's all. I'm fine. God, I'm sorry."

I breathe so much easier as I move to sit next to her. Then I pull her into my lap and crush her against me, my face in her hair.

"Don't scare me like that," I say. I mean it, and I don't care how fierce it comes out.

When her breathing is back to normal I lean to the side so I can catch her eye. I don't say anything. Everything I want to tell her would be too much. So instead I press my lips to her cheek, kissing the last of her tears away.

I love her.

I've always loved her.

I'll find a way to be able to do this forever, be the one to comfort her, to kiss her tears away.

"Gimme that food before it gets cold. My hysterics are over, I swear," Taryn says, making us both laugh.

****

I wake up tangled in my own sheets, wishing it was Taryn.

It's early, at least an hour before my alarm is set to go off, and as my eyes adjust to the gray light of the morning an idea starts forming. I may not be able to stay over at her place yet, but I can do more. Grabbing my phone, I head to the closet and get dressed as quietly as I can, letting Skye sleep.

Me: Can I drive you to work?
Taryn: But then how will I get home!
Me: I'll drive your car and leave it there with you. Then call a ride home.
Taryn: You sure?
Me: I just want a few extra minutes with you to start my day.
Taryn: Deal :)
Taryn: Can you bring me a donut too?

I get three donuts and a large iced coffee. The extra thoughtfulness, the time to slow down and think about her, gets me a kiss that could light the world on fire.

"If I knew all I had to do was butter you up with sweets and chores, I'd have been doing it all along," I say as we pull out of her driveway.

"Keep it up," Taryn says with a wink before starting on the first bite of her breakfast.

"I promise," I say, now feeling wonderful about my chances of winning her over.

Taryn
Now

Summer passes into fall, and as the leaves change, not much else seems to.

Well, I haven't smoked in weeks; that's one small change. I just haven't felt the need for it or for drowning myself in booze either. Instead I'm *feeling* everything, letting myself express all of my emotions—living in the moment and the experiences. I don't crave numbness or a place to float away to.

It's nice. Surprisingly so.

Sometimes I see just Austin for a day, or a few, before I see Theo. Other times I go back and forth from one day to the next. Rarely, though it still happens, I'll see both in the same day. I'm insatiable, if I'm being honest, and though it's a novel experience, feeling so heated for them all of the time has been one hell of a ride these last few months.

Theo's kept his promise, and he hasn't uttered a word to anyone. Who the hell knows why. If it weren't for our past...I still don't know exactly why he sticks around. For a while Maicy begged to be the one to tell Austin about Theo, but she stopped asking after I threw a bottle of booze at her head. It may have been full. And it may have only missed her by a couple inches.

I'll never admit that I was aiming for over a foot away.

She hasn't stopped making little comments about how Theo's better and why he deserves to be chosen. She's always wanted to see me end up with him, even before we started our little…whatever we have. And now, since it's a competition, a comparison, she finds ways to point out why he's better. Every day. Which is fine.

It's kind of cute.

When Theo's over, I can hear them joking, even after I leave the room. He makes a point to include her when we're at my house, and he's even invited her over to his with us. Austin and Maicy on the other hand, they coexist fine, but there'd be no love lost there in a split—not from either side.

I try not to notice Theo's kindness. I still don't know what I want to do or who I should pick, and if it doesn't end up being him, it'll hurt me a lot. I don't want to ruin him for someone who deserves everything he is, all of him. He started out better than either Austin or I, and I've known him longer.

But, even knowing that, I still can't let him go. I'm too fucking selfish.

Not that I didn't know that already.

And he won't walk away either. Every time I try to bring it up, he stops me. Last time he looked me in the eye and told me to "Shut the hell up." I'm not sure I've ever been more stunned. Maicy whistled and left the room as fast as she could. I wanted to fight with him after that. So bad. And I tried pushing his buttons, but he just shut down, unwilling to argue or listen to my warnings.

He knows I'm still seeing Austin; I've flat-out said so. And still he stays. Theo doesn't want to be pushed away, and I've stopped trying. So now, I don't bring it up anymore. Maicy's the only one who does— I think she's trying to protect him, or protect both of us, maybe.

And on the flip side, I can't seem to let Austin go either.

When I think about telling Austin I'm done, that I'm choosing someone else, something easier, I start to hyperventilate. We have so much history, and he's worked so hard to have another chance. I know he's not the same person who made that mistake years ago. He's changed. For the better. For me.

I can't imagine letting either of them go, and I got hives—I felt gross, all blotchy and red and itchy as hell—when I sat down with Maicy to try and make a decision. My stomach started cramping too, and I didn't even feel better after I threw up. It was miserable, and that's when I accepted that it's impossible to choose, at least right now.

So for the last month or so, I stopped trying to decide altogether.

I know I still need to. Just not right now.

It's been a couple months of having both of them in my bed. And all three of our cars. I started wearing skirts more often because it suddenly seemed more fun. Several uninterrupted, passion-filled—if only a little moody—months of mistakes, stupidity, and sheer bliss—getting everything I want, all the time. I'd go as far as saying it's been bliss; I've been *happy*.

There hasn't been more than forty-eight hours at a time that I've spent alone.

I know it's coming at some point. *I know, okay.* I know the other shoe will be filled with lead when it does drop. But today's not that day. And I just hope tomorrow isn't either.

Taryn
Now

Maicy texts me while I eat lunch at my desk, at work. I'm having Chinese food for another day in a row of I don't know how many. Just thinking about it made my stomach growl. I haven't even switched up the order, and I keep overeating.

But it hits the spot, so I don't really care if I'm getting into a weird routine. Though, my pants have started protesting. Speaking of...I sit a little straighter to get a little more room in the waistband of my jeans as they pinch. It works, and I take another bite of my noodles.

I finish after another couple of bites as my stomach starts to sour. I ate too much again, and the feeling makes me want to crawl into bed at home, take a half-day to nap off this food coma.

But I don't have time to debate it anymore as my phone starts buzzing.

Maicy: What's that book you told me to read the other day? The one with the girl?
Me: You're joking right...that's the worst description ever.
Maicy: Wait, never mind. I found it.
Maicy: And okay, what was that other book—the really deep one you loved?
Maicy: Jkjk found that one too.

Me: Omg
Maicy: Obviously I'm at the store. Need anything?
Me: Since you're in the books—grab me a new poetry collection.
Me: Oh, and antacid or something. I feel like shit today.
Maicy: What the fuck? You didn't even drink last night.
Me: Maybe it's all the greasy food haha I need to go on a diet soon.
Maicy: Kk got the liquid stuff (you said or something).
Maicy: And shut up you're gorgeous.

I put my head down on my desk, the wood cooling my forehead, and I try to think if there's anything else we need at the house.

But I can't think of anything; I'm distracted by my queasiness and the temperature in my office. This stupid building is always one extreme or the other. I have a blanket stored in the bottom drawer for when I'm sure my fingers will fall off and a fan stored for when I start sweating my tits off.

I sit up and turn on my fan on after thinking about it, then go back to breathing deeply with my head on the desk. The breeze cools my neck, and I start to drift off. My eyelids close. The fan continues humming.

****

Austin winks at me, trying to get my attention from my kitchen where he's cooking us dinner. I can smell the garlic and the sauces brewing. I almost start drooling.

I watch as his expression turns from expectant to pissed off, and I turn around to see what set him off.

Behind me, Theo's walking out of my bedroom, shirtless and in nothing but boxers. His hair is messed up; it's obvious that he just slept on it. And I look down at myself to see I'm in nothing but a white t-shirt of Theo's, his fucking last name across it from some sports team, leaving nothing to anyone's imagination with how worn it is.

Austin stomps over to us, his mouth open and prepared to start screaming, a fist clenched and ready.

****

"Shit," I say out loud as my head jerks.

There's a pool of drool on my desk, and my phone's going off again.

I check the time, and I haven't been asleep long. Although it scared me, I'm thankful Maicy texted again, or I might have slept through the rest of the day, drowning myself in my own nap drool.

Gross.

Laughing, I open the message from Maicy.

Maicy: What kind of tampons do you like again?
Me: I'm not out.
Maicy: Did you switch to a cup and not tell me or something? I've gone through two boxes since the last drugstore run.

Taryn

Now

I'm dizzy, as if I've pounded shots between bowls of bud.

She can't be right.

There's no way.

Me: I'm leaving work early. Meet me at home as soon as you can

Somehow I get to the store, purchase what I need, and make it to the house, but I couldn't tell you much about any of it. I don't think my memory recorded anything. *Autopilot*. I just keep telling myself over and over, and then over some more, there's no fucking chance. She's wrong; it's a mistake.

Or maybe I'm fucking crazy, imagining things.

When I get to our driveway, I can't park my car for shit. After three attempts to straighten it, I give up, just turning my car off and rushing inside the house. Maicy isn't leaving if she wants to anyway. Not if my fears are right.

When I get inside, she's laughing at whatever's playing on the TV.

I turn it off, and she glares at me.

"What's got your panties in a twist?" she asks, rolling her eyes at me.

I throw my bag into her lap. She jerks her head back a little, questioning my motives or, possibly, my sanity. I fall to the couch. I wouldn't call it sitting, since I just let my knees give out as my ass falls to the cushions.

"What?" she asks.

"Open it," I say. I don't want to say anything other than that.

The plastic bag crinkles, and I scrunch my eyes closed. The black gets darker and darker behind my lids until white spots start spreading. I watch fireworks go off as I hear Maicy gasp. It's quiet, but it's almost as if she's screaming it. I shrink inside myself more.

"No fucking way," Mace whispers. Her voice is what gets me to look at her.

"That's what I said. But...I don't know. You got me thinking. It could be—" I stop, not able to say anything more.

"Go now." She turns to the innocent-looking package then back at me before pointing to the bathroom.

"But I don't really want to know. If I pretend it isn't a possibility, then can't it just go away?" I know I'm being stupid, but I've never wanted her to tell me yes more than right now.

She stands and grabs my hand. "Nope. But I'll go with you."

I know I should be embarrassed, but I'm not. There's no room for that feeling right now. There's only room for worry, and there's so, so much fucking worry. We don't even close the bathroom door once inside. I drop my pants and sit on the toilet. Maicy sits on the edge of the tub across from me, just as unashamed.

If this were about something else, something not so monumental, I think I'd kiss her. Maybe never let her go.

But instead, I tear the wrapper with my teeth. I'd rather close my eyes, but I can't aim for the stick right if I do. So I follow the directions but flip the stupid thing over after the cap is back on, and I let it sit on the counter. I clean up and sit on top of the closed toilet once my pants are back up.

"How long since your last period?" Maicy has no judgment in her voice, and again, I could kiss her. "I know you've been using condoms." When I arch my eyebrow at her she adds, "I take out the garbage because you're too lazy."

I'd rather focus on the last part, but I know I can't.

"Close to two months, maybe more." I wince as she sucks in a breath. If I didn't know better, if I wasn't seeing the tension on her face, I'd think it was a sigh. "I don't always track it. It's never been an issue, like you said. And didn't even think about it till you said something today. I was so wrapped up in everything else. I just…I was a fucking idiot."

"You did something though." She means the condoms.

"Maybe not enough."

I hang my head.

"You don't know that yet," she says.

Well, let's find out.

I grab the stupid thing that'll determine my future, the rest of my life. I never thought I could hate an inanimate object, a little piece of plastic, this much before now. But I really fucking do. I hate this stupid thing. I hate it so much as I hold it.

I close my eyes and turn it over, breathing a few times before opening one eye to peek.

Then my heart flip-flops in my chest.

"Not enough," I reiterate.

"You're pregnant?" she shrieks. It's so loud, I drop the test to cover my ears. And Maicy bends over, grabbing it to double-check my meaning.

I bob my head after dropping my hands to my lap, then I start twisting them around each other until all of my fingers hurt.

I'm fucking pregnant.

There's something, a little parasite, growing inside me, taking over.

Maicy looks from the double lines to my face, trying to figure out how to react. Eventually she decides on getting up to sit on the floor right in front of me. Her hands go to my lap, stilling then holding mine.

I let this happen. I got pregnant, and I have no idea who the father is. It could be either. Even if I get it narrowed down to a window of a few days at the doctor, every space of time would have both guys inside me.

I'm not even sure it would help to know, if I want to. Because, at the moment, every option available to me feels wrong. Doing this, not doing it…I don't know. I don't fucking know. I can't breathe, and tears start choking me, blurring everything. Maybe this, right here, tells me I'm not ready. *I don't know.*

Maicy lays her head in my lap, and when she lets go of my hands I move one into her hair. I stroke her silky strawberry strands and look up to the ceiling. I move my other hand to my stomach.

So what the fuck do I do now?

Austin

Now

For a while now, life has been normal. It's been better than normal, actually; it's been pretty fucking great. I've somehow gotten away with zero sex with Skyler, even though I'm back from the hotel, and tons with Taryn. Even Theo begged off from his threat to limit our friendship based on my romantic decisions.

And I've fallen even further into Taryn. I didn't know that was possible.

I'm happy, stupid happy.

It's unexpected, especially since she's tested me for so long, but I'm content. Somehow.

I step out of the shower with a smile on my face, but that changes really quick. I have no time to react as my phone sails across the room and hits my chest hard, dead center. I try to catch it, but after I miss, it hits the floor. I step over it, not wanting to see a cracked screen.

"You've got to be *fucking* kidding me. You should have left her name as Theo in there." Skyler's blonde hair whips around as she storms from the bathroom, her shouting still clear as crystal as she moves to the bedroom.

Well, it had to happen sometime.

"I'm sorry," I say as I walk after her, dripping water everywhere, still naked.

"Don't keep lying to me. I'm a big girl," she says, sneering. It's not pretty on her.

I won't get angry. She deserves a whole lot more than I can give in the end, but at the very least, she's earned calm now.

"She's had a piece of my heart since the day I met her. And I never thought this would happen. But it did, and I *am* sorry you got hurt. That's the truth." She sits on the bed, and I pull a pair of boxers on. This scene shouldn't unfold while my dick is swinging.

"Was it already happening when I met her?" I'd swear Skyler's blue eyes flashed red, if it were possible. I don't know where the sweet girl I knew went, but there's no question that she's gone right now. Not that I blame her.

Maybe that's better.

"Yes." I sit next to her on the bed.

There's no point in keeping if from her anymore; she's right.

"The truth shall set you free," Skye scoffs. It's not the response I expected. "You know what a shitty person you are, right?" she says, turning to me. I don't argue, but I don't agree either. Of course I am, but she doesn't know how complicated it is. And she doesn't need to; it wouldn't help.

"She knew what was happening at the bar that night, didn't she? She probably looked at me with pity in her heart. Do you know how fucking stupid and horrible that makes me feel?" she says, quieter now.

"I can imagine," I say.

"No. You can't. Don't even pretend. You have no idea." I still don't look at her. I know it'll just make her angrier. I try to spare her what little I can. "You're the worst kind of person," she adds.

"I'm not arguing with you. I'm a shit. You deserve better."

Skye stands and moves in front of me. "You're fucking right, I deserve *so* much more." Her hands clench into fists, but she doesn't hit me like that night she's been talking about. "Nothing I did could have ever been good enough for you. I tried everything to make you happy. I went to therapy; I looked at couples and sex advice online. Nothing helped. You never even noticed. I became invisible." She sits on the floor, sounding utterly overwhelmed, trying to get me to look at her while she pours her heart out.

"When you started to pull away, I didn't smother you," she continues. "I tried to make you happy regardless of my wants and feelings. I put you above everything else. I almost got fired for it, did you know that?" She shakes her head but gives me no time to answer. "No, of course you didn't. I didn't matter anymore. Nothing else mattered, apparently. I walked on eggshells, trying to be perfect, and it was never enough. Now I know why, at least. But you know what I just realized? *You're* the one who wasn't enough." The fire is back; she no longer sounds defeated. "You found your whore, and from that moment forward, you changed. You became the lesser one in this relationship. *You* are the one who failed."

Finally finished, Skye stands and moves to her dresser, preparing to pack.

"Don't you say another word about her." My voice shakes. "This was my choice. I'm the one you blame. Say what you want about me. But if you say another word about Taryn, you won't like how much shittier I can be." I hear the threat in my words and choose to walk out of the room as Skyler gets her shit to move out.

"We're done," she says. It isn't yelled. She doesn't cry. It's a fact. A simple statement. Truer than anything else uttered in this whole breakup, in the whole relationship, I'd guess.

"Yeah, we are," I say.

Without clothes, I can't leave, and I'm not going back into the bedroom. It's too small of a space. I don't trust myself. I'd rather storm out and tell her to leave her set of keys on the table and be gone when I get back. But I don't. Instead I pick up my phone from the floor.

Me: Skyler found out.
Me: She's leaving. It's just me and you now. Are you ready?

I hope so.

But as the minutes tick by, and nothing comes through, I start to panic.

I wish Skyler would fucking hurry up, and my anger makes me wonder if she's going slow, stalling, just to piss me off. It isn't outside the realm of possibilities, but it also isn't likely. I'd like to think I know her, at least a little bit, and she probably wants to get the hell out of here.

There's no sense in prolonging it.

She's mad, and I wouldn't blame her if she is forever.

I can't. I never blamed Taryn.

But I want her out of here. I want to call Taryn, and I can't do that with Skyler here. I guess I *could*, but I won't. That's too far past the line of acceptable behavior. Not that my morals have been anything close to acceptable. But I won't do that.

If I could have everything I want, I'd have Taryn over here right after Skyler leaves. And I'd like that to be fucking soon. I haven't been able to have her here yet, and I want to see what she looks like in my bed. I'm pretty sure there won't be any sight more beautiful in the world.

I don't call, but I can't wait. I have to do something as my emotions start getting the better of me.

Me: Will you come over here?
Taryn: Give me an hour.

Taryn
Now

I have to tell him. I've already made my decision, so I have to.

I wish my timing was better, but that's nothing new. I suck at everything else having to do with feelings and relationships, so why on earth would I ever think I could get the timing down right? I really fucking wish Skyler had waited one more day before snooping into whatever gave her the truth.

As much as I want to hate her, to blame her for this, I just feel bad. She didn't do *anything* wrong. And I hope she finds someone that does right by her. She doesn't deserve what she got. None of it. After all is said and done, she's my *only* regret in all of this mess. A big one.

On the drive to Austin's, I go over so many possible ways to break the news to him.

Either you or your best friend knocked me up.

I'm pregnant, but I can't be sure it's yours.

No thanks, I can't drink. I'm carrying your baby. Well, a baby. It could be Theo's too.

Fuuuuuuuuck.

There's no possible way this'll go well. I park and sit in my car for a long, long time. I wish I could text him the news or let Maicy tell him. She begged me to let her, but I knew she'd be evil. Plus, I'm a grown-up now. Well, close to it, at least. I have to be, since in less than a year

I'll be shoved head first into grow-the-fuck-up-or-fail-miserably territory.

I looked online, and stress isn't good when you're growing a kid. So I try to relax, but it doesn't work. Eventually I just get out of the car, trying to breathe as slow as I can, knowing I'll be tense through this regardless.

When I get to Austin's door, I only knock once before he opens it.

"Why did you stay in your car so long? What's wrong?" he asks before I can even step inside. The crease above his nose is adorable and nerve-wracking at the same time.

"I…Umm, well…I don't know how to start this," I let the last bit out in a rush after taking forever with the first. Walking over to and flopping down onto the couch doesn't take as long as I'd like it to. Then Austin's looking at me, and he's expecting me to continue.

I don't.

"Tell me, Angel."

He's distracting, with nothing on but his boxers, and I can feel my hormones egging me on to ignore what I *have* to tell him. So I compromise with myself, if he doesn't kill me I'll try to get sex after he calms down.

"Okay." I do what any immature kid would do, I close my eyes, making the hard words a little easier to say. "So the thing is, I'm pregnant." I hear his breath stop. My heart beats faster, and I speed through the rest, wringing my hands, eyes still closed, tripping over my words.

"And, well, you know how I wanted things to be as fucked up as possible? I helped that along a little. I've been sleeping with someone else too. It started before we did." Like that'll fucking help him at all. I keep running through what I have to say, though. "I'm sorry. I'm so fucking sorry. And I know you'll hate me. I just needed to have you go from the worst to everything I needed, and I had to challenge the possibility in every way—on my end too—before I could trust my own feelings. I've been wrong about us before."

I pause to breathe, giving him a fraction of a moment to put a little blame on himself for years ago. It's shitty; I know it. But I do it anyway. And I hope it works. Then I push through the final part. "So, I know you may leave me after this. That's okay, though. I'm a horrible person, but I don't know who the father is." I finally finish.

Peeking one eye open, I see Austin's gaze trained on the floor. He looks so dumbfounded. His whole face is so smooth, like frozen ice, that I wonder if he's awake, alive. If there's emotion behind his eyes, I don't see it. Then he breathes, and a little life comes back into him. Mine eyes snap shut again in response to his starting to turn toward me.

"Who is he?" he asks.

Fuck.

I really, *really* hoped he wouldn't ask. I thought maybe the baby part would sidetrack him. At least I'm prepared with an answer.

"Does it matter?" *Please don't let it.*

"I just have this feeling I want to be wrong about." I feel one of his hands grab mine, and the other lands on my knee. So I look at him, and somehow—I don't get it—he's forgiving. The chocolate-brown of his irises waiting for me is warm. I almost wonder…but I try not to see the hope there.

"Theo." I spit it out before I can worry anymore, before I can stop myself.

It is what it is, and it's the truth. After all of this, I suppose he deserves the truth.

Austin doesn't flinch. I can't fucking believe it. He drops his gaze to my stomach and lifts the hand from my knee to hesitate in the area just around my belly. His eyes flick up to mine, and I nod.

He presses his palm to the bloat that's barely there, and it's a sweet moment. But then it comes to a crashing halt.

"Just so you know, I'm going to fucking kill him." His chilling words are made so much worse by his even whisper. They're almost a coo to the little baby in me. And he doesn't look mad, there's almost an upturn to the corner of his mouth.

"Don't…" I try.

"Shhh. I'm not mad at you. I knew there was time, I knew that there were people in your life since me. And I knew you wanted complicated. I knew everything I had to get us past to get over your walls. I agreed to that. And, baby, this is about as bad as it gets." Wow, still a better response than I'd expected. I can't believe I let two best friends each get ahold of half of my heart.

"But *he* should have told me. He had plenty of chances, and now we're going to have it out," Austin says, still quiet.

"No. Please don't," I beg, and I hear the tears in my voice.

He must hear the crack of emotion too since that's when he looks back to my face and raises the now-free hand to my chin. "You can't change my mind. So let's go into the bedroom and be together before I let myself come undone."

I'm not entirely sure what he means, but I let him pull me to my feet, into his room, and then onto the bed.

My clothes are off in a blink, less maybe, but Austin won't let me strip him of his boxers. He keeps looking to, and touching, my stomach, and I know he's torn between lust and a whole other batch of emotions not about me.

I can't take it anymore; I grab his face and pull it toward mine. When I have his full attention on me I say, "Make this about me. Need *me*. Be here with *just me*." I flick my gaze back and forth between his eyes, watching for understanding. Then he closes his and kisses me like he did the first night we sat on my couch months ago.

His tongue searches me for an answer. He pushes on top of me, a little too carefully for my liking, though I don't say anything, and cups the back of my neck with a grip that makes me moan into him. I start to melt, and it's what I needed.

He is part of what I need.

I pull his boxers down, and I think he's forgotten the little-huge thing growing between us—for the moment, at least—as he proves to me, without words, how much he still loves me, even though I'm the world's biggest fuck-up.

Austin

Now

Taryn stays in my bed, naked, for almost six hours. She lets me make love to her, not just fuck her, multiple times. It'll be a memory I'll never forget. It's also one I'm not sure we can top, though I know I'll try. Forever, if I have to.

It's not until her stomach growls that I remember, since she asked me to focus on her, that she's fucking pregnant. She's growing a child, and it could be mine. I jump out of bed then.

"What can I make you? Whatcha hungry for?" The worry in my voice makes the pitch embarrassing and high. I should've fed her so long ago. "Donuts again? Cheeseburgers? Chinese? Something healthier? I can order whatever," I say.

"I need to get home. Maicy and I have plans tonight. I'll be a little late, even if I leave now," she says.

I don't try to hide my frown.

I don't exactly argue either, even though I want to. I do have something else to do anyway.

"Please." It's all she says. With my jaw squared, she must know where I'll be going when I leave here. I'm sure she doesn't want to hear my answer, so I don't give it out loud. I do shake my head; I just can't argue about this.

She gets out of bed and dresses. I don't lie to her.

I get dressed too, ready to leave a minute after her. She watches me from the bed, not upset, but resigned.

I walk Taryn to the door, kissing her soft and sweet before opening it. I surprise myself as I kiss my fingers too then place them to her stomach. I never really thought about kids before a few hours ago, but now I can't stop hoping the little thing in there is mine. And, damn, I hope that's not just a caveman need to claim my territory. I mean, I don't think it is.

She leaves without another request, with nothing else said.

And I wait until I hear her car drive away before heading toward my own. On the stairs, I type out the warning.

Me: If you're, home stay there. If you aren't, head there now.
Theo: Should I be worried?
Me: Yep.

Austin

Before

I ruined myself.

As Taryn walks away with me still on my knees, I'm ruined. To the core. And I have no one to blame other than myself. Maicy comes out of the house and does her best to drag me back into her car. Reluctantly, I let her drive me home.

Home, where I'll be alone.

Alone forever. Because no one will ever stack up to Taryn.

Theo comes over once I'm there—I guess Maicy let him know what happened—and he spends way too much time talking me off the edge, talking me out of calling Taryn, talking just to keep me distracted. He convinces me that, even though I screwed up, everything happens for a reason, and I may not see what it is now, but there are reasons to keep going.

He tells me that if it's meant to be, it will be again.

Someday maybe, but not now.

He says everything right, but it's still not enough. I don't stop hurting.

"I think," I say through more angry tears, "I think ruined what we had because I never believed I deserved her in the first place. I was waiting for her to leave me; turns out I thought it would be just easier to force her."

He never answers; he doesn't need to.

I know I'm right.

Theo is the thing, the *one* person, that keeps me going while I realize Taryn'll never forgive me. He keeps me sane until I can get along on my own. It takes weeks, and I call Maicy too many times after Taryn's phone dies. But he's there for all of it.

Theo, my best friend, gets me through the hardest time in my life thus far.

Austin
Now

This time, Theo isn't outside when I get there. That might be smart. This way, hopefully no one will get arrested. I can't imagine Taryn would be too happy about both of the men she cares about—that hurts to admit even to myself, though I know it's true—going to jail for trying to kill each other.

Even with this anger bubbling inside me, Taryn stays my number one priority.

I can't let myself forget that. Ever. And especially now.

My fist lands hard on the door in several quick pounds. Theo opens it and steps aside. I walk in and head to his living room before turning to face him.

"My best friend," I say.

"I'm not sorry."

He looks me in the eye as he stabs me in the heart.

"No fucking way you just said that to me. I must've heard you wrong," I shout.

Most of my prior sense of responsibility starts to evaporate.

"I meant it. I fell in love with her long before you started seeing her again. Long before you ever even met her. I've been in love her as long as I've known her. Since the first day we met in foster care." I take a step back, watching the room shake back and forth. But he keeps going.

"I've been keeping her company for months, waiting for her to love me back. And I'm sorry you hate me for it." How can he be both sorry and not sorry at the same time? If he thinks he can confuse me out of my rage, he's dead wrong. "I never wanted to lose my best friend. But you know as well as I do, she's the only one out there worth losing *everything* for."

Fuck.

I wish he hadn't said that.

The red I'm seeing turns a shade lighter.

"I should've told you years ago. I fell harder for her somewhere between when you broke up and when she finally slept with me." That brings out a cringe, and I hate that I showed weakness, but he doesn't even seem to notice. "I tried to push it down, ignore it till it went away, but then it never did. I didn't mean to fall for the one person I shouldn't. But shit happens, and now, even knowing what will become of us," he shoves his hand toward me, meaning he and I, us, "I wouldn't do anything different."

I can't hear one more word.

So I do the thing I shouldn't.

I pull my arm back and then let it fly forward right into Theo's face. My knuckles land somewhere between his eye and his nose. It hurts bad, but I don't regret it. He deserved every broken blood vessel. His eye will be black for a week.

Good.

Fuck his face. Fuck the years of friendship, hiding a love for *my* girlfriend. *Fuck Theo.*

The worst part about all of this is knowing Taryn will be upset.

He doesn't protect himself, even though he had the time. He stays standing and doesn't move an inch in retaliation. He knew it was coming, and he took it. But that isn't enough.

The words fall from my mouth, each one louder than the last to cover the rush of blood in my ears, while he's still bent over, rubbing his eyes. "You're right. You should've told me before anything happened. Maybe then I could've forgiven you. But now I never will." I turn my back, the adrenaline crashing and everything going quiet again.

Speaking to the hallway before walking away, I add, "I'll *never* forgive you."

"I'm not backing down, you know. I'll keep fighting for her until she tells me to leave." Theo's voice is strong. I wouldn't be able to tell his nose was broken, or close to it, if I wasn't the one who just did it.

Those words hurt worse than any yet, and I don't know why.

"Well, then, you do it on your own." I breathe as calmly as I can, knowing what's coming next. "You aren't my friend, not anymore. You'll never be again." I can't turn around. I didn't think this would be so hard. I thought it would be like ending things with Skyler, easy because of what I still have, but it's worse. Way worse. "You may have taken away my soul mate, you know. She was supposed to be my forever," I say.

I take one step, but then stop to add the thing I can't ever take back. With this I'll be taking something away from Taryn. And she may hold it against me for a long time. But I can't keep it inside, and I trust I've come far enough for her to forgive me for this one little mistake.

"She's pregnant," I say.

I don't wait to hear what he might respond with.

I don't turn around to gauge his reaction.

I just walk away, from my best friend, for the last time.

Taryn
Now

"How's Tuesday doing?" I ask Maicy as she chugs a soda. Most of the time I try to pretend that I'm her only friend, that I'm the center of her universe. But I really need some distraction, and it's all I can think of.

"She's doing so much better. And not that I'd ever tell her this, but what happened made the podcast even more popular."

I nod, not really knowing what else to say, eating quietly again. I could ask about the others in that group, but I don't have the energy, the drive. So I keep eating Maicy's fabulous combination of take-out dinners—like me, it's her version of cooking—as slowly as I can.

One down and one to go.

Ugh, that sounds horrible, even inside my head. I cringe even thinking it.

She notices I'm stalling.

"You can't eat your way to finishing this. You have to actually tell him." She stuffs a whole wonton in her mouth at once, and I laugh. It feels good to laugh, if just for a second. Then she tries to talk around the cream cheese, and I laugh even harder. "Besides the first one went okay, and that was supposed to be the worst. Theo should be a breeze," she says, garbled, as crumbs fall onto the table.

She isn't wrong, and I wish I were as optimistic.

"Will you go with me?" I give her the widest, wettest, pouty eyes I've ever mustered.

"Fuck no," she says, choking it out.

"Why the hell not?" I ask. I really thought she'd go for it since she likes Theo best.

"Because you two are going to do the dirty afterward. I know you, and I know him. And even if I'm rooting for him, there's no fucking way I'm covering my ears in the living room, pretending not to hear you," Maicy says.

"I can control myself you know," I argue.

"Nope. No way." *Damn.* But a brilliant idea comes to me, and I text Theo.

Me: Movie at my place?
Theo: On my way.

Dependable, wonderful Theo. I hope he stays that way. I try not to worry.

"He's coming here, so *ha*," I say, thinking I've won.

But Maicy thinks quickly. "I'm out then. There's a podcast meeting I was going to skip. But have fun here." And she takes her fried rice and a fork with her out the door, waving with the other hand.

Damn again.

I keep eating till Theo shows up. My expanding stomach was full a while ago, but I can't stop picking. I'll be as fat as a house in a few months if I keep up this rate. Then I remember that's kind of the point.

Theo knocks, and I just yell for him to come in.

I can't stop myself from smiling when he locks the door and takes off his shoes before heading to the living room.

"What're we watching tonight, Pidge?" he says from the hallway.

I can picture how happy he is, even before he rounds the corner, and that does something to my heart. The very heart I wasn't always sure was still there.

"Anything you want," I say as he walks into view. He rubs his hands together and sits next to me, putting his feet up on the coffee table. "But I have to tell you something first."

Then I see the black eye he has.

"Oh shit."

Austin made good on his promise. I guess. And I regret the rift between them more than ever, wishing I could undo it. I should've told Theo first. There are so many fucking things I could have done differently.

I touch Theo's purple, swollen skin, wishing I wasn't such a walking problem. He squints at me, trying to read my face. He should be able to read my anxiety, but to my surprise he grins in response to whatever he's seeing.

"Tell me," he says, not explaining the bruise. We both know how he got it anyway.

At least Austin left the hardest part up to me.

I don't let myself over-think this time. I don't preface it with anything.

"I'm pregnant." I just blurt out the scary truth. His mouth drops a little, and then the grin he wore a moment ago turns into a wide, beaming bunch of confusion to me.

"Even if it's not mine, I'm sticking around. Nothing could get rid of me." He tucks a strand of my hair behind my ear, and I try not to melt into a puddle of relief. "The only way I'm leaving is if you beg me to. Repeatedly. Even then, it'll take a lot of work." His voice gains depth, more gravel, with each word, and I feel a special tingle that only comes out with him. Then he winks, and I almost explode.

I'm amazed at how appreciative I am that he keeps his eyes on me. He doesn't make this about the baby yet. He lets me feel my own feelings, about us. One of Theo's hands goes my hair, and as he leans in to kiss me, I watch the other twitch on his leg. It looks like he's tapping his pocket. That or he's having a spasm.

But I forget all about it when his lips find mine.

There are no more thoughts of the baby. No more thoughts of Austin. It helps that Theo doesn't threaten anyone else I care about. A nice change, even if the first one was all my fault and my shitty timing. Either way, he makes this about me, about us, and nothing else.

I swear I hear him mumble three terrifying words against my skin, though I choose to pretend it was a hallucination, a glitch in my eardrums. And after a few minutes of wonderful making out, I force him to pick a movie.

"There's plenty of time for you to drive me wild. Let's be normal for a minute," I say.

"Anything you want," he answers immediately, but he barely pulls back from the kiss—slow and measured— tempting me to strip him right here on the couch, not caring if Maicy, or anyone else for that matter, walks in. Knowing from the look in his pale eyes that he wants me just as bad doesn't help either.

****

Theo stays the night, and I wish neither of us had to work in the morning. Weekends aren't ever long enough. Granted, my weekend could have been a lot worse. But then again, everything can always get worse. If I've learned nothing else in my life, that's one lesson I can't ignore with how many times it's been drilled into me.

But while tangled in Theo's limbs, without the sadness or sobs I faced the first time I woke up with him, I let myself hope those days are behind me now.

Austin

Now

Monday morning I call in sick to work and start drinking with lunch. I kept a brave face for Taryn, but sitting alone here, I'm not sure what to do with myself. I can be a good father with her by my side, I'm positive of that, but I don't know what kind of stepfather I'd be.

And I can't even think about the worst possibility. I'd pack up and move, start over somewhere else, after committing assault again.

Today it's shots of vodka to numb the terror.

I shiver as my throat protests the liquid. My stomach isn't too happy about it either.

But I don't want to think about stomachs.

I take my bottle and stretch across the couch, flipping on the TV. Channel after channel of stupid shit sits before me. When did shows get so bad? Sitcoms are not what I fucking need right now, and that's all that seems to be on. Reruns and soap operas. So I leave it on the latter.

It's only a little better. That is, until some dark-haired hottie announces to her father that she's pregnant. Of course that would be on here. Taking another swig of my clear problem-eraser, I choke back a horrible scream trying to break free from my throat. It made it past my diaphragm, through my stomach, and almost got out. But if I start, if I let the beast of pain and fear out, I don't think I'd ever be able to contain him again.

So I try to stuff it deeper down.

Once the mess is to my toes, I take another drink.

****

I don't remember sending the first text, but I look at my phone and there it is. Maicy's name flashes on my screen, and my already-churning stomach does a move that doesn't speak well for my near future.

Fuck, fuck, fuck.

Me: Do you want to help me make a bad situation worse?

How do I manage to fuck things up so badly, so quickly? The night Taryn walked away the first time, it had only taken a matter of minutes to shatter everything good in my life. Almost no time at all was spent in that basement making the biggest mistake of my life.

And now it can't have taken more than a few seconds to type out a stupid message I can never take back. I see the indicator that Maicy's writing back, and I push through the cloud of vodka to type faster than her.

Me: I didn't just say that. I take it back. Don't tell her, please.

The little icon drops away as she deletes whatever she'd started with. Then it pops back up, and I hold my breath, waiting.

Maicy: How drunk you are right now will determine the level of furious I am.

Me: Very. And even more stupid.

Maicy: You got that right, fucker. She needs way more right now than ever before, and you've already had trouble in the past living up to what she deserves.
Maicy: So step it up or walk away.
Me: You're right.
Maicy: I know I'm right. There won't be any second helpful hints for you, so learn it now no matter how drunk you are or fucking leave. She can handle leaving better than a fuck up.
Maicy: That's my only warning.
Maicy: She can't emotionally handle a third chance. It's now or never.
Me: I fucked up. I'm sorry.
Me: I get it.
Me: It won't happen again.
Me: I love her you know. I'm not going anywhere.
Me: Sometimes I think she deserves better than me.
Maicy: Sleep it off, champ.

The part hurting me the most is that Taryn has feelings for both of us. She didn't sleep with Theo just to spite me. That might've been better. She may have started out just fucking him, but somewhere in there, she started to care.

That kills me.

I don't know if there's something deeper than bones, but if there is, that's where it hurts—it feels like my soul aches knowing I'm not the only one she's in love with.

She'd never say the word, but I know it.

Taryn loves me, but she also loves Theo.

I only stayed with Skyler at *her* request. I'd rather have walked away, but she asked me to stay, so I did. And even then, I just slept with her one time. Once in all those weeks, and while living together, did I slip and fuck my girlfriend. I think that's pretty amazing.

Who the fuck knows how many times she was with Theo.

I shudder thinking about it, and right away the stupidity of the decision hits me like a brick to the gut. I run to the bathroom, tripping twice on the way. I almost don't make it to the toilet. As I heave and retch, it feels appropriate.

I've lost my best friend.

He may also be the father of the baby growing inside the woman I'll love for my entire life. Even if she chooses him, I don't think I'll ever let go of the last spark between us. It's burned inside of me, branded.

I'm shit-stinking-drunk, and life couldn't get much lower than this moment.

But, of course, that thought comes too soon because only seconds after getting the last of this round of puke out, there's a knock at the door. A sudden, and irrational, anger flares, warming me. I don't want to see anyone, for any reason. But then, that fades away when I consider it could be Taryn.

I struggle to get up and to the door. Unlocking it is even harder. And when it opens, I almost fall over.

"Skyler," I say, choking on her name.

"You look like shit," she says. I'm pretty sure it isn't meant to be mean, but that doesn't make it feel any better.

Especially considering she still looks great, maybe even better.

I wonder if the world will stop kicking me down. I've already fallen face first and tried not to move, but that hasn't seemed to help. Not that I deserve the break, but I wouldn't mind it. Taryn always believed she didn't deserve to be happy, but maybe I was always the one with the curse and we never knew.

"What do you want? I'd like to get back to puking," I say, so drunk I'm honest.

"I forgot that brooch my mother left me. If it were anything else, I wouldn't have come. I tried calling you first." She walks in despite not getting the invitation. Shoulders squared, chin pointed slightly up.

I don't stop her either.

Letting the door close, I go back to the couch as she heads to the bedroom. I'd much rather she wasn't in my room, but I'm not searching for her shit for her.

"If you wouldn't mind hurrying up…" I shout, like the dick I am.

"You know, I am sorry I ever said anything bad about Taryn," Skye calls from the bedroom. My face flames hot again, and I can't stay composed if she does what I'm anticipating she will. "She did me a favor."

Skye walks back out into the living room. For a second, I wonder where she's staying, but then I know it doesn't matter. Even if it did, I don't deserve to know, to ask.

She continues, "We never would've worked, and I would've snapped my spine, bending backwards to try and make you happy. She may have been the best thing to happen to me. I'll have to thank her someday."

I have no response.

Skye can see it. I know as she smiles and glides out the door, leaving me in the pile of shit I've been wallowing in for hours. I wish Taryn were here. I wish even more that Skye hadn't stopped by. I could've sent anything to her in the mail.

I didn't kiss her goodbye or anything. No, I'll never make that mistake again. I didn't even let her touch me. But I still feel worse than I did five minutes ago when I was dumping my guts into the toilet.

So I take another swig from the bottle.

And I know I'll be back in the bathroom soon, but it doesn't matter. Nothing matters right now.

I need tonight to be wiped from my memory. I need to get all of this shit out of my system so I can move on and step up like Mace said.

I need to be someone to be proud of, to show off and appreciate. I need to be someone worth choosing. I need to make Taryn want to stay with me, no matter who the father is. I will collapse in on myself, self-destruct, if I can't get her to need me, to want me, to be the one she raises a family with. I want her to pick me over Theo, choose me over everyone else. And for all of that to be possible, I need to bleed the bad from my system. I have to flush it out with booze and vomit and the mountains of mistakes.

Then I can start fresh. Then I can be who she picks.

Austin
Before

I shouldn't, but I text Taryn almost every single day, not that my current girlfriend knows. Not that any of them have known. I try to resist, I try to go as long as I can without reaching out to her. But in the end, it's pretty much every day.

Or night.

Interacting with her at night has become sort of a routine. I need it now. The other night I tried to be better, to focus on dinner and the movie, on my girlfriend and our date, and tried to make it work without thinking about Taryn. I tried not to want Taryn in my head or my heart, even as a friend.

But it didn't work.

I can't sleep until I send her a message.

Me: Goodnight.
Theo T: Going to bed so early?
Me: Why, you bored?
Theo: T: How's what's-her-name?
Me: Okay.
Theo T: Just okay?
Me: Yeah. I mean she's awesome. I just...idk.
Theo T: Wanna talk about it?

Me: Here's the thing...
Theo T: Uh oh
Me: I would never cheat on her, but if I did, it would only be with you.
Me: It would only be you.
Theo T: ...
Me: I'm sorry.
Theo T: What am I supposed to say to that?
Me: Nothing
Me: idk
Me: I just wanted you to know.
Theo T: Well now I do.
Theo T: Goodnight.
Me: Yeah, goodnight.

If only she would've let me back in, let me make up for everything, given me one more chance. She could still be mine, still wearing her ring, and I wouldn't have to say stupid shit like this. We wouldn't have to pretend that being friends is enough.

Friends could never be enough.

Anything less than everything bullshit.

But most nights, if I'm truthful with myself, I'm just glad she lets me be her friend again, after everything. I shouldn't have said so much and chanced her leaving altogether because I can't keep my stupid emotions to myself.

When my phone buzzes again, I sigh with relief, so glad Taryn hasn't closed herself off.

But my smile fades when I see who the message is actually from.

GF: Want to hang out tomorrow?
Me: Sorry, I can't. Maybe later this week.
GF: Sounds good, just let me know when.

I need to break it off with her, I know I do. Just like I did with my girlfriend before that, and the one before her. I don't mean to do what I do, but none of them are Taryn. And I'm getting worried that no one ever will be.

I try to imagine myself happy with someone else, someone other than Taryn.

Me: I'm sorry. Really. Forget I said that.
Theo T: Already forgotten. It's fine.
Theo T: You should be sleeping, friend.
Me: I was worried.
Theo T: Seriously, go to bed. It's fine, I swear.
Theo T: Goodnight.
Me: Sleep tight.

I smile again, even if it's a small one.
Friends is better than nothing.

Taryn
Now

I have my first OB appointment today. It's terrifying; I'm terrified.

Did I mention this shit is terrifying? Well, it is.

I never wanted kids before, but once it happened I realized there was no other option than to keep it. Not for me, not right now. The need is already building, a connection strengthening every moment. And it's only been a week and a half of thinking that way, but it's engrained.

Thank fuck neither asked if was going to get rid of it. I hate to say it, but I expected to hear that at least once. Though, Austin did surprise me with his one request that followed, for an amniotic now instead of waiting to test for paternity after. It shouldn't have been a shock. The jealousy and need was written all over him, but somehow it still caught me off guard. In the end anything was better than demanding an abortion. And I'm considering it. I don't know.

Holy shit, I'm gonna have a baby.

I hope it's a boy.

My thoughts are so scattered, I'm glad as hell that Maicy's the one coming with to the doctor today. She asked first, and I was so happy about it. Both Theo and Austin offered to come, one even begged, but I held firm and said no. Both pouted about it. But I didn't want it to be about *them*. I didn't want to have to choose between them; I'm still not ready for that. And no way in hell was I going to deal with bringing both.

Chaos would've ensued. I don't need that shit today. Today is about me and my little bud of a baby. Regardless of who the father is, this thing is still mine.

I'm the mom.

That's one of the weirdest things to think about, ever.

I never thought much about kids or being a mom to one. I guess it was a conversation I was prepared to have eventually—but nothing had swayed me either way. Until now. And the word is like a flash of lightning each time I think it. *Mom.*

In a good way.

Unrelated, but important anyway—I really want to have someone over tonight. I haven't decided who, though. My desire has gone up. And come to think about it…that may have been a clue. I like sex and all, like anyone else, but I did it almost every day for a couple months and at my request. That's excessive.

My heart says to have Theo over, but my head is telling me Austin needs me more right now. Since Skyler left, he's been hinting I need to choose, but then the whole bun-in-the-oven thing threw everyone for a loop. I know he's having a really hard time. I do. That's why he said the stupid shit he did to Maicy. And that's the *only* reason he gets one pass for it. Just one. I was so fucking pissed, but then I slept on it, and I get why he's struggling. Even still, his pain, his struggle, it's not enough for me to give in.

Plus, maybe I should get through this appointment first and then decide later. See how I feel.

I hear Maicy's car rumbling outside, and she honks while I'm putting my shoes on.

"Yeah, yeah, yeah," I mutter, while locking the door on my way out, because she won't stop beeping the horn. Hopping into the car, I shake my head, frowning. "If I'm deaf by the time this baby comes out, then you'll be the only one to hear all the crying," I say.

She takes her hand off the horn like it's on fire. "Good point." We both smile as she backs out of the driveway and heads to the clinic.

Maicy blasts nostalgic music the entire drive, and we shout-sing every word. I laugh most of the time, still smiling when I'm not, and somehow I don't worry about anything. It's only when we park and she shuts off the car that anxiety starts to bubble in me.

"Is this really happening?" It's a stupid question to ask, I know.

I've peed on three sticks since the first one. This definitely is *really* happening.

"Yep, cookie, this is real life." She squeezes my hand before getting out of the car. I sit in my seat until she walks around to my side. "Open up, or I'll drag you out of there." Her smirk looks evil, so I open the damn door.

Leave it to Maicy to bully me into my gynecologist appointment.

****

The little heartbeat flashes on the black and white screen, and I fucking hate how choked up I get. Real tears fall from my eyes, and Maicy starts sniffling too. We're a regular bunch of babies.

"It's too soon to tell the sex. But everything looks good so far. Normal and healthy. I'll print you the picture." The technician is all smiles.

Both Maicy and I nod; I have no idea what to even say.

When the lady leaves the room, Maicy hops up onto the bed-table-thing with me. "I think Maicy would be a great name for a girl. And Mace for a boy."

"How would we tell you two apart when I'm screaming at you both?" I say.

"Middle name then," she says. *Pushy little brat.*

"Maybe." I say, winking.

Leaving the clinic, we stop at the front to make my next appointment, four weeks out, and I can't stop looking at my sonogram. Twenty-eight days never felt so long before.

"You should make a shirt with the picture right over your stomach," Maicy suggests when we get into the car.

"Only if you wear one too."

****

When we pull into the driveway Theo's truck is waiting on the street, empty. He's sitting on our front steps with a box in his lap. He's also wearing a bright smile, lighting up his piercing blue eyes.

When I get out of the car, I skip over to him, now in an even better mood.

I hand him one of the pictures without a word.

"Theo Junior, huh?" I can't be sure, but it looks like his eyes open a little wider, his smiles gets a little bigger. And these stupid hormones are going to make me crazy. I almost want to cry again.

What the hell.

"Mace already called dibs on the name repeat. So what's in the box?" I eye the simple, brown cardboard. There are holes but no labels. It's nameless, plain.

"Well, Mommy," he sets the sonogram onto the concrete next to him, like he's worried about being too rough with it, "I got you something to practice with."

Then I hear a pretty unmistakable noise from inside.

"You didn't," I say, trying to hide the excitement from my eyes. I have no idea where those emotions come from. A few months ago I'd rather have been high and wasted than growing a baby or adopting a cat.

So this is new, and maybe it's what being an adult feels like. *Weird.*

"I checked with Maicy first," he says, looking at her. She nods and goes inside, walking around us, while Theo continues. "Her name is Persephone—Hades's girlfriend by the way—and she's a year old. She's a little bit of a crab, like you, but I have a feeling she'll warm up real quick."

Theo lifts the top to the box so I can peek in, and I'm greeted with the largest amber eyes I've ever seen. She's curled in a corner, hanging out. She isn't scared or hissing, she's just sitting, looking pretty. I reach my hand in, tentative, terrified to scare her. When I'm close, she nudges her cold nose into my palm, begging to be scratched. Then her purr starts, and it's like a freight train.

"See, she already likes you. Your cranky spirits must be kindred." Theo holds onto my waist with his strong hand. He's warm too. "You can rename her if you want, but I think it fits."

Persephone's fur is spotted white and black. She has weird patches, and she's a little funny looking. But it's also the softest fur I've ever touched. And she never stops purring as long as I'm near.

Theo helps me bring her inside, and then he sets up everything from the litter box to her food and water dishes he'd had in his trunk. He's thought of everything.

"She's fixed, and I even bought some toys." My insides start to feel mushier than they ever have before. "You can't scoop her litter though, so don't even think about it. Either ask Mace, or I'll do it every time I'm here."

"Thank you," I whisper. I move up onto tiptoes and kiss his lips softly, then the tip of his nose. "She's perfect. *You're* perfect." I know saying it is unfair without adding that he's my choice. But...but I can't yet.

I know that makes me horrible.

"She's yours. I just thought it'd be a good fit. You're meant for each other."

He smiles and walks to the front door. He lingers there with his hand on the knob. I know he's waiting for me to ask him to stay. And I want to. Fuck, do I want to. But then I don't, and he opens it, and the moment's lost. He turns right before closing the door behind him and talks through the crack.

"I'll be back tomorrow to visit you four, with dinner. And I'm staying over," he says with a smirk.

Guess tonight is Austin's then.

Austin
Now

Taryn: You can come over tonight if you want. I have a picture for you.
Me: Leaving now.

After I changed her name in my phone, it started giving me a good feeling to see it pop up, like it does right now. But the warmth's followed by a pinch of nervousness, knowing I'll see a picture of a baby, maybe my baby but maybe not.

Since my low night, I've stressed a little knowing I'm going to get attached to the kid, not knowing what's going to happen. But those feelings, those rational worries, won't keep me away from Taryn. I still need to convince her I belong to her. She may not be mine yet, but I'll always be hers.

When I get to her door, I want to be able to just walk in anytime, unannounced. But that's not my reality, yet. So I knock and wait to hear the okay. Maicy shouts through glass and wood, "Come in."

I swing the door open to find a little furry thing winding its way around the shoes piled in the entry. It takes one look at me and runs away with an angry squeak. Maybe it was a hiss, not that it matters.

"When did you get a cat, ladies?" I say on my way to the kitchen. Taryn's munching on fruit when I get there, and I can't help but smile when I see her lips stained from the berries.

"Today. Her name's Persephone. Isn't she perfect?" Taryn beams.

Well, I wouldn't say perfect. Cats are tricky fuckers. But if it makes her happy…

"Post-appointment celebration?" I ask.

"You could say that," Maicy says. Taryn stands, heading to the living room.

"I'm sure you'll like her," Taryn adds, with three blackberries crammed in her mouth.

We get to the living room, and Taryn picks some romantic comedy. I can't help but arch my eyebrow at her.

"Who are you, and what have you done with my girl?" I say.

"Hormones," again Maicy answers for Taryn. "She's really weird now. She cries and everything, just like a normal person." Taryn sends a grape flying through the air and it lands right in Maicy's cleavage. Maicy picks it up and eats it. I bark out a laugh and settle in to spend time here.

I pull Taryn's feet into my lap to start massaging them, and I get even better responses than normal from it tonight.

Brownie points.

"Please stop having foot orgasms. It's gross. You're gross." Maicy snatches the remote and changes the channel. Taryn doesn't even argue. She's in heaven. I love that she's so happy.

****

When we head to the bedroom it's late, but neither of us have to work tomorrow.

I can tell Taryn wants to talk about something. She keeps fidgeting and sighing, but she hasn't spilled it.

So I take the bait.

"What is it? You can tell me."

She sits on the edge of the bed and curls her feet under herself. I drop next to her and grab for her hand, waiting.

Finally, she spits it out, "Are you and Theo okay yet?" Her eyes look so concerned when they search mine.

"I'm not talking about this with you. I know what the reality is. And I can accept it. For you. I guess. But I don't have to like it, and I don't need to have conversations about it," I say standing. I turn from her, moving to undress for bed, looking at the ceiling as I speak. I can hear her stillness, not coming after me, and a small wave of disappointment washes over me.

"I don't want either of you to lose your best friend because of *me*." I hear her drop backward onto the bed, probably on her back. And the catch in her voice hurts me again, but I don't turn around yet. I won't until the subject's closed.

"Nothing is your fault. He stopped being my friend because of *his own* choices. *Period*. And that's the last time we're talking about it. Okay?"

"Fine," she says, and then I turn around.

And I want to show her how thankful I am she let it go. So I turn around with a wicked look on my face, somewhere between lust and relief, I think. When I get to the bed, I drop to my knees and pull Taryn's toes out from beneath her. When her feet hit the floor I part her legs. But I don't undress her yet. Instead I stand back up and straddle her, my knees on the bed with no weight on her.

Trying to put the baby out of my mind, I keep my hands away from her stomach and look right into her eyes. I want it to be about us until it can't be anymore, since in the end, everything is up in the air until she's decided. And things might end.

The thought stops me for a second, as I hover over Taryn's warm skin, my lips at her collarbone, hands massaging her neck and shoulders. This could be over, sooner or later. I don't know what I'll do. But then she quirks her head to the side, and her eyes are alight with unspoken emotion, her lips are full and just barely parted. I push through my concern. Every second with her should be lived right.

Our lips connect, and the world fades away until it's just us.

Taryn and me.

Then only Taryn.

My emotions stir, and I start to come undone. What if this is the last time we'll be together? What if I'm losing her to my best friend?

Yeah, and what if the world ends?

Distraction. Distraction. Distraction.

I try to keep from what-if-ing myself to death by training my mind on her body and her movements, her beauty. But it's harder than it should be to stay in the moment. I start to feel lost. Eventually, Taryn grabs my face with both of her hands, tugging my head down until our foreheads are touching. She pulls me closer until I look at her.

"Where are you?" she asks.

"I'm right here. On top of you. Inside you." I smile.

But she doesn't return it.

"No, *where are you?*" She moves her left hand and puts it to my chest, her palm to my skin. Then she taps her fingers with her other hand to my temple. "You're off somewhere else."

"I'm sorry," I say in shame, closing my eyes. She should never have to ask that.

"Come back here, to me. Don't be sorry." She wraps her legs around my waist and tips her head back a little to give me access to her neck. When I move my lips there, her arms wind their way around my back, pulling me closer.

But I can't shake the worry sitting cold in my bones.

If it's the last time we ever have together, if it's the last memory we'll have in bed, it'll haunt me forever. We've had so much better. I really fucked it up this time.

Taryn
Now

Morning sickness can go fuck itself.

It's never just in the morning; it's all damn day. Twenty-four-fucking-seven, unless I'm sleeping or currently eating. I feel like shit, and I just want to sleep all of the time. This baby-making business is fucking tough. So much harder than I ever imagined. So many people do it, I just assumed it was okay. But fuck me, I was wrong. My back hurts, my stomach hurts, my head hurts; I have way too many aches and shooting pains. Plus, aren't cramps supposed to stop when you're knocked up?

Today I've thrown up decaf coffee, soup and crackers, and a grilled cheese. I don't even want to try eating dinner. I can't handle another thing I love being ruined by this little bud inside.

Though, maybe ice cream would stay down.

That does sound good.

A little gag bubbles up in my throat, and I cover it with a fake cough.

Maybe no ice cream then.

This baby is pickier than…well, than any picky people I know.

And you know what, that's another issue, I've realized. People talk about pregnancy brain, and it's absolutely a real thing. I put my car keys in the fridge yesterday when I got home from work. Maicy and I searched for over an hour until we gave up. We only found them when she went to grab a beer and they were right there, literally chilling, on the shelf.

Plus, all of a sudden, it blows not to drink or smoke. I mean I know I'd been on hiatus from both—I can't even describe how thankful I am for that—but now I could use the chill pill sometimes. But nope. And I don't complain out loud. But I miss both. A lot.

Did I mention getting fat sucks too? I can't use the pottery wheel anymore, and it's getting harder to back up when I'm driving. Plus, I have really cool clothes, edgy and funky. But now they're starting to get uncomfortable. I need maternity clothes, I know, but I've refused so far. They all look so weirdly shaped and plain... or—gasp—preppy. Nothing looks like me anyway. Instead I've gotten bigger, stretchy, workout clothes and tops two sizes bigger than normal. It'll have to do for now. I'm awkward and in limbo, but whatever.

These are the things that go through my mind while at work. Obviously, I should actually be working, but that's one of the perks when the boss raised you.

Speak of the devil.

"When's your next doctor appointment, pumpkin?" Cooper asks as he comes into view.

He's called me that since he's been in my life, and he's literally the only person on the face of the earth I'll tolerate it from. My mom called me "pickle" when I was a toddler, and I nixed that in middle school. But Cooper can pretty much get away with anything when it comes to me. My dad left when he found out my mom was pregnant; I never met him. And Cooper, one of my mom's best friends her whole life, had been in love with her for years, so he started proving he was worth her time while helping her get clean to get me back from foster care. When she did, when she chose him and got her shit together with him by her side, he raised me like I was his own. There aren't many men out there as good as him.

I curl my lip, trying to think of the date, but draw a blank on the specifics. See, what I meant about the pregnant-brain thing?

"Two-ish weeks. It's in my phone, I think," I finally say. His green eyes light up with my vague guess, though.

He stands straight, un-peeking his head from halfway through the doorframe, and his brown hair falls around his face. No dad but him could pull off hockey hair. He's nerdy and adorable.

"Can Mom and I come?" He smiles so big, his cheeks go up, squinting his eyes.

I want to say no. Because, duh, that's so weird. But he looks *crazy* happy.

"Only if you stay in the waiting room. Lobby. Whatever it's called." I shake my head.

"What's the point then?" Cooper slumps his shoulders. He's right, for that they could just stay home.

"I'm too old for that to not be weird, having my parents at an OB appointment. But feel free to pick me up at home after and take me out to dinner instead," I say, then smirk.

"Whoever said we were normal parents—or that *you're* normal for that matter." He changes tactics when I raise one eyebrow in response. "Okay, let's make a deal. We'll wait in the lobby, if we each get our own copy of the next printouts. Then we'll all go out for dinner." His dimples deepen with the suggestion.

"Deal." I nod.

He walks away without another word, so I don't have time to change my mind. Not like I don't see him every day of the week.

I'm thankful though, and I won't cancel on him. Their wanting to come to the doctor—it's a huge improvement from where we started off after I told them.

Taryn
Earlier

"So I have some news," I say to my parents. After telling Austin and Theo, this is almost as scary. I have no idea how Cooper or my mom will react. I'm not sure I'm ready for any possible reaction, but I can't hide it anymore either.

Sitting on their couch, looking out their French doors, I stall.

"Why do those few words scare the shit out of me, little girl?" My mom drops down onto the couch too, a bit too close. Leave it to my mother to have the exact right idea. She's been through too damn much not to see the dangerous possibilities ahead of me at every turn.

"Because they should," I say, closing my eyes as I lean back into the cushions, my head tipped up toward the ceiling, though I can't see it.

I feel Cooper eyeing us both, but he's refusing to do anything other than stand in the kitchen. "Get on with it," he says.

"So…" there's absolutely no easy way to say this. "I'm pregnant."

The shit hits the fan.

"Excuse me?" my mom says, and I swear she almost sounds like something hissing. Her smoker's voice is so low, it's menacing. "Did I miss the part of the conversation where you said you have a boyfriend? That you're engaged again? That you learned from all the mistakes I made?"

"Nice, Mom. So I was a mistake?" I look at her then, my eyes blazing with irritation.

"You absolutely were *not*. But having you so young? Yeah, that sucked. You know how shitty life was for a long time," she says, reaching for my hand. But I pull mine away before she can touch me. "How could you be so careless? You aren't keeping it, are you?" she says, reacting to my anger with her own. I wonder for half a second if she added that just to hurt me for not telling her sooner, for not letting her comfort me now, for whatever else.

"Kimberly," Cooper says. It's sharper than I've ever heard him speak to her, ever. And tears sprint to my eyes. I love him for sticking up for me.

"Just because you got knocked up at seventeen and couldn't stay sober long enough to take care of me until someone else came along to save you, doesn't mean I'll follow in your footsteps." I try so hard not to shout it at her.

"Knock it off. That was a low blow," Cooper says to me this time. I glare at him, even though I deserved it.

"You're supposed to want better for your kid than you had. And besides I've done my best to make up for everything I did wrong. You know that." I shrug, not willing to answer. "Who's the father?" She tries a new tactic.

"Well," I say but then stop. I'm not going to lie about this. She'll find out sooner or later that I don't know, and I may still have both in my life for the long-term depending on how it all plays out. So she'll have to make nice with either, or both, anyway. "That's the thing…"

"You've got to be fucking kidding me." My mom throws her hands up in the air, then lets them slap down onto her thighs. Her frown accentuates her crow's feet and laugh lines, and I have to turn away from her as a rogue tear leaks from my eyes. "Even I knew who got me pregnant," she adds.

"That's enough," Cooper says to her, walking over to the couch. He sits between us, one hand on each of our laps. "Both of you."

"I'm sorry," my mom whispers. It's not enough, not really, but I'd rather just get it all out now.

"I've been seeing Austin again," I say. "Shut up, I don't want to hear your opinions about that either, okay?" Cooper nods, and I don't even look past him to my mom.

"Do I know the other guy?" she asks.

"Theo," I say, looking to the tan carpet, following patterns in the variegated threads.

"I hope it's his," Cooper says. My head snaps up, and I can feel how wide my eyes are. "What?" he asks, with a hint of something hidden. "I've always liked him."

My mom surprises me by laughing then. I don't join her, but the sound helps a little.

"Are you both cooled down enough to be civil?" he asks.

I don't say anything. Neither does my mom, not for a while. And the awkward silence stretches longer and longer.

"Oh, come on," Cooper tries again.

"Ummm, it gets worse," I say. The caveat, the thing that goes along with two possible fathers. But I'm surprised, stopping, as I feel the room turn into a vacuum as all of the air is sucked out. After a moment of absolute silence, I can hear my mom's breathing pick up speed before she brings her free hand up to her throat. "Oh god, Mom. No. The baby is fine. I didn't mean anything like that. Shit. I'm sorry."

Her fear, her genuine concern for me, for the bud, that's what lets me finally forgive her attitude, her harsh words.

"I'm sorry," I say again. "I just meant that I'm not doing a paternity test till after the baby comes. I know the risk isn't super high, but there's no risk waiting until afterward. So we'll wait."

"I guess," my mom lets out a huge breath between words, "there are worse things than an unplanned pregnancy when you're almost thirty, have a job, and own a house already."

"No shit," Cooper says, blinking his eyes a few times in quick succession.

I can feel them both relax a little bit, and I let myself too. I never really thought about it all that much; I just took for granted that everything's fine with the babe. I shrug, the best indication that she'll get that I'm over it, the closest thing she'll get to another apology about the rest.

My mom follows suit, shaking her head without another argument.

"I think I like Nana and Bapa best," my mom says finally, and this time I do let out a little laugh.

Taryn
Now

I'm staying at Theo's tonight. Just driving over to him lowers my pulse and evens out my breathing.

I've been trying to do the every-other-day thing with both guys, trying to keep it fair, but leaving at least one night a week to myself. I need to recharge, and that part they've both taken well. But the rest…it's been tough, and I haven't navigated it well. But I *am* trying.

I slipped and let Austin know that Persephone is kind of Theo's too. He was so fucking pissed, he didn't text or call me, let alone come over, for a few days. The cold shoulder feels worse than an argument, and it was too familiar. Plus, I wish this wasn't true, but I've called both by the wrong name lately, so now I just always say "babe" to both. It's easier.

I want to make a choice. I want to do the hard thing, the better thing, for everyone.

But I feel like I need to wait. At least for a little bit longer. I know, I know. That's partially because I'm a selfish chicken-shit. But it's somewhat about my strong feelings for both. And what if I choose one but the other is the father? I don't want to be forced by the outcome, by the bud, but how can I not be at least a little swayed by genetics. I know—or, well, I think I know—both would raise the baby as their own, even if it wasn't and I picked them anyway. But with my heart still torn, I'm leaving it up to something big to decide, a sign.

And what's a bigger sign than a baby?

I honk in Theo's driveway, not even getting out of the car to knock when I get there. It just takes a second for him to come out, and his smile could split his face in two. It's contagious; I feel mine in my chest.

"You *are* hungry, aren't you?" he says as after locking the door on his way out, and heading to my rolled-down window.

"Fucking A right I am."

"Move over; I'll drive." Theo motions his hand for me to move and winks.

"Those are the kind of things a girl wants to hear," I say.

"A pregnant one," he adds.

I slap his shoulder when I settle into the passenger seat. My back hurts, so it's fantastic to sit back and let him worry about the traffic. "Are you trying to butter me up?" I ask, not really meaning it. Austin's the one who would try for brownie points. I close my eyes and let my head sink back against the headrest, settling into the moment.

"Don't be mad," he finally says, surprising me with his response.

My temperature shoots up, and I open my eyes, turning to squint at him, trying to decide if I need to panic. My heart has jumped the gun and it's already racing. Body says yes, but I try hard to slow my breathing and give him a chance.

He must see the fear in my eyes as his scan his face, and the red in my cheeks as he starts to back track as fast as he can. "No, no, no, it isn't bad, I swear."

"Then why'd you say it like that?" I whine.

"Because I know you, and you aren't going to like it, even though *I* think it's good."

"Go on…" I'm still skeptical. He's caught me in the middle, and though my pulse has stopped rushing in my ears, my palms are still clammy. I wipe them on my leggings, still waiting for more.

"I bought a few things. I'll show you when we get home."

"Oh, okay," I say as my blood pressure stops squeezing everything inside my chest. Shopping is never bad. Crisis averted. "You scared the shit outta me, jackass."

I poke his side as hard as I can, but he's made of steel and only laughs.

****

After dinner, Theo holds his hands over my eyes as he walks me into his house. His chin rests on the top of my head, and his feet are on either side of mine. It's a new feeling I can't name, having him surrounding me like this. A little scary, but also warm.

"Ready?" I feel each syllable, every letter, of his deep words in his chest as he speaks. The vibration against my back sends a sweet sensation through my spine.

"Obviously," I say, bouncing on my tip toes to press into his chin, so antsy. My tendency towards impatience has only increased as my hormones swell too.

"All right," he says as he moves his hands from my eyes. We're in the spare room in his house. It used to have his desk and a second TV. It was essentially a man cave, kinda bare but with a mini fridge dedicated just to beer. Why he needed that, I never understood. The whole damn house is his man cave since he lives alone.

But now...

It's a fucking nursery.

I suck in a breath and try to hold the tears in my eyes, pressuring them to stay put, while a similar pressure pushes against my lungs. The walls are painted purple, I can still smell faint traces of the fresh coat. It's more of a dusty plum than plain-old purple, with minty stripes, also dusty, on one accent wall. Turning, I notice that all of the furniture is a deep gray wood. There's a crib, a changing table, a gliding rocker, a dresser, and little gray accents like stuffed animals, a rug, and pillows. Letting my breath out, I walk over and touch the fabric on each soft surface. Walking around the room, I drag him with me, holding his hand in mine as tight as my knuckles let me. Screw the tears, they fall despite my protests.

There are two sets of sheets sitting on the mattress in the crib. Both have green or purple patterns. One is birds, and the other geometric shapes.

"I didn't know what you'd like best, so I went with both. Then you could decide." He's quiet as he speaks. His smile is hesitant. I know I haven't said a word yet; I'm not sure I remember how to speak at the moment. "The lady at the store said green and purple are both gender neutral. I started with just purple, but it didn't look very neutral to me. So I added the green." His eyes move around the walls and the furniture with mine as I take in every detail again, not wanting to stop touching, stop looking.

"Do you like it?" he finally asks, looking apprehensive.

"Are you fucking kidding me?" I answer, shoving my face into his chest and getting it wet. "I love it, you idiot!" Then I surprise him, which may be a mistake considering I could land on my ass, but I jump into his arms. He doesn't even totter, holding me up by my ass, and I kiss his face over and over and over.

"Now I have a question for you." But then I stop talking, and he lowers me back to the floor gently. As I leave it hanging, lines form in his forehead again.

"What?" he asks loudly, drawing out the vowel in hesitation. Serves him right.

"Can I bring Persephone over here? Mace sucks at mothering, and anyway, she's yours too." He smiles, relieved. "She loves you way more than Maicy anyway. And she deserves a cleaner litter box," I say.

"I'll make a deal with you." Theo lets just one side of his mouth quirk up, and I roll my eyes.

I didn't think he'd need any convincing, but I wait regardless.

"Name your demands," I say.

"You bring some things to keep here too. Some clothes and things you need to get ready, some of your books. *Then* it's a deal," he says.

I raise one of my eyebrows in thought, as he waggles both of his at me. It isn't as if we aren't together a lot. And it would be so much easier, especially as I near the stage of waddling versus walking. Plus it's simpler than him asking to keep things at my house. That would really piss Austin off.

"Can I buy a second body pillow?" I ask in answer. It's kind of a joke, but not really. I don't want to miss out on having one at both places, and it's getting dirty, carting it everywhere.

Theo answers with a kiss. It almost brings me to my knees. But instead he pulls me back up into his arms and carries me to his bed.

Our bed?

****

In the middle of the night I wake up, for the second time, to pee. And on my way back to bed, I pause by the baby's room. Hesitating at the door, rocking back and forth with one foot inside the room and the other in the hall, I can't decide if I want to go in. But hearing Theo snore gives me the confidence to step inside. Moving to the rocking chair, I touch the solid frame before sitting to test it out.

Yep, of course, it's amazing. I could sleep in this thing.

If I keep gliding back and forth, I will fall asleep, so I stand and move to the dresser. And damn Theo for shocking me again. My hand flies to my mouth when I see every drawer is filled with tiny little clothes. He's gotten onesies, socks, pants—so many adorable, soft, little things.

I look around a little more, amazed by his style and the attention to detail he's put into this room. I could stay here all night, but I do shuffle back to bed when my eyelids get heavy.

And just before snuggling in, I think about how different my relationship is with Austin. I've been trying so hard not to compare them, to compartmentalize, but I don't know if that's the right thing to do. Maybe I *should* be comparing.

Navigating both is treacherous, almost impossible, especially when trying to also navigate my own heart, and the other fast little heart, which I'm looking forward to hearing more, somewhere below mine.

My side hurts a little, somehow a simultaneous pinch and ache, reminding me that I'm never alone anymore, not with the little bud swimming around inside.

Maybe it can tell me who to pick.

Austin

Now

I need to do something.

I'm not doing enough.

But I have no idea what Taryn would like, what she'd want or allow me to help with. Not to mention, I don't even know if now is the time or if everything should wait until closer to baby's arrival. And self-criticizing won't help. But action will.

Walking into a store covered in pink, blue, and fluffy animals is intimidating as shit. And still, I'm trying here, even if I should have done it sooner.

I don't know what half of these stupid things are.

I know I decided I have to do something, and that's totally the right call. But standing here, I wonder why the fuck I thought this was the best place to make up for my shitty behavior. Shopping here is mortifying. Everything looks foreign. And she's not going to forgive my petty silent treatment if I get something stupid.

I wish I could just shove some cash at Taryn to start a bank account for the baby. That'd be so much easier, and actually helpful, logical. Though, easy isn't enough to make up for the worthless dick I've been. And I don't want to make things worse than I already have. But…what do babies even need besides diapers and clothes? *Damn it.*

The longer she's pregnant, the more unsure, the more scared, I get.

Standing in front of an entire wall of different types of bottles and pacifiers, I start to panic. I can feel the sweat beading on the back of my neck, so I try moving to another part of the store. But the clothes section doesn't help either. Nothing in this store is going to calm me down. It's a million degrees in here, and my heart is beating harder the hotter I get.

This is dumb.

All of the thoughts bouncing inside my head start to converge, overlapping each other.

What if I'm a terrible father?

What if I'm not the father?

What if I'm a stepfather? Would it kill me to see Theo in the face of that baby every day? But wouldn't it kill me even more to be asked to walk away, despite not seeing my own face reflected back?

Shit. The what-if-ing again is making everything worse, and I turn to run out of here.

"Can I help you find something?" A way-too-cheerful department-store-something comes over and smiles at me just before I bolt, forcing me to freeze. I want to punch her in the face. I don't even know *how* I need help.

"I don't know." Truth, right there. I don't know much about anything anymore. *Anything.*

"Well, what are you looking for?" Her teeth are too white, and her smile is forced. Her gray eyes are dull, or maybe just sort of disengaged. I'd guess she doesn't want to be here either.

"I'm not sure yet," I look to her obnoxious name tag covered in fluffy clouds with her name in baby pink, "Mabel. I'll come find you if I think of a specific question."

Translation: go away.

Thankfully she does after nodding enthusiastically, head bobbing so hard, her heels lift up off the ground. She'd be a decent actress if it weren't for those eyes. But her departure only increases my annoyance.

It does nothing in steering me toward an appropriate purchase, which I'm focused on again. So back where I started.

I know what I need to do, but I *reallllllly* don't want to do it. I have the actual urge to stomp my foot, but I resist since I'm not a toddler. So instead I walk around the store, two laps, trying to pick something on my own. But everything I grab seems like it's either wrong or could already have been purchased by now, or is just something a boyfriend doesn't get for his maybe-baby.

I dig my phone from my pocket and sigh as I go into my contacts, sucking it up.

At my ear it rings and rings…and rings. Then voicemail starts, and I hang up. I'm not leaving a message. The robot lady can suck it. Instead of giving up, since there's no way I'll accept failure at this one simple task, I call again. On the last ring before I'd get voicemail again, he answers. I almost sigh in frustration, but stop myself just in time. I don't think that would get me the help I need.

"If you're going to threaten or yell at me, I'm hanging up right now," Theo says.

What an encouraging opener. Fuck, this sucks worse than I thought. *Taryn's worth it, though.*

"I'm not. I need your help. Can we call a truce to at least be civil, if not friends?" I ask, and that feels like the biggest concession I've ever made in my life. It hurts my pride a little to even offer it.

Again, Taryn.

"I can probably do that, as long as you don't take another swing at me. Next time, I'm not going to just stand there, not even for her." He sounds wary, and I guess I can't blame him.

"Civil then?" I ask.

"Civil," he says.

"All right, I need your help," I say—I hate admitting it, I don't want to, but I've already made the call, knowing beforehand I'd have to actually speak. So I swallowed my ego and agreed to not hate him, even if I can never go as far as liking him again. This is just another nail in the coffin of my pride, but it still sucks as much as each before.

"Fine. Name it," Theo replies. He sounds a little sour, a little superior too, but the words are right. It's not what I thought he was going to say. I swore I'd get lip, or at the very least, hesitation. But instead he's ready to help, even if it's with attitude.

Great.

"I'm in this stupid baby store," I hear him try to cover a laugh with a cough, "Asshole," I say. Then I sigh before moving on. "I have no idea what to get. I don't even know what most of this shit is. Tell me what to buy, something she doesn't already have," I say. It's begging, if he listened closely. And it hurts me somewhere deep, somewhere I can't even describe—I can't even locate it—admitting he knows the answer and I don't.

"Don't get furniture. I know for sure she's covered with that." He pauses to think. I hate the waiting. I hate that my success in this rests on him and how willing he is to give me a helpful answer. Tapping my foot, I try to slow my breathing. "Get something that'll make her life easier."

"Gee, that's specific." I roll my eyes, not that he can see.

"Let me finish. I wasn't done. I have something in mind—it's perfect—unless you want me to buy it for her," Theo says, threatening only in words. "I've been planning on it, so that's fine."

"Nooooooo," I draw out the word with another loud sigh, not caring how annoying it sounds. Or obnoxious. I'm glad it gets Theo to laugh because at least it makes one of us willing to. My stomach is still in knots.

"I just need to look up the brand name." I hear him typing on his computer. He's at work, and it finally hits me that he's helping me when he doesn't have to.

"Thank you," I say.

The simplest words are hardest.

"Don't mention it," he says, and I know I never will. He gives me a foreign-sounding name; I'm assuming it's the brand he was looking up. He sounds sure of himself, proud. Too bad I have no idea what the fuck he's talking about.

"What the hell is that?" I ask.

A mom and her toddler turn around and walk the opposite way they were heading, to avoid me. *Whatever.* I didn't even say "fuck."

"It's a sling," he starts. I suck in a breath to ask what a sling is for, but he beats me to it. "It's a piece of cloth she'll wrap around her body to carry the baby in. That way she can have her arms and hands free to do other things. It's better than the other brands, and it's customizable since it's super long and can be worn in different ways. Plus, it's just one size. So no guessing or getting it wrong."

He's gonna be an amazing dad.

My heart falls past my feet, well below the concrete. It burns up in the Earth's core, blackened and shriveled. What a fucking shitty realization to have in the middle of a baby store. About someone else.

My best friend will be a better father to the kid that's hopefully mine.

The jealousy is so strong, it turns everything green, a shade so bright I worry I'll never see anything but the one color again.

Still, he didn't do anything wrong, even though I do have the urge to hit him again. He helped. More than I expected. So I suck up my hurt and my misplaced anger, shoving them into the black hole occupying the spot where my heart used to sit.

"Thanks. A lot."

"Don't worry about it," he says.

"No, I seriously mean it. Thank you." I stress the words and try to put feeling behind them. He didn't have to do this, any of it. It won't do anything for him. And we both know if the situation were reversed there's no way I would have done what he did. I wouldn't even have answered.

Better father *and* better person. My eyes narrow at the dead space in front of me.

Just great.

"Anything else?" he asks, his voice strained as it comes out rushed. I can't blame him for wanting to get off the phone.

"Nah, that was it." I want to leave it there, but I know I can't. I need to extend the same kindness—or at least an approximation of it—that I received. "Talk to you later," I say, proud that I didn't clench or grind my teeth in the process.

"Till next time," Theo says, then hangs up before I can.

Feeling unsatisfied, I make my way back to Mabel, the unhappy clerk. "I know what I'm looking for now," I say. Then I ask her about the specific baby-carrier, and her smile falters.

"We don't carry the specific brand, but we have similar wraps."

"Sorry, I need the exact one. Any idea where I can find it?" She looks annoyed, like she isn't supposed to send customers to other stores. "My girlfriend really wants that one, and I'm so lost." Maybe she'll take pity on me.

"Let's look on the computer up front." She winks. Shameful, but it works.

****

Two damn stores later I have the stupid thing for Taryn. I got four of them, every one a different color. I spent a small fortune. But Theo's right, it will make her life a hell of a lot easier. I also bought a card that seemed mushy enough to show my heart was in it but not so much to push my less-than-romantic girl to groan. *Hopefully.*

Finally, I'm doing something right.

Taryn
Now

"You know, you can try getting a hold of me before the sun goes down if you want to hang out. If you want to catch me before I already have other plans," Austin says.

"I didn't see a text from you during daylight either." I glare at him as I answer, trying to swallow my frustration. His gift was so fucking sweet, and still he knows how to push my buttons in the perfect—wrong—way.

"Fine." He sighs and puts his hand in my hair. It's heavy and warm, tangled in the wet strands, but I'm still annoyed. And his conceding only makes it worse. Dick.

I want to argue more, but he cuts off my thoughts as his fingers move against my scalp, rubbing and scratching until the rude words I was beginning to piece together are all forgotten. My skin tightens on itself as I get goosebumps from the massage.

"You're good," I say before dipping my head beneath the bubbles and into the water of my hot bath. His hand is pulled down with me for a second, getting his sleeve wet.

Good.

Okay, so I can only handle the high road for so long. Just a few seconds it seems.

"You look good all wet," Austin says as I pop back up. I roll my eyes, and he frowns.

As he pushes up his sleeve, still leaning over the tub, I catch a glimpse of his version of our tattoo. With that, I breathe in, holding it for a moment and then two before exhaling it back out, trying to re-center.

"Sorry," I say. And I am. I don't mean to negate his compliments, ignore them like a bitch. It's not a blasé attitude, like I know he thinks it is. It's just hard to agree. "Can you grab my body wash?" I ask him with my hand held out over the side porcelain lip, dripping water all over the claw feet, the tile floor, and his socks.

"Can't you just be done?" Now it's his turn to roll his eyes, but that's okay, and I start to narrow mine in response. He just laughs and hands a few bottles over, having no idea which is the one I need. He keeps hold of the loofah, pinning it to his chest, knowing I need it too.

I open the bottle, vanilla and oranges wafting around us after I do, waiting for the sponge to put it on. With a smirk dancing on his tempting lips, he dangles it above my head, wanting me to stand up for it.

After a staring contest he finally drops it into the bath, splashing everything in the process. Temptation to fake soap in my eye is strong, but I resist. After all he's trying for playful. But when he looks at me, hungry for my skin, my company, all of me, something sparks in the air, a welcome change.

Everything inside me tingles.

"I'm sorry," I say again. "Off few days." It's not an excuse, just an explanation. I still don't want to get out of the tub. Even if I want him as much in return. "Here," I add, handing the sponge over and leaning forward to give him access.

Except Austin doesn't take it right away, and my elbow starts to get sore from bending, pushing against the tub, my hand feeling like it's filled with lead.

"Well, forget it," I say. And I sink deeper into my bath, until my lips touch the water, my hand hovering just above the bubbles.

He takes it finally, just before I let it drop, and I keep my eyes closed. But I'm not moving again, so he's still lost his chance. All that I hear for a few moments is his breathing. Then I hear cloth falling onto tile, and Austin's toes slide past my hips as he gets into the claw foot with me.

"I love you."

"I know," I say after blowing a frustrated huff out across the bubbles between us.

"And that's why…" he adds.

"Please don't." *I can't take it.* I know where he's about to go, I can feel it, and I just can't have the conversation one more time before I'm ready. I can't do it again. I can't choose, choose one, choose to commit. Not yet.

"Taryn," he starts, softly, and I open my eyes. He looks determined, but nothing else.

"I don't know why you insist on repeating the same argument over and over. If it's not good enough for you, I understand. But I'm not there."

"Not yet," he says.

"I don't know when I will be." I try to smile, though it's not a great one.

How he's so confident in himself, in us—in me—I'll never know.

"Not yet," I add.

"So…we're exclusive now, right?" he asks with a smirk, and I splash him. Bubbles land on his chin as he smirks at me, making a lot of things feel just a little bit better. "But really," he starts.

"Shut the fuck up," I say as I lean over to his side of the tub.

My lips find his, like they're drawn there by a magnet. Where they should be. Water upends out of the tub, and I hear it, but I don't care. His hands are in my hair again, I'm tingling and warm, and my brain is quiet. His is too, I'd guess.

The sounds of Austin's enjoyment pushes me onward. He may not like my evasion, but the end result is, at least for the moment, enough. He grabs my chin with one of his hands, dripping with suds, and lifts my face until I open my eyes; they flutter. His are half lidded, but they're burning holes through my already heated skin.

But when he opens his lips to speak again, I don't let him get anything out before pressing mine back down to him.

The reckless passion flows as he grants my tongue access. It's an invitation he could never pass up. Then he's pushing me back until he's pressed into me. The faucet bites into my back, and I feel it like ice on my spine, but somehow it's a welcome contrast. My legs wrap around him, and my hands dig into his back—matching the pressure of the metal against mine.

It's wild and deep, but it's a fast burn. It's hard to breathe through the nonexistence of space. He always wants me closer.

A groan escapes his mouth as we move, sending more and more water onto the floor.

My breathing gets loud, and my moans follow after, until the bath is half empty and the rug is soaked.

The match sparks, then burns out as I finish a moment before him, my nails making red lines all over his shoulders and back. And it's over.

The water, what's left anyway, cools down right after we finish, and I stand. Too fast, too eager. Austin's eyes trail the drops falling down my skin, and for the first time in a really, really long time, I feel embarrassed. Vulnerability pulsing just below my skin, so hard I can feel it in my wrists. I know I *shouldn't* be embarrassed. But there it is, like a piece of trash sitting in my stomach.

Unfulfilled; the nasty little word creeps into my mind, unbidden, and burrows into the newly-made memory tonight, in the bathroom together, here in the tub. It doesn't fit, but it won't go away.

"I can still wait," he says with a smile, unaware of what's running through my stupid brain as I just stand here, naked. Like a moron.

I feel like shit, but I have nothing to say, nothing he wants to hear anyway. So I turn and get out, reaching for a towel instead.

Austin stands behind me, the water draining at his feet, and he smiles at me in the mirror.

Mine in return is pitiful. But I try.

Taryn
Now

The sharp pains start in the middle of the night.

And by sharp I mean like a stabbing, searing pain. They were short at first, just a small burst, so I thought I'd imagined it. Maybe it was part of my dream and the fear of it woke me up. But then it happened again. And now I know it's not stopping, not made up.

Of fucking course it's the one night this week I decided to stay alone. Maicy is off with some bearded dude she met at a coffee shop with seating on the floor. I didn't see him, but I would bet money he has a man bun.

So I'm alone, all alone, it's straight up impossible to ignore that something is wrong. Bad wrong.

I've never been a crier, well not before bud, but right now, I can't stop.

This doesn't feel right, and I'm terrified to get up. The fear has me frozen in bed, wishing that I won't feel another thing, and I could just go back to sleep. I swear I feel like ice and fire at the same time. I don't know if I'd make it all the way to the bathroom. Plus what if I'm overreacting? I've never been a worrier, so this is foreign anyway, and I never thought I'd be pregnant either.

But I have lived inside this body my whole life, so I definitely know something is off.

"Oh my fucking shit. Ouch!" I yell. I can't keep it in anymore when another shooting, piercing pain moves over my back, stomach, and uterus at the same time. Following it is a dull ache, reaching from my spine to my toes. I remain rigid, blinking into the darkness, willing my equilibrium to return.

Talking to myself isn't going to get me anywhere, so I reach for my phone. Of course I proceed to drop it on my face before I can hit a single button.

Are you fucking kidding me?

I would laugh if this wasn't so scary. Then I hesitate when I unlock it. Which of them do I call? I'm not ready to dial for an ambulance, I don't think I'm exaggerating, but I don't want to be alone for that. But choosing which to reach out to, it seems sort of important; it holds no finality for me, I don't think. But they won't see it that way, I know.

When another stab makes the tears double, I stop worrying about their stupid fucking feelings and realize I need to care more about myself and the little one. I click on Theo's name, and he answers in one ring.

"What's wrong?" he says before I can even take in a breath to start speaking. He sounds half asleep while the other half is ready for a heart attack.

"How did you know something was wrong?" I ask, trying to mask the shaking in my strained voice.

"What is wrong?" He ignores my question, enunciating each word slowly—so he doesn't start yelling, I'm sure—determined to get his own answered. I hear shuffling. His voice is stronger, louder, the sleep already gone.

"I think…oh shit, I think I need you to take me to the hospital," I say through a sharp breath. The words terrify me, no matter how true they are. And a sob catches in my throat after I finish. Swallowing hard, at least I stop before it becomes a wail. "Fuuuuuck," I say with another wrenching stab of pain.

"I'm leaving." He sounds worse than I do somehow. I can hear his engine starting, and the distinct whine of tires not ready for peeling out but having to anyway. "Do you want me to call Austin?"

Maybe there's a little finality, however unanticipated.

"Probably." I cringe. I should have thought of that, already asked him to.

"I'll tell him to meet us there." I hear honking, though I have no idea who is even in his way this late, and his voice is almost as unsteady as mine. He's being strong, though. And he'll have to be for a while. I'm ready to break down. "Hey, Pigeon…"

"Yeah?" I ask as I slowly sit up. I'll need to change. I can't go to the hospital in boy shorts and a sports bra. But I stop, unable to do much else after I'm sitting. When I try to stand I fall back on my ass.

"No matter what," he pauses, "I love you." His breath is uneven.

Holy fucking shit.

"Hurry," I beg, without saying it back.

"Almost there," Theo says then hangs up.

All I do is sit here, gripping the edge of the bed, wishing that this wasn't real—it was just an awful nightmare. Hoping against hope, in desperation, I'll wake up soon. I'm in the second trimester. The books say the risk isn't as high in the second trimester.

I cry harder, knowing I need to calm the fuck down.

So I start counting the moments until Theo shows up.

One: Maybe I brought this on myself.

Two: Maybe all the drinking and smoking for years has caught up with me.

Three: Maybe this is payback for being such a pain in the ass my whole life and acting out.

Four: No, I don't deserve to lose this baby.

Five: But I still might lose it anyway.

Six: Maybe I'm overreacting.

Seven: Or maybe I don't deserve to be happy.

On eight, Theo uses his key to rush into the house.

"I'm in here," I say from the same spot I've been since we hung up. "But I need help getting dressed." The vulnerability washes over me in waves, knowing I've never felt so useless in my own skin. I've never needed help with much of anything. But I can't even stand on my own.

I can't support myself, not now.

Theo rushes and I hear a "shit," as he trips in the hallway. But then he's in the room, right next to me. There's no hesitation, and he's masking his fear behind a stiff jaw and focused eyes. He slips an arm behind my back and under my armpit, helping me up.

"The closet." I point even though he fucking knows, can see, where the closet is.

He pretty much carries me over there then leans me against the dresser to pull out items at random. He still hasn't said a word.

"Breathe," I say, reminding Theo. He only nods. I was hoping for a comment or at least a halfhearted smile. Instead, nothing. He tosses me yoga pants and an orange shirt. I'll look like a pumpkin, but whatever. I'm not complaining. Then he stands there looking helpless.

And my heart breaks a little more.

"Help me put them over what I'm already wearing." There's no sense in wasting time to change underwear when the doctor'll need them off anyway.

Again, Theo just nods.

"If you don't say something soon I'm going to punch you right in the throat," I say. He's kneeling at my feet, helping me into the legs of my pants, when he looks up and finally attempts something other than detachment. But his weird, lame smile fades quickly when he gets to my knees with the stretchy material

"There's blood," he chokes out, looking at my shorts.

"Not what I was hoping for," I admit. "Just get me dressed and we'll get there. Nothing we can do about it right now." Now I'm the strong one, tears dried up for the moment. It's like only one of us can be freaking out at once, and it's his turn. That's okay. Actually, it helps a little.

But just a little.

"We'll get through this," he says, then grabs my face after moving the shirt over my arms and head, kissing me harder than he ever has before. "No matter what happens, you *will* get through this." His words bounce on, staccato, dripping in strength and security. Yeah, who the fuck was I kidding; *he's my rock.*

"Thank you for not saying it's going to be all right," I say, then put my arm behind his back and grab the hem of his shirt in a fist.

"It's stupid to make promises you aren't sure you can keep," he says. And something opens up inside me. I'm not sure what, but I can feel it anyway, even unnamed.

I say nothing, though, as more pain rakes through my belly and down my thighs. My teeth are clenched so hard against each other, I may end up breaking them. Theo gets me to his car as fast as he can, the two of us limping and readjusting over and over. It's excruciatingly slow, but at least we don't stop. But when he opens the passenger door, I hesitate.

"I don't want to ruin your seats with blood. You love the truck." I look to him, unsure of what to do. "I can wait while you run and grab a towel."

"Shut the hell up, and sit down," he says. It's almost a growl.

I shrug, still feeling bad, then half-laugh and regret it when it hurts like a motherfucker. So I do as I'm told. I shut the fuck up and sit down on his seat. "I'm paying for any cleaning it needs."

"You're so stubborn," Theo says. Then he peels out of my driveway, heading down the road.

"Go the speed limit. It'll only make it take longer if you get pulled over," I say, trying to be rational. We'll be there in just a minute regardless, but he's not paying me any attention. Well I take that back, he's not paying those words any attention. He's looking over at me ever few seconds to make sure I'm still in the car, or breathing, or something. I don't know.

When we sit at a red light he pulls his phone from the cup holder. I hear a few rings and a soft beep. "Austin, I'm at the hospital with Taryn. Something's wrong. Get here." He hangs up, throws his phone back down, and grabs my hand. I just sit here, trying not to think about anything at all. It doesn't work very well. But then we're pulling up to the ER entrance, and he's getting me out of the car. The phone doesn't come with us, but I don't say anything.

Inside he helps me sit down and checks me in, taking my wallet for my insurance card.

A little voice starts to say something in my head, a word I don't want to think, one I wish I didn't even know, but I squash it. This is not the time. Twenty-something weeks left. Not the time at all.

The tightening starts again, pressure builds like cramps, knotted and hard, deep below my belly button. Squeezing my eyes shut, I try to prevent them from bursting me open.

Thirty.

Twenty-nine.

Twenty-eight…holding Theo's hand, I make it down to zero, but the pain isn't over. My toes curl, and I lock my leg at an odd angle, trying anything to help reduce the ache in my gut. *One* breath, *two, three* breaths, *four* in, *five* out—and all the way back up to fifteen. My phone says it was four minutes since the last one. Forty-five seconds long.

Two sharp, cramping pains later, we're in a room, waiting for the doctor. Every patient in the lobby looked at me with narrowed eyes, flared nostrils, pursed lips, when my name was called. I stood up to leave, hunched as the second wave of cramps subsided, wishing I wasn't here to be called at all. If only they knew what was going on, they'd rather sit and wait.

A nurse, I don't even catch her name, gets an IV going. She misses my fucking vein on the first try, and I squeeze Theo's hand to keep him from screaming at her. "It's fine," I say to him, despite exactly nothing being fine.

"Sorry 'bout that," Miss No-Name Nurse says after the needle is finally in the right spot.

Then she checks my blood pressure—it's high—and leaves the cuff on.

When she starts putting a monitor around my stomach, Theo can't hold it in anymore.

"When will the doctor be here?" he snaps.

The nurse, a middle-aged woman with silky blonde hair and kind eyes, isn't phased at all. She just smiles at him and walks toward the door. "It shouldn't be too long now. Click the button if you need anything," she says. Then she's gone.

I wanted to ask what the monitor is for, but I was too scared. I'm not sure I want to know, and I'm thankful as fuck that the screen it's connected to is faced away. I'm too afraid to look, to have Theo look even.

I think I want a couple more minutes of hope, a couple more minutes with the possibility that this is all okay. Maybe not normal, but just outside that realm, still in a safe zone. And at this moment I don't give a shit how stupid that is.

The dripping of the IV pumping into me is something to focus on, at least.

Drip.

"Are you okay?" Theo asks in a whisper, flexing his fingers between mine.

Drip.

"No," I say, without elaborating. I know he'll understand.

Drip.

I still don't turn to him, even though I should, even though I want to. I just watch the droplets falling.

Drip.

"I love you," he says again.

Drip.

This time I do turn to him, and there are tears in his eyes. That's what does it.

"I don't know if not knowing or actually finding out scares me more," I say.

Theo nods; he understands me.

Then the cramps start again, deep and aching. I grunt and pull Theo closer until he gives up and gets into the bed with me. We don't talk anymore. I keep watching the liquid drip down, down, down into the tube, into me. I think Theo watches too, but I don't turn to check.

I count the drips, like I counted the breaths before, like counting the moments between lightning and thunder. But really, I'm counting space between pain, the moments of hope, fleeting, between reminders of what I know, deep inside, is happening.

The time ticks by, counted in cramps and tears, seconds of nothing added to seconds of pain to mark the time we're without a doctor, still. Theo's leg starts to jiggle, shaking the whole bed and both of us in it. The line in his forehead deepens as his fingers tap, tap, tap on the railing next to him. His nails are too short to connect with the metal, thudding, instead of clicking an erratic rhythm. Another nurse, a meaner-looking one with nothing to say, takes my temperature and pulse and something about oxygen, her scowl telling me more than her silence. Then she leaves us to sit once more. Just waiting.

Still waiting.

"I'm going to find someone." He lets go of my hand so gently I almost don't realize, then he hops down and stomps out of the room. The door slams toward closed, but stops just short of latching. A line of extra light cuts across the too-white wall, and I stare at it, listening. Right away I hear voices in the hallway, one I know is Theo's. I try to hear words, but mumbles and vibrations are all that come through.

So I switch, trying to block it out, straining to clear my head.

When that doesn't work, and I'm still sitting here alone, I do what I did in bed. It's the one thing that's helped much tonight. So I go for round two.

One: I'm not sure I was ever meant to be a mom anyway.
Two: Either way, I just want the pain to stop.
Three: I really wish Theo would hurry.
Four: Will they blame me if I lose the baby?
Five: Whatever's going to happen, I wish it would just be done already.

On five I regret half of what I just thought. I'll take the pain if it means I get to keep him. Or her, whatever; I'll take anything if it means I get to meet little bud in a few months, crying and pooping and all. And they can blame me all they fucking want. I grew up; no more living in the smoky past. This wasn't on purpose. If either of them want to leave after this, fine. They can shove it—and their judgments, their rejections.

The only person I vow to love forever is this little bud—if we both make it through tonight. Clutching my stomach, I feel another ache start to build. My insides turn inside out, knotting around each other and cutting off circulation. My body tries tearing itself in two as I sit here with my hand on my belly button, crying into the empty room. I will the pain to subside. Wishing my pleas are enough to pull him through.

Him.

I don't even know yet, but it feels right.

Before I can wonder if I'll make it far enough to find out, there's a soft knock on the exam room door, so quiet, I question if it was on mine. But then it's opening, after barely a pause. A young female doctor walks in, followed by Theo, and, surprisingly, Austin, behind him. I blink a few times, trying to catch up.

The doctor's jaw is clenched, and I catch her left eye twitching. "Hi Taryn, I'm Jessica."

She hesitates, like she's about to give her last name, but thinks better and stops there. She's right if she's assuming I don't give shit, and won't remember even if she gave it. *Doctor Jessica.* I want to sneer. And I would any other time. But right now I'm tired of being snippy. I'm just tired.

"If you want to be alone with me, these two can head back to the lobby." She turns to Theo, and her shoulders rise practically up to her ears.

Dr. Jessica looks young. Time hasn't pulled the color from her cheeks or the pity and kindness from her eyes. Some people would worry about a young practitioner being incapable. But she calms me instead. She has to understand me better than some old man, with wrinkles and liver spots on his too-cold hands, would. *She has to.* Her hair's bright red—box number 564—in a short, angled bob. Her eyeliner is dark, thick, and I can see three spots in each ear for missing earrings. She's the kind of person I'd want to hang out with.

I take back my bitchiness from before. She's still starring down the guys, and I already like her. With her arms crossed she looks back to me.

"They can stay. If they're silent," I say, looking at each one in turn. Theo's emotionally drained, his eyes drooping a little, and Austin's somehow scared and pissed at the same time. His arms are shaking even though they're pulled tight to his chest, one over the other. Not that their emotions don't count in here. Just not yet. "For now," I add.

Dr. Jessica nods once then sits in her swivel chair. I adjust, painfully and slow, while she scoots over to my stirrup-ed lower half. The air feels colder, drafty beneath the paper sheet. My toes somehow seem to start sweating, and if I were standing I know my knees would give out.

I squeeze my eyes shut, until it hurts, then they bounce back open as Jessica place warm fingers on my ankle.

"Just breathe," she reminds me, and I could kiss her.

Her chair squeaks as she moves again, rolling a little closer still. And after I look from her hair to the sheet, I notice the blood on the sheet.

Just a drop, but it's so dark, so final. Then, as my heart starts cracking down the middle, I look away, to the ceiling.

This suck so hard.

"If either of you stare too long, you're out," I whisper, sort of trying to be funny. They both look wide-eyed, though. Nothing but hard lines and clenched muscles.

I exhale, long and slow.

As Dr. Jessica does what she needs to, my body starts reacting, changing and fighting against me. It's like my skin is cramping and tearing at the same time, not just my muscles. My chest feels tighter and tighter; while there's enough for me to breathe, it feels like it's moving through a straw.

Then my thoughts—about the pain, about the bud, about the boys—it all just stops. I could swear I hear a poof, and for a moment I feel lighter. The constant stream of worry and what-ifs were threatening to consume me, but I think my brain may finally be revolting. Unwilling to focus on anything but the physical, I feel the cold metal, the latex-covered fingers, the draft in the room from the vent above me; I hear all four sets of lungs breathing in and out. And I feel a trickle of blood, warm at first but getting colder as it drips, trailing down my inner thigh. I know it's blood without looking; I just know. But, for the moment, there's no room left for emotions. But that's okay right now.

After the exam, Dr. Jessica swivels up toward my head. She pulls the curtain over to block both guys from our view. It's not like they can't hear us, though, and both shuffle their feet back and forth. She sits right in front of me and looks me straight on.

"Taryn. I'm *so* sorry." She says it quietly. But there's so much emotion in her voice—in her eyes—it's like she's screaming, and all of mine comes rushing back.

No, no, *no.* This isn't right. Her big, dumb green eyes look sad. I don't want to hear what she has to say next. She shouldn't need to be sorry. *No, no, no, no, no.*

"I know how awful this is to hear, and it's going be even harder to process," she says this because I've started shaking my head, thinking somehow I can shake it enough to change her mind, to change what's happening. "But there's no heartbeat. And you're losing tissue."

It's over. I was right.

I never should've let that horrific word flit though my mind earlier.

I thought it into happening.

I choke a little on the lump that's landed in my throat, my chest, somewhere it shouldn't be. I hear two quiet breaths from behind the curtain. One raspy, the other stuck after coming out halfway.

I can't deal with them, with anything extra, right now. I'm already past the point of breaking; I have no idea how my body is still held together, how my mind hasn't run away screaming. Picturing those two, faces so different, kills me. I know how they feel without needing to see it. And my heart breaks even more.

Closing my eyes, I ask the thing I know I have to. No matter how terrible of an idea it is, no matter how much I shouldn't.

"Can I see?"

And Dr. Jessica shows me in black and white a little blip that should be moving, should be beating, but is still. The world goes grayer as all of the color fades around me to match the still screen. And I move my eyes to Dr. Jessica's badge—the safest spot I can think of. Where no one can reflect my own pain back to me. Where I don't have think about absence instead of presence. And while the trickle of fluid still comes out of me, soaking into the white sheet, a new cramp starts, building until I have to grip the side of the bed to stay conscious.

"Can they go now?" I ask after the pain ebbs away, just loud enough for Dr. Jessica to hear. She closes her eyes and shakes her head a bunch, up and down like it's on a spring, clearly wishing I'd sent them packing earlier.

She doesn't move the curtain the rest of the way, letting it remain in purgatory, but walks around it, leaving me feeling somewhat concealed, like that's somehow safer. I don't know why it feels better, but it does. And I love her for it.

"Okay, it's time to give her space," she says to the guys. But then nothing happens. No one moves, and as the seconds stretch, sticky with resistance, my head starts to hurt. "Out. *Now.*" Her voice is harsh this time. She's pissed now, and for just a second, just the fraction of a moment, I smile. Then I regret it right after.

After three sets of feet move out the door, and grumbling follows in the hall, only one pair comes back into my room, softly, slowly. The care in those steps makes it worse somehow. They sound like they're trying to keep me from breaking down by keeping quiet. They're gentle, unlike everything else I need to hear. I cling to them, even when Dr. Jessica rounds the curtain again. I echo each step she took inside my head over and over as a beat, like drums, in the background of the conversation of here and now.

"Taryn." Dr. Jessica sits down, close to me again. My eyes move from the wall ahead to her face, but it looks blurry. "With the amount of bleeding you're having, I want to keep you overnight." I nod once. Argumentative instincts gone. Her face is even blurrier now, and my cheeks are cold. The rest of me is burning up. "If no more tissue passes, then tomorrow we need to do a D&C. Do you know what that is?" she asks. I don't answer, don't shake my head, just stare ahead at her perfect name. She must understand, has to, because she continues. "It's a procedure to ensure everything needing to leave your body does." I'm thankful she doesn't say 'baby.'

"We can talk about any questions you have, but first I'm going to get you a room for the night, bigger and more comfortable than this one. We'll do some blood work when you get there. But before I leave this room and get everything in motion, I want you to know, this isn't because of anything you did. Do you understand me?"

I close my eyes, a shaking breath escaping me.

"I won't be able to tell you exactly what happened. I so wish I could. Likely there was something wrong all along. But no matter what, this early, *believe me* when I say this, there's nothing you did or didn't do that caused this. There's nothing you could have done to stop it. This *is not* your fault," she says. And she grabs my hand. Hers is colder now but so steady and strong. I nod, trying to believe her, at least appeasing her.

"I promise I'll be back; I'll be with you all night," she says. Finally I look back to her sad eyes. "Are there any questions you want to ask me, before I get everything going?"

I have a million floating around, waiting to make it from my brain to my mouth. But that's a long journey right now, longer than normal.

Did I deserve this?

Just why?—stands out strongest.

But it's not the one that leaves my mouth, even though it's what I'd planned to say. "Can I have a hug?" Dr. Jessica's eyes look a little glassier, watery maybe, but she doesn't cry. Instead she wraps her arms—inside scrubs, inside a white coat, protected by layers—around me and squeezes, harder than she should as a medical professional, I'm sure, but not hard enough to make me forget, to make it go away. "I'm sending your men to the family waiting room on your new floor. They won't be allowed to see you until *you* tell me you're ready."

Then Dr. Jessica leaves me to be swallowed up in my own black grief.

When the door closes behind her, I start shaking. It starts small, like I'm cold even though I'm still sweating. But months, seconds, lifetimes later, my entire body quakes. My teeth chatter, and my hands won't steady.

The tears get fatter, dripping down numb cheeks, but this is the as-calm-as-it's-going-to-get before the huge fucking storm ahead. Lightning, thunder, and steel-bending wind should be expected.

And I keep bleeding, crying into the quiet of my lonely room, my hope fading with every tick of the clock.

Austin

Now

I pace back and forth while Theo sits and stares off into space. He hasn't said a word since we left her room after hearing…

I want to be in there. He wants to be in there. But we spend all night, and all day, just doing nothing in the waiting room. Staring. Sitting. Freaking out. I drink coffee; he zones out in his own head. I tap my foot and watch the news; he just stares, stares, stares, blinking and breathing.

I'm helpless. I feel hopeless—empty and hollow.

But neither of us ever leave the room for longer than a food run or bathroom trip. Not even when the others show up.

Taryn
Now

I'm in the hospital less than twenty-four hours, but it feels so much longer. It feels like a lifetime of heartache, one I'll never be the same after.

I bleed. *Red and sticky, my hopes trickling out at the same time.*

I break down inside. *A black hole widening, consuming me.*

I don't think I ever stop crying or falling apart. *I'm not sure I'll ever stop.*

I have the D&C.

A stupid tiny little voice whispers in my head, and the beat of footsteps continues its rhythm like a heartbeat song, pushing me to believe maybe the doctor was wrong. Up until the procedure, I wonder if maybe my body will stop bleeding, stop fighting against me, and the bud will end up being okay, somehow survive and continue growing, proving everyone wrong, that the vitals were just hiding.

And I never let anyone into my room.

Dr. Jessica makes sure I know they stay—both boys, Maicy, my parents; they all stay. The entire time. They wait for me to call them in, though I never do. I just can't. I want to, but...

No one leaves anyway. And I love them for it. Every single one. But I still can't see them. I can't do anything, but they wait for me to be ready, thinking and hoping I'm stronger than I know I am.

Austin

Now

Taryn's been home for an entire day, and I just can't wait any longer. I tried, and I'm done.

I shouldn't have to.

I need her, and I'm sure she needs me too. I haven't talked to Theo since we left, and we barely spoke a word to each other there either. I knew he was waiting for the okay from Maicy to go over there; she told us both the same when she agreed to text us as soon as Taryn was ready. So I should wait.

But fuck that.

At my car, I drop my keys. Twice. My hands may be shaking, but I don't look down to see, I don't want to know. Nothing's been right since that night; nothing works quite the same. But I'm ignoring all of that. It'll be okay once I see her, when I can hold onto her.

I know it will; it has to be.

And in the car, on the way to her house, I smoke three cigarettes. Chaining them like I did the night she let me back into her bed. There's no sweet with the bitter this time, though. The chilled air pelts my face on the drive, every window in the car open. By the time I get to Taryn's, I'm worked-up and wide awake.

She'll let me in, and we'll get back on track. Maybe she'll move in with me if I ask her tonight. That would be a silver lining, something to take away from all of this mess. And I grasp the happy thought as I pound my fist on her front door.

"Go away," Maicy shouts from the other side. "I didn't say anyone could come over yet. Get back in your car and drive home."

"I'm not leaving," I yell right back at her. She's not allowed to decide my future.

"Oh, yes, you are," she says as she opens the door just a crack. She has a lighter in her hand, like that will scare me away. Doesn't she get it? I'm not going to let this tear us apart.

"*No. I'm. Not.*" I shove the heavy wood into her chest, and Maicy falls back onto her ass. "Sorry. But you were in the way," I say as I step over her on my way to Taryn's room.

Her door's open, and I linger in the opening for a moment before entering. She's curled in a ball on her bed, blanket up to her chin, tissues everywhere, the TV playing, though it's barely audible. She's wearing the same pants she left the hospital in two days ago—a corner of the fabric peeks out from under her comforter. Those pants, I know they're the same ones, stained with blood. Theo washed them while she had her procedure, but the spot wouldn't totally come out. I wish she was wearing something else.

I grab the doorframe to stop myself from falling.

Just before moving, I hear Maicy stand up and lock the front door, but she doesn't come rushing in to drag me away. It's all up to Taryn now.

"I'm not sleeping, you know." Taryn's voice sounds small, like wet paper that was supposed to hold powerful words but got left out in the rain by carelessness, lost its ink, lost its meaning. "You can come in since the watchdog hasn't chased you out yet."

"I heard that, and I'm pretending you didn't just call me a dog." Maicy walks by, and she sits on a chair in the kitchen, out of sight but within earshot. Of course she's listening to make sure I don't upset Taryn. She's a great friend.

"Sit." Taryn lifts her hand and lets if fall to the bed. No strength behind the movement.

"I wanted to be with you. I wanted to help…" I say, leaving off the period on the thought, leaving it open ended. But I have no idea what else to add, so I let it linger out there, hanging in the air, unfinished.

"You can't help," she says matter-of-factly, her eyes still on the TV.

"Look at me," I try.

She won't.

"I'm sorry you came. I'm not ready to see anyone. And I don't want you here." The tears in her voice cut me straight through. I feel my own coming on, and I try to swallow them away.

"That's it." Maicy says, already in the doorway. "No more."

"But I…"

"She said she doesn't want you here. That means you leave, *now*." Her voice is cold. It brings out an acidic rage I didn't know I was building inside.

I get to my feet and in Maicy's face in only a second.

"Make me," I say, clenched.

"I'm not above calling the cops." Her phone rises from around her hip into my face; I didn't see she had it before now. And it's already lit and dialed, she'd just needs to hit send. Girl's prepared.

Turning to Taryn, I ask, "Are you sure? I'll do anything I can, even sitting next to you. I'll stay silent, I swear, and I can just hold your hand even." The desperation in my voice should be embarrassing.

Should.

"Please just leave. I'm not ready." Her eyes close and a tear runs across the bridge of her nose, down her cheek, and onto the sheets she's swaddled in.

I don't argue.

I want to, but I don't.

Austin

Before

"Just let me in the damn door, Angel." My throat hurts from yelling for so long.

"Why should I? You're a fucking idiot. Go away," she says. Then I hear Taryn stamp her foot like a child. Despite my irritation, it makes me smile.

"I'm not arguing my being an idiot. We've established that. I want to make up for it, apologize, move on." I know my words are useless. She's too fucking stubborn. But so am I.

"Apologies are shit," she says. "Just lot of useless shit."

Eloquent.

"I'm going to sit here until you forgive me," I say, sliding to the floor outside the bathroom and sitting right against the door, making a point to let my head fall back into it heavily so she knows.

"You'll be sitting there a long fucking time," she mumbles.

I hear her kick something. And I know she's right, this may take a while. I never should've let my stupid anger get the best of me. Insulting her was the dumbest thing ever, regardless of her low blows in the argument. I knew better, and I still let her get me to that point.

I should have walked away a moment sooner, taken a breath, so that she didn't have to.

"I told you to go away. Leave me alone. I'm not ready to calm down," she says, trying to sound even.

"I can wait till you are." I'm composed when I say it, and she huffs in response.

I hear shit being knocked around, and I sit there, waiting.

It isn't until later, when it's been too quiet for too long, that I suspect something's up. Grabbing a paperclip, I unlock the door from the outside. The window's open, and Taryn's gone.

"Fuck," I say to no one.

She'd rather run away than deal with a problem.

Austin
Now

I shouldn't have gone there. I should've listened to Maicy and waited for the okay. Taryn's shattered spirit and empty voice were way worse than my sitting at home waiting. Seeing her so...it was terrible. The unknown wasn't as bad as the sad real-life scene. I imagined anger, sadness, all of the normal reactions. And not that hers wasn't normal, but I just hadn't expected to see the strongest person I know curled in a ball, absolutely shattered and hopeless.

Not that I want to, but he shouldn't have to suffer the same, so I text Theo.

Me: She's not ready. Wait for Maicy's okay.
Theo: Thanks for the warning.

I can't tell if his answer is sincere or sarcastic, but I suspect the second. Fine, let him walk into something he can't recover from. The way he just sat there in that waiting room, I bet seeing the beaten shell of her normal self will hurt him even worse than it did me.

His thread of composure is already thinner than mine.

Fuck.

My fingers twitch, too empty, too useless.

So I stand—it's jerky, like I just learned to walk—and stomp to the kitchen. With laser focus, I grab what I want, and when I'm to the living room, fall back onto the couch. I unscrew a new bottle of whatever the fuck was in the cabinet. It's dark and burns the whole way down. This time I won't text Maicy. Skyler won't come over. It's just me and this bottle of booze left to commiserate together. The night couldn't get more pathetic, more perfect, for what I need.

Shot after shot goes down, and with each comes another burning doubt.

Should I be back there, fighting for the woman I love?

Shot.

Don't I deserve to grieve too? The baby was mine too, maybe, and now we'll never know.

Shot.

Is there something she could have done differently?

Shot.

Will I lose her now?

Fade to black out.

Taryn

Before

"He's two years older than us," Maicy eyes me while slurping her slushy in her seat, being as loud and obnoxious as possible. I don't look at her; I keep my eyes on the theater's screen.

"So what?" I ask, faking nonchalance. But I actually kind of love that she's interested.

"So he's older. He's best friends with Theo, someone whose opinion you can trust. And he's hot. I mean they both are, but *he* won't leave you alone." She grabs hold of my shoulder and tries to shake the sense into me. "How many times has he asked you out now?" she says.

Maicy wiggles her eyebrows. The excitement in her voice makes me betray myself as a smirk tugs at the corner of my mouth.

Damn.

"Four," I say.

"And you haven't said yes yet…why?" she asks, incredulous.

"You know love is fake. It's an illusion created for people to hold reality at arm's length. It's a chemical shift that always shifts back. We tell ourselves we feel love so we don't have to feel lonely. And romance is just a ploy to get laid," I say, finally turning to her. She's heard this speech a hundred times, maybe more. She knows why I feel this way, why I try to get her to understand. She'll never get it like Theo does, but she tries. And still she scoffs every time I tell her the hard truth.

Not that that ever stops me. I'm sure she'll understand it someday if I keep repeating myself.

All excitement strips from Maicy's face, leaving annoyance.

She rolls her eyes.

"Even if that's true, and I'm so not saying it is," she sighs, "but even if it was, then why not sleep with him at least? Get laid. Don't you think he's sexy? I mean if you wanted either of them, you could have them so fast." She grins, wiggling her eyebrows up and down.

I throw a handful of popcorn in her face.

"Yes. He's hot, okay? But he hasn't worn me down yet," I answer right before the previews start.

Saved by the trailers.

****

After the movie, Maicy's forgotten about the drama that is my life, for the moment at least, and she's going on and on about the actor we saw and his "delicious abs." I guess she's the one who should be getting laid.

I'm perfectly fine on my own. Always have been, always will be.

I don't even see him, distracted by Mace's droning, until he steps right in front of my path.

"Hey, beautiful," he says.

My eyes widen, and I feel the burn of Maicy's stare next to me. She's swooning, probably smiling like an idiot.

"Hi," I say.

"Articulate," Maicy mumbles, and she gets an elbow to the chest for it.

"Fuck," she says before taking a step back.

"Fifth time's the charm, right?" he asks.

He counted too.

Austin's smile is huge, and his hair is falling into his eyes. God, he *is* sexy. He could be a decent distraction from the monotony of college, of life, I guess. He does seems to want it enough. I look at those dark eyes, filled with hope at the moment, and they seem genuine.

This time it's Maicy who elbows me, to say something.

"Okay, okay fine," I give in. "But don't say I didn't warn you." He deserves to know. "I don't make promises I can't keep, and I won't promise we'll last," I say.

"We'll just see about that." He winks and walks away. Over his shoulder, heading into the lobby toward Theo, he adds, "I'll pick you up tomorrow after your last class." It isn't a question; it's somehow a fact. I narrow my eyes, trying not to smile. *This one is too smart.*

And...we have our first date set.

Theo's face frowns then hardens as Austin reaches him. He never should've let us meet after they became friends. Austin's dangerous for me.

"Why'd you say all that negative stuff?" Maicy asks as we walk out of the doors to the parking lot. "You could've scared him off."

"That was the point." I say, looking at her. And she shakes her head, baffled by my stupidity. Only it's not stupid. "The other four times I said no should've already scared him off," I say, getting into her car.

But she'll never understand, not from the outside, not until she's forced to.

Her walls haven't been built yet.

Taryn
Now

Maicy locks the door behind Austin, yelling something incoherently as she kicks the solid wood, and I let out the wail I was struggling to hold inside. It's not a sound I've ever heard come from a person. It's hollow; it's lonely; even objectively, it's heartbreaking.

He shouldn't have come. I wish he hadn't.

Fucking selfish asshole.

In trying to make himself feel better, he's set me back.

The sobs continue to break into and through me, deciding when and how hard to strike. My head aches, my body's sore, and my heart won't stop cracking away, piece by piece. The shards wither, sent to the pit of nothingness where my soul drowns.

I'm pretty sure my eyes will never un-swell again. The crying hurts both my lungs and my throat too, but the physical pain doesn't make the tears stop. I probably deserve it anyway for letting the little bud fade away, out of existence. I could've done something different, something better; I just know it. No matter what Dr. Jessica said.

But Maicy doesn't run back to me after kicking his ass out. She moves gently, letting me have my time to get some of this broken-down rage, this fiery sorrow, out alone. In the kitchen I hear her fill a cup with ice water, grab a fresh package of crackers, and then she comes into the room. She sets everything down, before crawling into bed with me.

"It'll take time. You're allowed all you need," she says behind me, her arm tucked around my hollow body. "It's okay to be broken, to be miserable. Let it out." Turning up the TV, she just lets me cry.

And I do. I *do* cry.

I cry until there's nothing left, and then my body just shakes like back in the exam room at the hospital. This circle of events has gone around a few times, though. So I don't expect it to be the last.

It hurts, it sucks, and I'm falling apart.

It's a real shame how much can change so quickly. I'd been on the verge of...

Maicy and I both flinch when there's a knock at the door. She swears in a string of jumbled syllables as she gets up from my bed, careful until her feet hit the floor. He's suicidal to come back so soon. It's as if Austin is intentionally trying to make it worse. And if that's the case, I hold zero sympathy for the harsh regret I'm about to make him feel. It's not as if I didn't just go through a horrific enough experience.

Get a clue, buddy.

But I don't hear yelling when Maicy gets to the entry. She opens the door and there's mumbling. Oh God, don't let my parents be here. They should know me better than that. They, of all people, should understand that I need the time I need. They're supposed to be waiting for the okay from Mace too.

As I keep worrying, footsteps pad toward me, only one pair. Before I can guess who I'll see, Maicy hangs in the doorway. She's not stepping into the room, but not leaning out in the hallway, lingering somewhere in purgatory.

"Theo asked if you'd like company. I told him you have *me*." She glares toward the entry for a moment, but not with the same fire as before. "He insisted I ask anyway. He said he just wanted to check, make sure you're okay, and he'll leave if you don't need him."

Need him.

Those two words open up the tiniest speck of warmth, of light somewhere in me.

It doesn't spread, doesn't grow. But it's something. It's a start.

I nod and wave my hand for her to let him in. Maicy's eyes betray the littlest look of disbelief, unadulterated shock, but she walks back toward the doorway without a word. She wanted to argue, to tell me I'm not ready, but she wisely thought better of it.

Then two sets of feet make their way back to me. Four swishes of sock on wood, one much heavier than the other.

Theo doesn't stay under the doorframe when he walks up; he moves right to the bed, no hesitation, and gets in behind me, taking the spot Maicy had been lying in. His arm—warm and strong, the opposite of how I feel right now—comes over my body and rests at my heart. I can feel the pulse in his wrist against my skin, and I use it as a marker of my own.

Mine still beats then.

Maybe they beat together.

I choke back something putrid when I realize it was supposed to be three beating as one, not two.

Maicy comes in too and sits on the floor in front of me with Persephone in her lap. I grip Theo's fingers hard. He thought to bring her over. Persephone, who can't judge, who just loves because she's loved.

The sight of her fur pops another speck of light into the black all around me. Two little holes of dangerous, and addictive, hope. Two that weren't around a few minutes earlier. Then Persephone sees me and hops up onto the bed. She curls in a ball, after circling twice, right in the crook of my neck.

And she purrs.

The sound of her, the constant vibration, carries me into sleep with one hand in Theo's and the other draped across Maicy's shoulder on the floor.

Taryn
Now

"**I** saw my painting hanging on your wall," Maicy says, her eyes averted as we gather everything we need into a huge box she picked up from the liquor store earlier today. When she told me her plan, it was like fate. I can't believe I hadn't thought of it before, on my own. And I'm itching to finish getting ready and outside.

But now, now all I can think about are her words—about the artwork she created for me.

She made me something with dark colors and hard, angled swipes. I don't know why, but the moment my eyes landed on the canvas I knew it was a picture of little bud. Though, it doesn't look like a baby, or a womb, or anything real at all. But still. Still, I knew.

"Because I love it," I say.

"I didn't plan on making it when I started. It just kind of came together. Then it felt perfect."

"That's because you're fucking brilliant," I tell Maicy.

"I mean, didn't we already know that?" She smirks, tossing her gorgeous hair over her shoulder as she carries the heavy-as-shit box into our backyard, not letting me help at all.

"Duh." And I smile. It feels weird, a little off, but I try anyway.

"Okay, chicky—here's the deal," Maicy says as she sets everything down at our feet. "I'll hand you one at a time. You can just drop them, throw them, whatever you want. But the one thing I want you to do, if you're okay with it, is say something with each."

My head starts to tip toward my shoulder at the same time that my eyebrows pull in together. "Say what?" I ask.

"Anything," she tries.

There are still question marks in my eyes, all over my face, as the lines crease deeper into my skin.

"So like…here." Maicy bends down into the overstuffed box and pulls out a tiny dish I made in the ceramics studio. It's got a chipped edge and the glaze bubbled up and cracked in a few spots. "When you break each one you can say something that you're bottling up inside. Something that you want to burn up and let go of. Something that you can't keep a hold of anymore. Then it'll be gone," she says.

"You do that one first," I tell her.

"That's not the point of this…" I watch as Maicy's shoulders work their way up toward her ears, and the corners of her mouth turn downward.

"I don't care. Everyone has frustrations, things they need to let go of. Right? So, show me."

She nods, her fingers moving over the bowl she's still gripping onto as she thinks.

"Okay," Maicy says before swinging her arms up over her head. Her angry face is just as sweet as the one she uses to butter someone up, and there's a little pang in my chest. Then she starts to swing her arms back in the other direction as her mouth opens wide. "I'm so fucking sick of getting rejected by art dealers and critics," she shouts as the hardened clay smashes into the ground.

"That's the prettiest sound I've ever heard," I say as my eyes follow the glittering pieces scattered across the grass.

"Who doesn't love the sound of breaking glass?" Maicy smiles as she walks over to me.

Then her hands are on my shoulders, pushing me closer to the box. And when she lets go there's a new strength in my spine, in my hands that had been shaking before.

"The rest are yours," she adds.

"I'm sick of fucking up," I scream—taking my cue from her—as I throw the first piece, aiming for where Maicy's landed so I can hear an even louder smash.

Grabbing another, there's a tingling in my fingers as I think about what to try and let go of next.

"I've never missed anything more than I miss that baby now."

This time I don't yell the words. They're even, almost monotone, and so much quieter. But somehow they feel stronger, truer, as they explode on the ground.

"I wish I could go back and fix everything, undo the loss."

There's no shaking in my fingers anymore. And my words are as solid as the pieces I'm picking up before flinging them down.

"I'm terrified of making the wrong choice now," I say.

Smash.

"I don't want to ruin something else, anything else. I just want to be happy."

Crash.

Maicy holds me from behind as I keep going, not saying anything, not judging, just standing with me, supporting me.

"I deserve to be happy."

Crack.

My heart feels more stitched together as the shards pile higher and higher at our feet.

"I'm terrified that I won't be able to move on, to get past this. All of this shit. I'm petrified that I'm going to let these mistakes define the rest of my life. And. I. Don't. Want. That."

Shatter. Smash. Crash. Bang. Implode.

I let out a sigh, something that almost lifts me off my tip toes and up into the air. It's so different from the sounds of the breaking, of the shattering, but it's better. It's lighter, better held together.

"That was…" I try, when everything we dragged out here is in pieces. But the right words won't come, and I close my mouth eventually without finishing.

"Cathartic," Maicy says as she moves her arm up and around my shoulder to steer me back toward the house.

****

"You can come over, I promise. This isn't a punishment. I just feel better around him," I say, trying to make Maicy understand. After a few days and nights here with Theo, I know he's what will help me heal. Even more than Maicy's outside therapy session. I don't know why, and I'm done trying to figure it out. It is what it is, and it's helping. Maicy was the best, until better showed up with Persephone in tow.

The two of them are what could fix me, if it's possible anyway.

That doesn't mean I don't need Maicy too, but not as much, not right now, for once.

I need Theo.

I can break down in front of him, and it doesn't make it worse. I don't feel bad when he gets up to grab me what I need like I do with Mace. I'm still half of what I used to be, and I want to be around the person who makes me want to be whole again. If I stay here with Maicy, I won't want to do anything but maintain and survive.

"Can I come over *now* then?" Maicy's foot rises and falls to the floor in time with her *now*. A tantrum is brewing, but I won't stay to see it. "I don't want to be here alone. I'm sad too," she says.

"Tomorrow," I say, straight-up ignoring her ploy to make me feel guilty.

No one is sadder than me in this situation, so she can shove that right up her ass.

Squeezing her shoulder is the best she'll get as I move to leave. I don't want hugs from anyone. Well, almost anyone. But she won't put up with that, especially since I'm leaving for Theo's. So she kisses my cheek before holding the door open.

"I'll be there for lunch tomorrow. Don't even think about changing your mind," she says, glaring.

Then I walk out the door and into the soft light of morning as Maicy lets our front door close behind me. It's a new day, I tell myself.

It's a new day.

Theo holds my door open as I get inside.

In the truck I feel infinitesimally better heading toward his house. Nowhere is easy; nowhere feels right. Though everywhere seems a little better with this guy. I reach over and grab onto Theo's hand, intertwining my fingers through his.

It's funny, I sobbed with both him and Austin that day, but one made me feel worse, and the other a little better.

Austin

Now

The stinging in my chest, the hole somewhere inside, it won't go away with just booze. I've tried for days, and it isn't enough. I started smoking pot again too, and that wasn't enough either.

So I sit here. Empty. Hurting.

Taryn won't answer my texts either. Though, I don't stop sending them.

Me: I need you.
Me: I miss you.
Me: I'm hurting too. I want to be with you.
Me: Please? I still love you.

Nothing back.
Then minutes later, something…

Maicy: Leave Taryn alone. She'll reach out to you if she's ready.

One little word sticks out, and it stabs me like a knife, just like she wanted.

Subtle, malicious.

I hate seeing someone else's name pop up. Why can't Taryn just answer me? I could help her piece it all back together. I do still love her. That wasn't a lie. I love her more now than I ever thought I could, but I'm not so sure it's enough.

I don't answer Mace. She should keep her nose out of it. But then my phone beeps again, and I can't stop myself from opening it. I'll read every message coming through, just in case it could be Taryn.

Maicy: I'm going to push her to get a restraining order if you don't ease up.
Me: I get it.

The drinking isn't enough. The green isn't enough.
And the unanswered messages make everything worse.
So tonight I'll try something else.

****

A car drops me off, since I've already littered my coffee table with empty cans, and I walk inside to the loud, dark bar, full of opportunities. There's so much skin showing, even through the haze of my buzz, and I know I'm in the right place. Everything's dark—black paint and black floors—and hot. But that's fine.

And right away an opportunity walks up to me with heels, a short skirt, and an almost empty drink in her hand.

But her hair is dark and long like Taryn's.

Fuck no.

I shake my head, and she pouts but walks away.

Heading straight to the bar, I sit down and look around after ordering. Blonde. I want a blonde tonight. So whenever a girl who isn't blonde comes over, she gets the boot. They don't even stay long enough to share their names.

Names don't matter to me anyway.

I won't remember it, plus I don't actually give a shit. There's just one name in my head, and, though I can't erase it unless I latch onto another, I can't let it go yet.

"You look like you need cheering up," a strong, feminine voice calls next to me.

I turn, and blonde hair is all I see.

"I do," I answer.

Standing to leave, I offer her my hand. I don't want to sit here any longer; I want to go home and forget. I want to feel better. Surprisingly, she follows. No more words exchanged. Either she needs the same or she wants to feel good, fast.

Either's fine with me.

In bed she's different. She feels sort of wrong. But I push through that and the booze, trying to feel something. Trying to escape the abyss. Eventually, I get into it. It's not the same, but it takes me out of the here, out of my problems, a little out of my grief. It's not enough, but it's something.

"Oh, Taryn," I mumble into the dry, blonde hair on my pillow.

****

I repeat that night, every night for two weeks straight.

Every time, taking home a different girl. Every time, uttering Taryn's name. They all make me feel a little better. For a little while I forget. But then it comes back, when I've finished and they're leaving—some apathetic, some angry—and I'm emptier than before. So I go back again the next night, searching for something I'll never find, not where I'm looking, at least.

Every day between the hollow nights, before whisky and vodka and gin say hello again, I drive by Theo's. I see Taryn healing a little more while I spiral deeper down. She's staying with him when she wouldn't even let me sit with her. In her bed, in her house. She couldn't stand the sight of me. I heard her cries after I left. I stood on the doorstep and listened to her heart break more.

And now she's living with him.

I know she's pretty much living there because she hasn't left in two weeks. That's not just a vacation from her problems. That's uprooting to a new home.

At the bar again tonight, I chat a redhead up. She's perky and ready to go home with me.

I almost don't get my address out to the car's driver; it's hard to focus. I've had too much to drink. But somehow, he gets what I'm saying, and we're to my door in minutes. I'm glad I didn't have to hand over my license to get us here.

And on the way upstairs, Redhead is kissing me in places that make my mouth open, little grunts coming out. She's good, better than most of the other girls recently.

In the house, on my couch, she straddles me with lust flaring in her eyes, and I have an idea. I pull down her shirt, ripping it a little, and move her hands inside my pants. With one hand I pinch and tickle her skin until she's giggling with pleasure. My other hand grabs my phone and calls the one person I'm supposed to be ignoring while she fills my head all the time.

"It's three o'clock in the fucking morning," Taryn says, slurred. She must not have looked at the phone's screen before answering.

"Do you hear this?" I ask, full of cruelty, wanting to hurt her back.

I attack Redhead's skin with a ferocity that's grown inside my anger. She coos and laughs, either unaware or not caring about what I'm doing with the hand not on her, while tipping her head back. When she moans my name, I'm finally satisfied.

"Fuck you," Taryn says through the phone still pressed hard to my ear.

That helps even more.

But then I hear rustling, and I shush Redhead so I can make it out.

"I know you're hurting, but enough is enough. You've crossed the line." Theo's voice doesn't sound sleepy. He sounds like he could punch a hole though my face. "*You're* done now."

The line dies, and I feel worse than before. I've lost the will to fuck Redhead. So I send her home, unsatisfied and finally furious. But I don't care.

After she's gone, something starts simmering in my bloodstream, and I can't see straight. There's a bubbling in my throat, just at the back of my mouth, and there's no way I can keep it in much longer.

Words fly from my lips that don't even make sense as I start shouting, screaming.

"Fuck," I yell, as my fist makes contact with the drywall next to my TV.

Panting, my wrist and knuckles raw and pulsing, droplets of blood coming to the surface around skin that will surely bruise. I plop back down onto the couch and wrap up in my misery. Now I understand what Taryn always said about the lies of love.

Taryn

Now

I watch fringe and cleavage twirl on polished floors as couples compete for the honor of last standing and a useless trophy.

Sit through the news of abusive daycare workers, of high school car washes, of hoarding and dog bites and Florida men running through parking lots naked.

Ignore the urge to give money I earn to companies making pink razors at a mark-up instead of toward my water and gas bills.

Persuaded by pleas of donations for sick animals and those who can't care for themselves, meant to bring tears to my eyes with sad, slow music—but who am I to help anyone else.

I look at, look past, channel after channel of nothing, hour after hour of wasted time.

And the grease on my scalp, in my hair, makes its way toward the ends. A stink—somewhere between desperation and sorrow, in the ballpark of completely given up—builds on me, under my arms, making its way to my nose, to the rest of the room. Closer and closer, it rises, begging me to shower. But I don't. The couch, it's safer, even if it shouldn't be. I pretend not to notice. Instead I roll over, pulling the blanket higher, giving myself a few more hours, a few more days, before I really have to do something about it. And I fix my eyes back on the screen once again.

I wake up to the shouting between spoiled sisters too rich to be arguing about anything, but yet they continue in high-pitched tones and fake tears.

Fall asleep to the sound of sizzling bacon and a voice way too excited to be talking about the meat and wine pairing.

Wake up to cheesy music and glances into the distance with long pauses. To over-dramatized plot lines with twists like amnesia and long-lost twins.

Fall asleep to young couples buying their first homes in neighborhoods they can't really afford, complaining about the color of the paint on the walls.

Wake up to black and white movies, with too many gun shots, big hats and leather boots, and racist undertones in the saloons and brothels.

Fall asleep to clips of medical procedures bordering on the disgusting, clips of redecorating on a budget, of deconstructing and rebuilding, of how-to explanations for painting, of interventions and cat-whispering and ways to unrealistically lose weight that won't stay off forever.

Wake up to more bullshit, to a scripted reality that's nothing like real life. And still I keep watching.

I wake up to the same sad, shitty life that won't fix itself. To the same problems I had yesterday and the day before that. To the same emptiness, focused on what I lost. Thursdays, then Sundays, every fucking day is exactly the same, even when I will it to be different, when I feel like this. The only thing changing is the weather outside. And I'm still not ready to face it yet, not really, not like I should.

Most days I'm better. Really, here with Theo I'm almost back to me. Most days.

But today and days like this, maybe once a week still, I can't face anything. Somehow a weekend slips by this time with Theo coming into the living room and leaving again without our saying a word to each other.

I barely notice.

And somehow it's Sunday night, the sun setting behind his huge living room window. My eyes itch, and I'm sure they're as red as my dry throat. As I struggle to push myself up to sitting, the room seems to tip to the side, trying to throw me off balance.

I barely catch myself, one shaking hand on the edge of the couch, from face-planting onto the floor—or worse the corner of the coffee table. But I do, catch myself that is, and that's what's important.

"When is the last time you ate?" Theo asks from the shadows of the hallway, making me jump.

"I just ate," I say without emotion. I'm pretty sure I just did.

"No."

As he walks into the living room, hands shoved deep into his sweatpants' pockets, I see the hard line of his mouth, the crease in his forehead, the worry in his eyes.

"No, you haven't eaten since yesterday. Yesterday," he says, strained, as he moves toward me on the couch.

"That can't be right," I argue, looking out the window.

"Well, it is."

"Then why did you even ask, if you already knew the answer," I say with venom in the stiff movements of my mouth.

Theo sits down on the couch in a rush of air and muscle, letting all of him fall hard onto the cushion nearest my feet. "You haven't moved in hours, haven't eaten in longer. Listen…I know you're hurting —"

"Stop," I shout, moving to sit on the very edge of the couch, ready to get up and run if needed, if he says too much. And I didn't mean to yell it, I swear I didn't. But the fear building in my chest, the pressure and anxiety pressing into my lungs, my ribs, with each of his words rushed me, raised my volume. "Please don't," I whisper, trying to end this now. "I'll go make something, okay?"

"You know the food isn't the real problem." Theo looks at me finally, and it just takes me a second to break the eye contact. He looks so hurt, like *I'm* hurting him. "You can't keep doing this. Every time I think you're going to be okay, you scare me again."

"I'm trying; I am." I can't get above a whisper anymore. There's a blockage in my throat, a mixture of terror and pain and something else I can't pinpoint.

"I know, Pidge. I know you're trying. And no one is *ever* going to blame you for being sad." He stresses the word, like if someone tried to blame me, he'd make them regret it. And the room around us goes blurry. There are waves in the TV, in the carpet.

I lean sideways, letting myself fall against Theo's warm chest. And I can feel each of his breaths, hear his heart—quick and rough.

"But," he adds.

Shaking my head, I try to stop him.

"You cannot take the blame. It was horrible, and I'm still devastated too. But it wasn't your fault. And you need to start living again, let yourself be happy again, at least sometimes. Preferably…happy with me."

When Theo finishes, he's breathing faster, like he just ran a race—I hope it was toward something instead of away. And the tears finally break free from my lids, from my lashes. They start streaming down my cheeks, warming and then cooling them.

Theo's arm winds around my shoulder, squeezing my arm. But then his fingers get gentler, until they're not touching me anymore, and I freeze. Something inside my chest gets hot, until it's boiling, and I have to bite my bottom lip to keep everything inside.

"Nothing?" Theo asks. "You have nothing to say to that? I need something…"

"You do make me happy," I try, knowing it won't be enough.

I'm right. Theo shoots to his feet, and I almost tip over in his absence.

"Pigeon, I can't take this. You know I love you. I love you so, so much." Now he's the one yelling, pacing back and forth in front of the coffee table, just out of my reach. Despite the words, the big L, and the meaning in his eyes, I can't stop the simmering inside me.

"Then why does that sound like an ultimatum, like a threat?" I mumble, trying to cut into him, trying to make him feel how I do.

He stops moving, looks hard at me until my cheeks heat up. I can feel my neck turning red in the process.

"Pick me," Theo says as he slams his fist into his chest, once, twice, three times with deep thuds that I swear I can feel in my own body.

"I'm not ready," I tell the floor.

"I know." His two words are so defeated I look back up, the corners of my mouth turning down as more tears fall. "I know you're not. And honestly, I don't know when you *ever* will be."

The words fucking hurt. He says them with such heart, such love, without malice, like he should. That makes it so much worse.

"I…" but I have no idea what to say.

That's not fair.

You're wrong.

I want to be better.

Nothing seems right, either it's not enough or it's not true, even if I want it to be.

Theo walks over, around the coffee table, and sits on the edge of it right in front of me, our knees almost touching. His hands find mine, and I don't want to look into those sweet eyes. I don't want to hear anymore.

"I want you to choose me, only me, not Austin." Theo sucks in a breath before continuing, and it's like time stops. I start shaking, my breath coming in little gasps. "Love me because I've loved you longer. I haven't made the same mistakes. I haven't hurt you and pushed you away. I've kept my mouth shut most of the time, but tonight, right now…I have to say something just once. I deserve to be your first choice, not a back-up plan."

"Are you kidding me?" I spit out the words, with venom on my tongue. "Are you fucking serious right now?"

It's too mean, what I want to say. But I don't stop myself. I should. He should stop me.

But we both just sit here, letting me make it worse.

"I'm literally still healing, still bleeding sometimes. I just lost my baby, our baby," my voice breaks, and I have to swallow a few times before I can continue. "You just pointed out that I haven't been taking care of myself; I can't do anything right. Why would you put this on me right now?" I choke on the tears gathering in the back of my throat. But something black, something mean, pushes me through so I can continue. "Why do you even want me? Why do either of you? I sit here, and right now all I can think is 'What is wrong with you, with your judgment, that I'm not *your* back-up plan?' Of all people, I should be the conciliation prize."

Theo drops my hands, and they turn to ice.

This is it, the moment he'll finally leave me. I know it. He should have a thousand times already.

"You want to know what's wrong with me?" his volume picking up again, trying to get me to listen. "I've pretty much always been in love with someone who doesn't love anyone. Not even herself. I don't even know if she *can* love anyone, if she wants to try. But here I am, still fighting for her. You need to wake up and see that."

"So, you're leaving? Is that it? You're sick of waiting, right?" I ask, looking back at his face, my heart breaking in the silence. "I wouldn't blame you. Everyone does. You know that better than anyone else," I scream.

It's my turn to stand, to walk away. I can't be near him if he's going to leave. I can't look into his eyes as he looks away.

I can't.

Before he can answer I hear a buzzing, and it breaks into the room like a wrecking ball. Instead of answering me, letting the phone wait, he pulls it from his pocket, and a weird little smirk moves across his lips.

Without thinking about it first, all of the air leaves my lungs and my legs collapse from under me until I'm sitting on the floor.

"So, who is that?" I ask, closing my eyes before he can answer.

"It's Maicy—" he says without hesitation. I'd have expected him to waiver, to try to convince me he's different, like he just said a minute ago. But I cut him off before he can say anything else. I don't want to hear the rest.

"My best friend?" I ask. "At least Austin fucked a stranger."

Theo narrows his eyes, and I watch as every muscle of his tenses and his eyes turn to fire. Even his ears get red. At least we can both explode this way; maybe it's better.

"If I haven't given up yet—if I haven't left in all this time—you need to realize that I'm never going to. *I'm not him*," Theo says as he walks over to me.

He drops his phone in my lap and then stomps toward the front door. He says, "Read it," over his shoulder before slamming the door as he leaves.

I wait, not daring to look down. And I listen, but he never starts the truck. He doesn't drive away.

Finally, when I check the screen of his phone, when I read Maicy's text, the tears come faster than they did before.

Maicy: Hey, is Taryn okay? I've bugged her all weekend, and she hasn't answered a single text or call. I just wanted to check on her. I know you've got her, but I just couldn't help asking.

Fuck me.

Taryn
Before

Make-up goes on top of t-shirts, on top of bras and underwear, on top of worn jeans with holes that weren't there when they were new. A blanket almost as old as me sits on top of everything, with a bottle of perfume I haven't opened in years—but that I remember smells like my mom when she was sober—and threadbare socks and a poem written just for me and everything else that I have to my name underneath it.

With everything inside I finally take a slow breath, calmer now that it's set in motion, now that I'm going to make it happen.

"Pigeon…" Theo says behind me.

Well, shit.

"Don't." It's all I get out; nothing else will come from between my lips. There's so much more I should tell him, things I'll never get to explain if I don't do it right now. And still…and still I can't get myself to turn around. I can't make my mouth open wider. I can't get the information out and to his ears so he can try to understand.

"You can't go," he tries.

And then his fingers are reaching for mine, his shaking—the only thing betraying his calm voice.

"It's like you don't know me at all," I say, trying not to shout as my shoulders inch farther and farther upward and my lashes close. I don't want to see his face. I already know what's waiting for me there.

But still, Theo pulls where he's holding me, tugging just my pinky finger until I turn around.

"Telling me——"

"Not to do something, that you can't, is the fastest way to get you to jump head first into doing it. I know, *I know*," Theo finishes for me.

Instead of laughing, like I'm pretty sure he'd been hoping for, I fall backward onto the hard, lumpy mattress that I've been assigned to for the last few weeks. All of the bravado I'd been holding onto suddenly gone.

My eyes still closed, I breathe out a puff of air that sounds something like an angry sigh.

"I'm going," I say to the back of my eyelids.

"Why?" Theo asks as he sits next to me, with his grip still tight around my finger.

"You know why." It's true. He's the only person who knows—not even Maicy; she wouldn't get it. She tries to understand, always listens and feels so fucking much for me. But she's never been here. And she never will be.

"Tell me again." Theo lies back next to me, and I try to picture what we look like here next to each other on thinning sheets that at least are clean.

"I can't stay here. Not one more night. Because every morning I wake up there's a few seconds, a moment in time, that I forget where I am. I forget how shitty everything is. And then it all comes crashing into me. That's worse than never forgetting. It's like torture having to remember every morning, each one worse than the last. So I just can't. I can't live here anymore with ten other kids," I try to explain. And I feel Theo tensing, finally getting me to open my eyes and look at him.

"Shut up. You know I don't mean you," I add.

"I thought it was getting better since we were finally placed together." Theo's eyes are on the ceiling as he says it. There's a wish in his voice, in the words. It's painful to listen to, but I try not to push him away.

"It was. It has. I don't know," I say. "I mean it's better *and* it's worse."

"Pidge, that doesn't make any sense." There's the hint of a smile on his lips, but it's sad.

I wish I'd snuck out before he found me.

"It's better because you're here. That's true. But having one of my best friends with me here just reminds me that I'm not with my mom. And you're leaving soon anyways. Your aunt is probably only weeks away from picking you up and driving you away from me. And then what?" I ask him, turning onto my side and facing his profile. He mirrors me, his icy blues boring into me, begging me to chill the fuck out. "I'm so angry all the time. I wish I wasn't. So… if I get away, if I get out of the system, then maybe I can let go of some of that anger, this rage," I point to my chest—an approximation of where my heart might be, if it's still in there. "Be better," I say.

It made sense in my head—somewhere inside all of that jumbled mess seemed coherent when I was planning, when I was packing.

"Where are you going to go?" Theo asks, a crease forming between his eyebrows as he gets down to the details.

"Anywhere else," I try.

"That's not a real answer. Where do you plan to run to?"

I bite my lip, knowing I don't have an answer. I didn't think that far ahead. "I thought…" I thought it would just all come together.

"There's nowhere you can go that will erase your anger for your mom and her mistakes. I don't think a location exists that will make you miss her less, that will make you calmer about this situation, about how life's been unfair," Theo whispers. "Because it's not fair. And you should be angry. Anyone would be." And the second part is quieter than the first.

Maybe he thinks that if he says it quietly it will hurt less.

I hate that he's right.

"Where will you go?" he asks again. "Really? Tell me your plan. Please." His eyes widen as he begs me to think it through, to be smarter. To listen to him. "I want to know."

"A motel," I say—the first thing that comes to mind. And I try to mentally count the money in my wallet, wondering how many nights I could pay for there.

"Before too long, you'd still end up on the streets. And that's worse than here. So much worse," Theo says. I don't ask for more information; I don't want to know how he knows that. But I can't look away as he blinks a few times, trying to brighten the dark spots from his eyes, not letting them harden.

"I hate it here," I admit. And I surprise myself as I reach for his hand, tucking my head under his chin at the same time. I let Theo wrap me up in his arms, and I swallow down the sobs that want to break free. "I hate it so much."

I don't cry. I won't.

"Know how I know that's true?" I feel Theo say it as much as I hear it, while hiding in his chest still.

"How?"

"Because I do too." I want to laugh at his answer. But nothing comes out. "I know it sucks, but if you stay, we can get through it together. We'll have each other here," Theo says.

I let scenarios run through my mind, wondering how fast I can run, wondering what kind of job I could get that would pay enough for me to manage on my own.

"I don't know," I finally say. And, boy, is it the truth.

I can feel him thinking; the cogs inside his head reverberate everywhere, as loud as if he were yelling at me. His thoughts stutter then start up again. It can't be good, whatever he's coming up with, but I don't have anything else to fill the space, the silence that gets longer.

"Well, then Pidge, it's too bad you didn't pack faster. Because if you go, I go too. I'm not staying here without you, and I sure as hell won't let you head out there on your own. So either way you're stuck with me. Just let me know what we're doing." Theo's voice gets surer with each word, like it was just an idea at the start and a solid plan by the end.

"*What?*" I pull backward, out of his arms so that I can see his stupid face. "No, no, no." My head shakes harder with each repeat. "No you are not," I yell at him.

"And who's going to stop me?"

It was a fine plan for me, the aimless one, always annoyed and making life harder for anyone near me. But him? No. Just no.

Theo sits up, ready to block my path if needed, I'm sure.

"Friends for life," Theo says, trying to make his smile look happy.

"Pain in the ass for life," I mumble, sitting up and tucking my hands beneath my thighs.

"Then what's it going to be? Do we stay here together or leave together?" he asks.

Letting my eyes drift away from his, I tip my head back until the back of my neck folds in on itself. The ceiling isn't stained. There aren't any bugs skittering along it. This place doesn't even have a lingering smell. It's not the worst place I've stayed—we may be forgotten sometimes, but we're not mistreated.

I sigh, already knowing.

"I nominate you to unpack my stuff," I say, still to the texture above our heads.

Then Theo's smile is finally real when I look back down to the warmth of his face—it's wide and reflected in the sparkles that are back in his eyes. He starts pulling things out of my bag without complaint, and the guilt washes through me like air into my lungs.

"Damn it. Stop, I didn't really mean for you to do that." I walk over to him, putting my hand on top of his.

He doesn't stop, though he lets me help him put everything away. Defeat creeps into me as I try to ignore it. And I know I'll be able to push it down eventually. Because I can stay if it's for Theo. He doesn't need to make a mess just before he gets out.

I know I couldn't have stayed for me, and I'm not sure who else—if there's anyone—that I would stay for. But it's Theo. He's not going to a creepy motel where we aren't safe, and he isn't sleeping in an alley when we run out of cash.

Never.

"You know, your mom has been clean the last few times. She's even been on time," he says when we finish, and I've put my bag under the bed again. "I heard her talking to the social worker too, they sounded positive. So, who knows, maybe we'll both get to leave soon. The right way."

I wish I was as optimistic as him, that I still could feel that way. But I don't argue.

Taryn
Now

"I'm sorry," I say the moment Theo comes in the front door, not giving him a chance to breathe, let alone say anything after his walk to clear his head. At least I'm hoping that's all he was doing for the last hour while I chewed on my nails and flicked through meaningless pages of black words on cream paper, through channels upon channels of bullshit. Every moment I wished I could rewind just a little and do it differently, better.

"Come here." He opens his arms and rushes to me as I all but run to him.

Theo's eyes are red, puffy, and his throat sounds raw and clogged. But I barely get to see as my face goes into his shirt, and I'm gripping around his ribs as tightly as I can, tighter than I ever have before.

"I'm sorry," I say into his chest.

Then I say it again.

And again.

He doesn't say anything, and the relief I'd felt starts to disappear.

"I'm sorry," I repeat, repeat, repeat.

Theo shakes his head, then bends down without letting me pull back, without warning me. His forearm goes under my knees and the other stays behind my back as he lifts me into his arms.

And he walks slowly down the hall to our bedroom—where he shows me that he understands, that he can wait at least a little while longer. Even if I don't deserve it. He uses his fingers and his mouth, and the rest of him to say what he can't seem to put into words right now. Taking a page out of my own book.

I may be the best person in the world to understand the silent speech.

****

Something stirs in my ears, my chest, or my head—I don't know, after my eyes flutter open, what it was. But then I'm awake, knowing right away that it's the middle of the night. Just like the first night I'd spent here with the baby's room set up, I walk toward that closed door. Only this time it's different. Theo has had the door closed ever since we— I—got home from the hospital. In his truck on the way over, I'd worried about my reaction to the precious little clothes and the furniture he'd worked so hard to put together. But, of course, he'd already thought of that.

It's been closed ever since.

But tonight, for the first time, I try to open the door. Holding my breath, my heart stuttering against everything else in my chest, I twist the knob. But it's locked. I shouldn't be surprised, and I definitely shouldn't feel relieved. But for a second both cross through me. I settle on understanding. It actually looks like a new knob; I doubt the last one had a lock now that I think about it.

I'm not sure what's right in this situation—not that I ever know what is—but I'm guessing Theo knows better than me.

After a sigh, I sneak back into bed, knowing he has my heart in his hands. Letting that sink in now. Even if I should have before. With weeks past, and *so* much shit in the rearview mirror, I think I'm ready for one thing I should have already done. Maybe not for everything. But this, at least.

"I want to sell the baby stuff," I tell Theo while he pretends to be sleeping, breathing quietly to himself. But I can tell. His chest stops moving, and his shoulders square up near his ears.

I hope it's from shock instead of something else.

"Are you sure? What if…" But he can't finish.

"If similar items are ever needed," I say slowly, careful not to say the wrong thing, as I keep my eyes on the dark ceiling. I don't need to start crying. "We will buy new. Everything in the room right now will always be sad. It will always be for…someone else." I rush the last sentence out, but it's enough to relax Theo a little.

"If you think you're ready," he says. He starts to turn, but I push forward and hug him tight before he can finish. And it's a hug that's warming, it's not something too touchy, nothing to make me squirm. It feels good to do something right.

****

There are a bunch of people coming over today to look at, and hopefully buy, the stuff from the locked room. Theo put it all up for sale, and he priced it to go fast, hoping that, with the holidays so close, we won't have anything left after today.

I've steeled myself. I'm hard as nails, a badass who doesn't care.

That's what I'm telling myself over and over, willing the words to be true.

This will be fine. It'll be easy.

Then when it's done, I'll finish moving on.

"You okay? We can tell them we changed our minds. No shame in it, Pigeon." Theo wraps his arm around my shoulder while we sit on the front steps. It's cold, and the breeze makes me pull my hoodie tighter, crossing my arms as protection.

"No, to move on I need to get rid of it," I say. The words are all breath and not conviction. But I do mean it.

He shrugs, trusting me for some stupid reason.

As the first car pulls into our driveway, *the* driveway, I flinch. "Don't let me change my mind. Even if I cry, make sure we keep going," I say to Theo as car doors open and close. "Be my rock," I add.

"For always," he says before standing to greet our customers.

If someone asks why we're selling this, I'm going to lose my shit. I never thought about the fact that we don't have a toddler around or any clear reason to look at and just know why we're selling brand new stuff.

I eye the couple, both near their late thirties, and I try not to get jealous about her huge belly.

I was supposed to have that.

"Everything's right inside." Theo points. Everyone follows him. "Did you find the place okay? Sometimes GPS gets people lost." He takes the lead and allows me to watch, silent. I try really fucking hard not to glare at anyone.

"No problem at all," the wife answers with a warm smile.

I hate her.

"You guys were interested in the crib, right?" Theo asks them.

I try to stand in the corner, but he pulls me to his side. I don't have to interact, but I'm not allowed to skulk and scare them away either. I get it. He's doing a good job with my request, even if I hate it.

The couple lingers and talks too much, but they're nice. They make me sad. At one point I think I see her stomach move. Picturing the baby swimming around in there, I wonder what it would have felt like to be kicked from the inside before I lost mine.

Then I excuse myself to the bathroom. And I cry.

Just a little.

When I come back out, they're leaving, and I'm glad to see them go.

"One down, seven more to go." Theo wraps his arms around my neck, breathing into my hair to warm me up, as we stand outside again to wait, starting the whole damn thing over. More, more, more of this.

Ugh.

"This kind of fucking sucks," I say.

"I knew it would," he says against my ear.

"Smartass."

I try to stiffen, faking an attitude, but really, it makes me feel better. His humor, his laughter, like Maicy's, it makes life better, easier. It gives me reason to let the little, and the big, shit go. It sparks the little embers of feeling inside me again. They're already threatening to catch fire.

Ten minutes later, after I've made lemonade, the next couple shows up. They're gray-haired. Looking for gifts for their second grandchild. Somehow that's easier, not having what I'm missing rubbed in my face.

But they're also here for the wraps that Austin gave me.

Theo told me I didn't need to sell them. Those could be the things we kept, "Just in case," he'd smirked. I argued it all had to go. Now, though, fear clenches my organs. Maybe not fear, maybe regret and guilt.

I can't even try.

I pull Theo down to whisper in his ear, "Sell them. I need a little break." He kisses my cheek and shoves me out the front door. I'd rather watch TV, but I walk down the sidewalk.

It's fucking cold, and I wish I'd brought my mittens as my chest starts to shake, rattling my teeth too. But I don't stop. I think about everything while I walk; I think about nothing.

This day is going to be long, and I'm so sick of long, hard days already.

I still haven't gone back to work yet; Cooper won't let me until he gets the okay from Theo. Who knew my stepdad got to decide I needed a babysitter? I waffle back and forth about which is better—being allowed to grieve in my own time or being bored as fuck, sitting on my ass for too many hours.

Maybe I'll start exercising again.

"They bought two of them," Theo tells me when I get back after a lap around the block. "And they were the only ones interested in the wraps. What do we do with the other two?" His face is tight, like he's done something wrong. He's waiting for me to explode somehow. I can feel it.

I think for a moment, sighing. He could have planned it, I'll never know.

"We'll keep one. I'll give the other back to Austin. He can do what he wants with it, sell it." I don't know if he'll want it, if he'll be pissed I sold the others.

Maybe I'll mail it to him, saving myself the horrible experience.

Theo agrees. And we keep going through the motions. Six more cars come and go.

I stay inside, in the room, for half. The other three times, I make an excuse to leave. Theo never gets mad, never rolls his eyes; he puts up with it. He didn't even want to do this, but I've been convinced he'll do pretty much anything to make me happy. I have no clue when he fell in love with me, but I suspect it was long before I ever noticed, before I gave him the time of day.

I'm such a bitch.

When all is said and done we have a thousand bucks in cash. I bet we lost double that, or more, but now it's done. Theo counts it out and gives me half.

"I have an idea." He smiles with his voice.

"Sounds dangerous," I say.

He grabs my hand and pulls me to the door, outside the house, and up to the truck. I follow, nothing tells me not to, not like it used to. He hasn't steered me wrong yet. Amazingly. Other than Cooper, he's the only one. Even my mom can't make that list.

Grabbing my face, he tips it up to look at him. "Do you trust me?" There's a nervous hiccup in his words that makes me melt.

"I do." I breathe in, slow and deliberate. "Even if I shouldn't." I hope he takes it as the joke I intended. Then after a second thought, I add a wink.

He shakes his head at me and points to the passenger side. I obey, despite every instinct in me screaming to be a stubborn child. Doing the opposite of what I'm asked will be a habit I might never break, no matter how much I grow up. But I suspect Theo doesn't expect me to. While he drives, I watch his face instead of the scenery. It doesn't take long before we're parked again.

I finally look out the windshield and see the tattoo parlor Austin took me to so many years ago.

"What are we...?" But the words fall short in my mouth, not making their way out. I know what we're doing here. I know what this gesture means. The only thing I don't know yet is how I feel about it.

"This is how I want to spend my half. You don't have to do anything. Honestly, that's not why we're here. But I'd like you to hold my hand while I get mine." His voice rings confident and steady now. One look in his eyes says just how much he's thought about this.

It's his *first* tattoo.

I'm not sure I've ever seen him happier either.

Inside we say hello. "Theo, I'm glad you convinced her to come." It's the same artist, Jason, who did my first. Austin's friend. I guess that makes him Theo's too.

"He tricked me," I admit.

"Smart man." He elbows Theo's side as we walk back to a chair, and I wonder how long this appointment has been set. I don't dare ask.

Jason pulls out two sketches and lays them on the back-lit table for Theo to inspect. They're simple, thin lines in solid colors. He nods his head, but holds up a finger to wait. After looking to me with big-ass question marks in his eyes, he waits.

I will not cry. I can't be that girl.

Even with hormones settling down, I can't be that girl. Not here. Not right now.

I bite my tongue and shake yes. They won't take long, so I hope I'll have time to build the courage I need to keep it together.

Jason sets up. I don't tense, though it takes effort.

We sit in silence. Jason's focused, so he doesn't notice the silence. But when he's ready to go, and the buzz of the needle sounds, he starts getting chatty. "You never told me what these are for," he says to Theo.

Theo doesn't hesitate. He smiles. I never realized before how often he smiles. It's most of the time, even when life's kind of shit. "That one," he points to the red Q that is now purplish on his body, waiting for its permanent ink, "is to match hers. Because she's *my* queen of hearts." He doesn't sound possessive, even though he emphasizes the *my*.

Jason starts giving it its permanence over his ribs, on the side of Theo's body.

Then Theo moves his hand for me to come closer until his lips are next to my ear, and he whispers, "I wanted it to always remind me how I'm enough for you. Not just a backup, not a comparison or conciliation." I gulp, watching Jason raise his eyebrow, but he asks nothing. "The placement is because you walk beside me. Not in front, not behind. Always next to me." When he's finished he nips at my ear lobe.

The first is already finished. Thirty seconds for a lifetime of remembrance.

It gives mine a whole new, double, meaning. Bitter and sweet.

I'm surprisingly okay with it. More than I thought I'd be.

"And the other…" Theo says, while Jason changes from red to black for his needle, starting with the second tattoo. It's simple outlines of hearts. Three of them, descending sizes, one inside the next inside the next. He cringes, squeezing my hand, as the hum of metal finds his skin. It's on the inside of his arm, where, when it sets against his side, it'll meet the Q. Both sensitive areas. "And the other is because her heart keeps mine beating." Jason smiles. I'm so thankful he doesn't bring anything unbearable up.

Again, Theo says the last part only to me, "And the littlest is to never forget what we lost." When I pull back, the smile he wears isn't touching his eyes, but confidence shines from them anyway.

"Jason," I finally say something.

"Taryn," he says back.

"Have time for one more?" He nods, I smile, and Theo tries not to smirk. *Yeah, yeah, yeah.* "I want that one," I point to Theo's arm, "In purple. Right here," I point to the spot, a few inches below the bottom of my bra, dead center, a little below the tip of the V of my ribs.

"Why purple?" Theo asks.

"The color of the room," I whisper.

****

The tattoo didn't hurt. Not physically. But then again it wasn't my first, or second. I've never gotten one with someone else, other than Austin. The fact that he thought of it, and brought me, it's kind of amazing, and I'm not sure why exactly.

In the car on the way home, I play with a penny I found on the ground by his truck, letting it slip between my fingers over and over. It's soothing. A thought, an easy way out, tickles the back of my brain, and I start tossing the little copper piece into the air and catching it. Maybe I can just flip a coin, have the decision made for me. As easy as that.

So I do.

The penny goes up into the air, spinning over and over, top over bottom.

Heads for one, tails for the other. But when I see what's face up on the top of my hand, something sinks in. Panic. My heart starts beating at the back of my throat, and I know. It's so fucking clear.

I know what I don't want.

Then, I let what I've been thinking since he explained the three hearts sit on the tip of my tongue. At a red light I almost say it, then stop myself. Too many times I open my mouth then close it, having done nothing but breathe. Theo waits. I know he's seen my fish impression; his eyes are shifty but not sneaky. But he's shut up, like me.

When he turns the car off, I just blurt it out.

"I was wrong about love not existing before," I rush. His head turns to me, with his eyes wide. "Because I loved that baby before it was even born. And I miss it."

"Me too, Pidge," he answers.

Leaning forward to hug me, he smothers me in his arms, his scent, his warmth.

So I jump.

"And I think I love you."

His breath pauses for a moment before he answers, "Me too, Pigeon. Me too."

Austin
Now

Taryn's chosen Theo. Probably.

For now.

She's only said one thing to me since that night, since I called her, since I pushed too far. She sent a single text, just one, and it broke my heart. I didn't know that three little words could be so painful, but when all she typed out to me was that she forgave me, I lost it. I expected a fight, or worse. I expected more than that. But with everything she's been though, we've been through, with the anger and the confusion, it must have been easier for her just to sweep it away, to forgive so she didn't have to talk about it.

So, yeah she's probably chosen Theo.

But there's still some hope.

It may be just a shred, but I'm clutching to it like the last piece of toilet paper in the middle of the woods. She hasn't *told* me she's picked him. Actually she hasn't said a word to me since the night I called her and...the night I might have ruined everything.

But no news is good news, right?

I don't think I could cling harder.

I've been a better person since then. Sort of. The night I called Taryn was the lowest point in my life. I still kick myself for it every damn day. It may have been the last nail in the coffin, the breaking point that I'll never come back from.

Or it could be the last thing she forgives me for, but that's a little harder to believe.

I stopped drinking after that mistake. It showed me how low rock bottom could sink me to and how big my problem had become. I could see the bottle hanging above me, swinging in the air above my head, ready to help me crash and burn.

I stopped drinking, but I'm still fucking different women every night.

It's hard to go cold turkey on it all at the same time.

But every face looks like hers when my eyes are closed. Every name sounds like, "Taryn." Every night with someone else, without her, is as lonely as the nights in bed alone. My chest aches, and my head swims.

All of the adventure, the single nights of sex, they don't help me feel better.

I'm starting to wonder if Taryn was right all along, that someone can be as broken as she always claimed to be. I never believed it before. I just thought she'd been hurt and never finished healing. But maybe some things can never totally heal.

Maybe it's possible to always be missing a piece, always need gluing back together.

If she never comes back, if we're over for good this time, if she chooses Theo and leaves me alone…*I'll be wrecked.*

But I don't want to be.

I want to be with her.

Taryn
Now

"Can I come over all the time?" Maicy asks with fear on her face, moisture in her eyes.

"Whenever you want," I say.

"You promise?"

"I do." She looks unconvinced, so I try again. "You know I don't promise things I don't mean. Besides, I stole a few things from your closet, that way you'll have things to wear at my place," I tell her with a wink.

Cooper and my mother bought my house from me, at a damn good price, and are renting cheaper than I did to Maicy. They made me the offer when I mentioned how much of my time I'd been spending at Theo's, after Cooper finally let me come back to work this week.

And now I'm moving in with Theo. Totally. For good. It's been a couple months of his helping me heal to get it right and give him what he deserves.

It's weird to leave my house. Weirder to leave Maicy.

Obviously I'll see her, at my new place and at *hers*.

But it'll be different.

Theo told me when I was complaining about change yesterday, "Nothing can stay the same forever." It was a simple statement, one

I'm sure I've heard a million times. Yet that time something was different. It sunk in.

Maicy squeezes me tight, too tight, like it's the last time she'll ever see me.

"Get in the damn car and come over now. We'll watch a movie. You can help me put my shit away." I can't drive away and watch her get smaller. I know Theo won't mind.

****

I *reallllly* don't want to do this.

"Stop shaking your head, Pidge. You told me to make you. I promised, and I don't back out of promises any more than you do." Theo holds firm.

"Fuck that. I lied. I don't wanna. Don't make me," I say. Pure complaining, my insides wriggling and writhing against what's so fucking uncomfortable, and my voice echoes every bit of that out loud.

"Too damn bad. It's ringing." He shoves my phone back into my hands and walks into the bathroom, locking the door.

If I hang up now, he'll just call right back.

"Hello?" Austin answers.

Too late anyway.

"Hey." It's all I say. *Idiot.*

"Hi." He does no better.

"Meet me for coffee? How about Perk-alot-Latte?" I ask, my voice all over the place, following the lead from my heartbeat, making me itchy and tingly.

There's a whoosh, maybe the wind or maybe his exhalation. Then, "I...yeah, I...okay. When?" he stumbles.

"Now. If it works for you."

Say no, say no, say no.

"On my way." He hangs up the phone without a goodbye. Probably so I couldn't change my mind first. Smart guy.

"I hate you," I call to the chickenshit behind the locked door on my way out of the house. "I'll be back soon."

Yeah, yeah, he promised. But that doesn't mean it was a smart promise. He's sending me to have coffee with the one who got away. *Twice.*

He has absolute faith in me. More than anyone else ever did.

More faith than I have in myself, than I've ever had.

I agonized for days before asking for his strength to make me go through with this. I worried, arguing devil's advocate with myself, if I should see him once more or let it go without even saying the words.

The thing that pushed me to this decision, though, was that I'd made this mess to begin with. All by my stupid self. I called him that night. I wanted all of this to be messy. I got what I wanted, what I deserved.

So he's earned a real goodbye, as much as it'll hurt. As much as I'd rather cut off a toe than be brave and do it. I set my overstuffed purse on the passenger seat of the truck and drive to the coffee shop, getting colder and more anxious the entire way.

When I park, he's already there, two cups at the table.

He ordered for me.

Somehow that makes it just a little worse.

Fuck, fuck, fuck.

My breath won't slow down, so I suck it up and get out of the car. When I slam the door Austin looks over. I see the frown for a second or two before he smooths his features out. I shouldn't have driven Theo's truck. *Dumb.*

My bag feels heavy walking to him. My feet feel like they're the wrong size. My head doesn't seem connected to my neck anymore. If I could turn back at this point, I would.

"I got you a black and white hot chocolate. No whip." The optimism in his voice hurts my insides. He holds my cup up then sets it back down as I sit in my chair. It feels too close to him. My foot is in dangerous, boundary-crossing territory.

We aren't here to play footsie.

I open my mouth to start rambling, but he says something first. "So how have you been since…everything?" Austin's hand inches across the table, and mine fall from around the base of my cocoa into my lap. He looks stung, retracting his fingers.

This isn't a good visit. Stop making me feel worse.

"I've been better," I say. "I'm getting better," I add.

In other words, I'm not as bad as I was.

"I'm really sorry about…" again he looks lost, "everything."

"There's a lot for both of us to be sorry for," I say.

"Well, I should be sorrier. I screwed up more." His eyes aren't on my face. He's looking at the tabletop like it has all the answers, like it can convince me to stay.

"That's true." I try to sound light. It only kind of works. When he still doesn't look up, I pull my hand from where it's pinched between my knees and put it on top of his. That gets him to finally look at my eyes.

There's no running from the sadness there, and when his eyes mirror mine, I think he might get what today is about.

"Taryn, I…" I hold my other hand up, appreciative that he didn't call me a pet name but not wanting to hear something that will make this harder.

"Can I go first please?" I ask.

Austin nods. Now he looks as scared as he does sad.

Fuck the hard parts of life.

"First, this is for you." I turn and pull the last baby wrap out of my bag. The weight still left hanging on my shoulder is surprisingly different. Some of my guilt and fear sat heavy in the material. Now I'm passing the burden onto Austin, like a coward. "I'm sorry, I sold the others before I realized I should return them." Half-truth.

"I don't want this," Austin chokes out, while trying to give it back. But my hands are between my knees again, getting red, so I won't take anything. I shake my head violently to drive the point home.

"It's yours. Return it. Sell it. Keep it," I suggest.

"I never wanted things to turn out like this. I never expected they would." Austin's speaking to the table again. His shoulders are slumped his eyebrows are furrowed, and he looks, sounds, utterly defeated. His eyes are almost closed from the weight of his lids. I breathe deeply, trying to find what I need somewhere inside me to finish.

"I never wanted it either. But I've never expected happy endings for myself, so I guess I should have seen it coming." I don't mean to sound harsh. "I warned you from the beginning what I couldn't promise. I always felt off, like something was wrong with me."

Austin narrows his eyes. I try not to flinch. Anger was always going to come, right for my heart. And I understand it.

"I could have helped fixed you," he holds onto the words for as long he can, and they sound like they're laced with every mistake, every missed opportunity, every single bad part about us. They *were* meant to sting, to feel awful.

And they do.

"That was always your problem." Mine are meant to rival his. "Your mission was always to fix me, to un-break everything in me that was torn apart. That would never, and will never, happen. All along you should've been helping me, pushing me to fix *myself*. No one can fix me but *me*. I had to put the pieces back together myself." The sentiment may damage him, but I hope he learns, grows from it.

I want that for him.

"I never tried to fix you; what are you talking about? You were always perfect, that was the point," Austin says, not getting it, making my heart squeeze tighter.

"You did, though. You put so much pressure on me without even knowing it. It wasn't on purpose, not ever. But I still felt it, all the time." I sigh, feeling awful. "I hated that I felt that way, and I tried to deny it, but the force of it, of your expectations, never went away. I couldn't ever live up to your version of me."

"That's not fair." His words are just a whisper, so quiet he might have hoped I didn't hear.

So I keep going, trying to get my point out before my strength is gone. "You wanted to do everything for me, give me the world, make everything better. And that was never going to work. I love you for it, but it's not what I needed. Our biggest problem was that I wasn't able to do anything for myself, I didn't have the space, the encouragement. You didn't push me to figure my own shit out, instead you tried to do it all for me." I feel exhausted after finishing, knowing he still isn't going to get it. Suddenly, I don't think he's ever going to no matter how many times I repeat myself or restructure, reword, around the same meaning.

"When? How?" Austin closes his eyes when he says it.

"All the time. Every day," I say. It hurts. Everything inside of me, from my breaking heart to the edges of my skin, raw and exposed, hurts. "When we fought and I ran, you just let me. When I pushed you away because I was scared of getting hurt you just let your own arms stretch farther. I needed pushing back. I still do. And when my past affected our present, our future, you never tried to learn about what had scarred me. You let me bottle it up, no questions. You didn't want me to have to do the work I needed to. You just wanted to erase it, gloss over it. But even as messy, as fucked up, as those truths of me are, they needed acknowledging, they needed working through, healing from."

I run out of words, out of energy, and I don't think I've ever wished for the end of something so much in my life.

"What can I do? How can I be enough? Where did we go wrong? Why is all of this so hard?" Austin asks like shots from something fast enough to reload itself. There's no time between each for me to even blink, let alone take a breath to answer.

When he's finished, though, when I do have time to speak, the answer is already on my tongue.

"Because life," I say.

For too long we sit in silence, uncomfortable as we're both fidgeting. I start and stop too many times in the minutes we let slip by. Minutes we'll never get back. Empty minutes we'll remember forever.

"Can't we ever make it right?" he asks so quiet, it twists the knife deeper.

"No." His head pops up, and there are tears in his eyes. "I can't get through what I need to say if you cry." A strong man breaking down will make me fall so apart. Every fucking time. "Please," I whisper.

Austin blinks a few times. Closes his eyes. Takes a few breaths. Then he looks at me and nods.

"We can *never* make it right," I have to say it out loud, more for myself than him. If I never say it, then we'll both hold onto the *maybe* we used to. "We're toxic together. It always goes bad; it sours. Even if we start out good, it can't stay that way for long. It never does; it never will." *I hate this.*

"I don't believe that." His voice is stronger, almost piercing as it rushes through me. It makes me want to change my mind, even if I can't. He continues, "We're a lot of things, but toxic isn't one of them. I think…I know that we can make it work." He isn't going to hear me, feel the weight of the truth in my words, unless I pull out the worst, the truest ones. The ones I've always wanted to, and still want to, hide from.

"Every time I look at you, all I can see is heartbreak." Tears fall down my cheeks as I take the next breath. One slow, cold drop at a time. I wipe them away, fast and rough, almost slapping my face. But I can't dry the sadness that's behind them. I can't make my voice stronger. I can't make this any easier, for either of us. "I see my shattered heart in your face."

Austin sucks in a breath.

If I don't put every single thing out there, I'll regret the unsaid things forever. I don't have any room for regret left. I've used it all up.

"My heart shattered when you cheated," I tell him. "It may have already been falling apart, but you smashed all of the pieces into dust."

There's a sound, something like choking, but I ignore it. "Though, that's not all I see."

Austin starts to shake his head, like it'll block the sound from entering his ears.

I keep going. "I don't just see the betrayal. I see the doubt I let fester for too long. I see the baby I lost that might've been yours."

"Why don't you see that when you look at Theo?" he interrupts. I get it, but I wish he hadn't. "What did he do right that I didn't? Why am *I* so wrong?" Austin's voice chokes on the words, on the idea.

It's hard not to gag on my feelings, on the pain. But I push through, as best I can anyway.

"I don't know," I admit. "But I see a future when I look at him, not a broken past full of mistakes. Maybe it's because he knows more about why I struggle, because he had the same shit going on back then. Maybe it's because of that, that he knows how to push me to work on my shit instead of fixing things for me. Or maybe it's none of that, I don't know. I wish I did, but when I look into Theo's eyes I see happiness, I see possibilities and hope, not everything I've lost," I get out. I don't add the rest of that sentence, but he understands anyway.

"I lost it too, you know," he says.

"I *do* know that," I say. I don't know if I'll ever be able to make him understand. "There is no way I will *ever* forget it. I can feel it every time I think of you, every time I see you. Every time I'm near you. I feel the shame of not being able to do the one thing I wanted to do. My body is supposed to be able to do that, to create and nourish life. But I failed. I lost that baby, and I will forever blame myself."

He starts to open his mouth again, but I cut him off. "Every time I look at you, all of that comes back. I feel the pain as strongly as I did that night when I had to watch the blood and tissue fall out of the one place it was supposed to be safe. I will never forget how I felt after losing him," I say.

Him.

I don't give Austin time to question. "When I look at you, even now, I see a crumbled relationship that can never be fixed again. It was good once," I admit. "And when it was good, life felt fucking perfect. But there were always problems. They may have started small, but they grew to something we could never get over. What happened," I say without actually saying it, because I know he knows what I mean. We'll both always know. "Was something that proved what I had believed for so long. That betrayal…I can *never* get over our damage."

I know he wants me to stop, to shut up if I'm not going to change my mind. But I can't.

I can't.

"I see unfixable things. Things that would just continue to tear us apart until we're unrecognizable. I would hurt you later if I wasn't hurting you now. You are worth so much more than I can give to you. There's nothing wrong with you. And maybe I'm okay now too. But together *we* are broken." I try to gulp down the lump that won't go away, even though my eyes have dried. "I'm so, so fucking sorry for even trying to fix this." I wave my hand between us, almost knocking over my cup. The distraction pauses everything, and I catch my breath. My hand shaking, clutching the edge of the table.

"I still love you. I'll always love you," Austin says with a steady voice. It sounds so much clearer than mine.

"But I can't separate the past from the present. For me it's too hard. I can't let go of all the wrongs we've done." I can see in his face, he thinks I'm just talking about his mistakes. "*Both* of us. It was always easier for me to run away than face a problem. And I expected problems. I never stopped waiting for the final one, the one that would break us up."

Austin grabs my hands before I can pull them away. He holds tight, his eyes frantic. "I'll be better, I swear." Somehow with those five words, my tears find a home once again. He sounds like a child begging for something that isn't possible. He looks lost, like he'll never be found, never be okay, again. "I'll make everything right."

I move my head slowly. He heard the words. He listened. But the finality, the meaning, it slipped past him before he could catch it.

"How?" I demand. "How can you make everything we've been through and done to each other all right?" Without an answer, I go on. "I don't want you to love me because of it. But I don't want you to love me in spite of it either. I just *wanted* you to love me. For who I was before *and* for who I am now." Two little extra letters, -ed, past tense. Two tiny little additions that change the meaning of everything; no longer what I want, but what I *wanted*. "And now… now hearing those words from you, hearing you promise to change everything, it doesn't feel the same. It's not enough."

The breeze flutters by, catching my hair for a moment, reminding me that the rest of the world is still continuing, unaware of our heartbreak.

He squeezes my fingers before I pull them from his grasp, bringing my eyes back to his.

"You make me want to be a better person. I *am* better with you." He starts to struggle for air, and I don't want to be here anymore. Claustrophobia hits me hard and sudden, even outdoors. My pain is crushing me into a tight corner I can't possibly survive in. But he still won't let go. "I can't make it without you. You'll always be my queen of hearts." Together we both shake, our bodies resisting the words coming from or toward us, grasping for a hold on what's left or trying to push it away. Then he continues, "*I need you.*"

I almost change my mind.

I know everything I've said is true; it's right. But this is fucking torture. Austin has been a fixture in my life for so long, I'm not sure I'll ever figure out how to let him go, to forget. And watching him in agony, all of it my fault, it's horrible.

"You don't, though. You've convinced yourself that you do. You need *someone*, but that someone isn't me. It hasn't been for a long time," I say, and then he lets my fingers slip away from his, scorched by my words.

"You really don't see the same loss when you look at him?" he asks. "Are you picking him then?"

"Does it matter?" I ask. "I'm picking me." I lower my voice, "I'm just not picking us." I try to make that enough.

Please let those words be enough.

Still, he won't stop. "So you're choosing Theo," he says again. I don't answer; he doesn't need the sting of it. The silence is enough. It screams my answer.

I keep trying to explain, even if it's a waste of breath. "I came across a quote once that said 'if you love two people at the same time, choose the second. Because if you really loved the first one, you wouldn't have fallen for the second.' It makes a lot of sense if you think hard about it. I never got it before all of this, but I do now. I understand and believe it." I just want him to understand.

"Yeah, and you're my second," he says with a horrible sliver of hope that's worse than anything else yet. The tiny perk in the corner of his mouth is awful. It cracks something inside me.

"But you're not mine…*he* is," I choke out. This is all so much worse than I prepared for. It's one of those moments, a splitting of what could have been. It's something I'll never, *ever*, forget.

Austin's face crumples, and as everything about him compresses in on itself, I know I don't want to hear what he's about to say. I know, but I can't get myself to leave before he does. "What is so much better about him? What does that relationship have that ours can't again?" Austin asks. His voice tearing me to pieces.

This is the worst thing I'll ever say.

He'll never forgive me. But I guess that's the point.

I know I have to.

"With him, I do want to fix myself. He makes me better because he doesn't see me as perfect. He pushes me. He sees the real me, and because of that I'm able to be a better me with him." I try to breathe, and it's so hard. This is where I lose every bit of respect for myself. This is the moment I will never be able to forgive. If only he wasn't forcing me to finish. "With him I have something I never thought existed, something I was never sure about with you. Something I hoped for all the time, but it never came. And no matter how close we got, I was never really certain." His eyes narrow. "I love him." Every word comes our quieter than the last, but I know he hears every single one. "And I don't love you. Not anymore."

Austin doesn't say anything. He sucks in a breath, wounded.

I have one more thing to add. It won't make anything better, not easier either. But now that I've thought about it, there's no going back.

"I can be your villain; that's fine," I let out in one breath. "But I want you to hear me and know, you aren't mine. Not anymore. Not ever anymore."

Austin's still silent, until he stands.

He leaves his coffee on the table as he gets up and walks away from me.

I hate that I watch him go. I follow every step until he's in his car. Then I watch him pull out and drive away.

He never once looks back.

****

"Can I help you with anything?" The friendly employee is too loud, too nice, too cheerful. He makes me feel hollow. There's such a contrast in our features, and my frown deepens the longer this day continues.

"I need a new phone. And I want a new number with it too," I manage to say it without struggling. New number, new life. Austin's is already deleted from my phone. It felt like deleting him from my life.

After everything is purchased and activated, a numb feeling washes over me. I wish I'd been numb before. This feels too little too late. And it doesn't last long.

I cry the entire way home.

Austin

Now

I left my coffee sitting there.

I left Taryn sitting there.

I felt her watch me leave, but I couldn't bear to look.

I went home, and I packed. I shoved everything I own into suitcases and boxes. I loaded it all into my car, and I stayed at a hotel that night. The next day I went back to pay what I owed on rent, and I gave my notice.

I can't live there anymore. I can't be anywhere we've been together. I can't chance running into her. I can't continue living being worried about breaking down, breaking apart, if I see her. It would hurt too much.

That day hurt too much.

Knowing she'll always be the one who got away, that I might never let her go, hurts too fucking much.

Now I'm in my car driving away from the one place I've ever lived. I need a new city, a new state, a new life, just new. *New.* But there's only one way, in the direction I'm headed, and I have to pass the beach I dreamt about only months ago. The beach where Taryn ran away from me, where I caught her before she disappeared. The dream should've warned me.

As I pass the last few hundred feet of sand, I toss the baby wrap out my window. It's the last thing I needed to get rid of. It was the last thing I still had that she's touched.

But it's gone now. And hopefully so is she.

Either way I'm fucking gone for good.

Taryn
One month later

Taryn

Another one

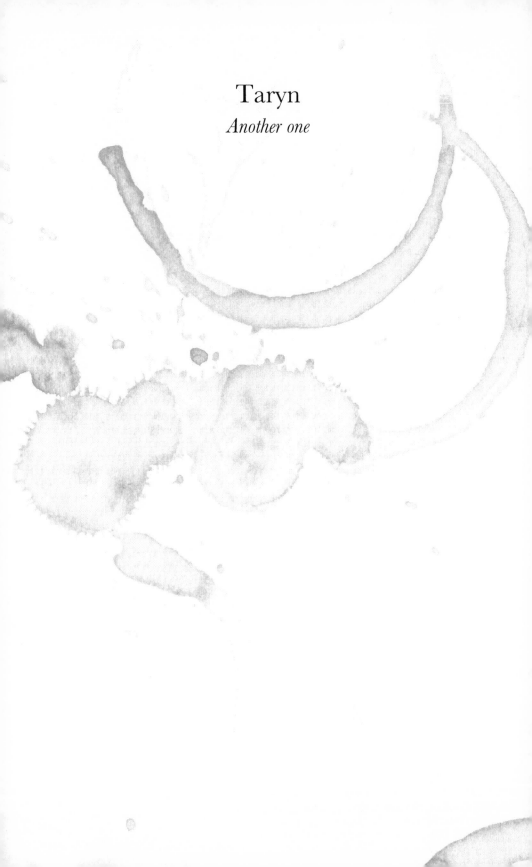

Taryn
And another

Taryn
Four months

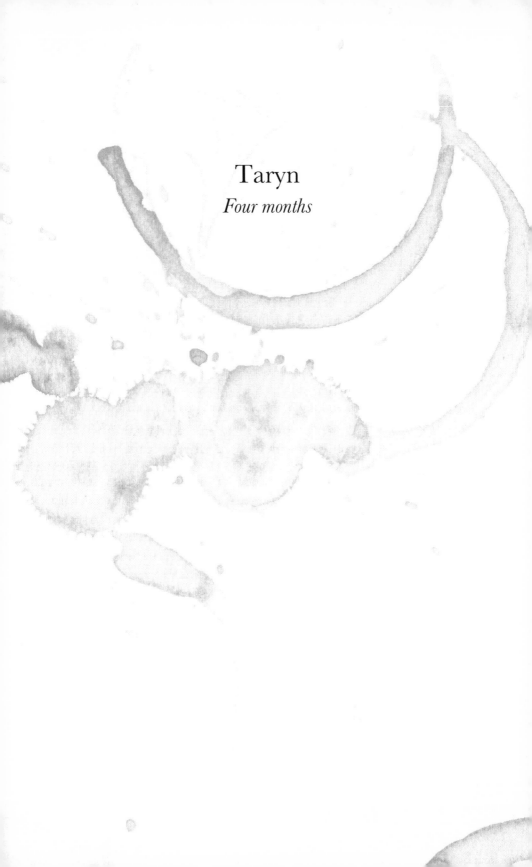

Taryn

Another month goes by

Taryn

Six months later

Taryn
Now

I haven't heard a word from Austin since that day. The spring came and went. I lived my life with Theo. I thought about Austin plenty but less as the days and months wore on. I was serious about how hard it is to separate the past from the present. I know the difference between the two, and I don't want the past, but I can never completely forget it. It will always have happened. It will always be there, affecting the present, the future.

I changed my number.

I let him go.

I've never reached out.

Theo and Maicy both mentioned he moved. Theo tried to be sly about the announcement, pretend it was a side note in passing. Maicy may have added something along the lines of "good riddance." I didn't ask either of them where he went. I don't want to know.

I don't need to know.

The past is impossible to erase or wipe from memory, but the further back it gets, the easier it is to stop holding onto.

There are still times I think about him. It would be impossible not to. We had too many years with each other, physically or longingly. In my heart he'll always stay a friend. I doubt he feels the same, but it's nice to pretend sometimes. I might think about him, but I don't ever dwell, not anymore.

I did that for way too many years. Dwelling, obsessing, letting it haunt me—it's what led to trying again. I couldn't let him go when I was still trying to hold on. Now when a thought comes I let it happen, and then I let it pass.

As much as I'd like to beat myself up for calling him that night when he was at the bar, for letting it go on so long with our dysfunction instead of moving on after the first split, and ultimately for trying again, I can't. I got so many good things out of that hard and shitty situation.

I wanted something beautiful from all of the mess, all of the fucked up ugly.

I got a baby. I wasn't able to keep him, but for a short while, I was allowed to be happy experiencing it. I also found how to love again. Theo proved it's not always fake. He showed me how to fix myself, and I did.

Like the lotus grows from the mud and the phoenix rises from ashes, I was able to make a few beautiful decisions while surrounded by a lot of horrible ones.

I also started writing again after I left the hospital. Theo suggested that I keep a journal to help keep my thoughts in order, in one place, while I physically healed, to help me heal emotionally too. He's one smart fucker. It helped. A lot.

So I kept up with it. I wrote through the loss of baby bud, the loss of Austin, and the loss of the way I used to see myself. I still write in it, almost every day. Theo's never asked to look at it either, which I can't quite wrap my head around. If he were writing in a journal, I'd want to see his musings, his secret thoughts.

But he doesn't.

And he's never peeked without permission either. I don't think.

When I started it, I'd hide it in a different place every day. I was weird and secretive, thinking if he saw the oddities in me, he'd run, leaving me worse off than I was after right after the hospital. I even took pictures on my phone of how I placed the damn thing in hiding. That way I'd know if he moved it an inch.

He never did, not for months.

Now I keep it on my nightstand, in plain sight. And if he asked to read it, I'd let him. If he asked me to look at something from the pages, I already know what passage I'd choose.

****

I hate admitting I'm wrong. It's one of my many deep-rooted flaws. I know there's a lot wrong with me. I'm fucking stubborn, impossibly so. But when I do admit a mistake, when I can allow right to replace error, I let it wash over me, overtake me.

I admit I was wrong about love for too long.

It isn't fake, not always. It's rare, but it can be real.

Romance, love, it's what you make of it. If you're convinced it's all shit, then it will be shit. If you don't allow it in, then you'll never believe it's real. You can't feel what you push away.

Love lives, but only if you let it.

You get out what you put in, the good and the bad.

Granted, the good may not wipe the bad away, but each helps rein the other in. There's some sort of balance, though you may not always see it. People make mistakes, and others do bad things on purpose. Shitty things happen without warning and for no reason. Good things die. Horrible things flourish. But the reverse is also true.

Sometimes good things die to let other good things, different-than-you-expected things, live and take hold. Nothing is ever perfect, never. Everything good takes work, but sometimes it's worth it, even if it's not what you were rooting for from the beginning.

Life is hard.

It needs a lot of effort.

But giving up solves nothing, not like you want it to.

We don't always want to put up with the struggle, especially after we've been taught there's always a bubble just waiting to burst in your face. When we're holding our breath, knowing something terrible is about to happen, it gets too tiring to wish for anything hopeful.

Believe me, I know.

I've learned, though, the struggle is worth it.

We change, we grow, when we come out of something horrific wishing for better.

I always thought hope was dangerous. I thought if I dared to hope for the things I'd been shown over and over I wasn't allowed to have, to feel, it would hurt worse than just not getting them in the first place. Hoping for something I thought I could never have seemed so much worse than just convincing myself I didn't want it.

I did want those things, though.

It's only possible to lie to yourself for so long before you catch on and see through the bullshit.

But now I know.

Now I know what real love is, and it's absolutely worth every piece of the pain from before.

Now I can feel the truth that lies in love every single day.

That feels like a really stupid thing to say, but no matter how much it embarrasses me to admit, and I'd never say it out loud, it's a fucking brilliant truth. Love is real; it's actually possible, and so many other important truths live inside that notion too.

Love is worth a lot.

It's more than just the warm liquid that wells up inside your chest, the tingles that sit heavy in your stomach. It's so much more. It's every mistake that led up to the moment you felt it. It's every broken heart that broke you or the ones you handed out in retribution. It's every memory, every event that came before. It's everything stirred together.

You get out what you put into love, and sometimes it isn't real. Sometimes it's faked or imagined. It's always confusing. But the possibility is still there. It can be real. You just have to reach out for it.

****

"No don't get up and help. I'll cook the entire meal by myself." Theo walks past the living room on the way to the kitchen. He stops to plant a soft kiss into my hair, after winking at me.

"You just love to hear yourself talk," Maicy says to him while she paints my toenails. I let her do it, only after she begged for way too long, but I made her do them black.

"Hell yes, I do." He laughs while banging pots and pans around.

The TV is quiet, but I can still hear it over Maicy's rambling.

"I think I like him..." she babbles on and on about a new guy she's been seeing. For the first time in a long time, I'm genuinely interested in her love life. She's happy, and the idea doesn't revolt me. I don't think she's deluding herself either. And if it doesn't work out, that's not because it isn't possible.

It's really fucking weird.

Despite her excitement, I worry a little. He'd better be good enough for her. I'll need convincing. She deserves more than she knows.

"Umm, what the fuck is that?" Maicy interrupts her own story with the question. I look up to where she's pointing.

"Oh...*that*. Yeah, don't ask."

"How the hell do you expect me to just pretend that's not there? And how the fuck do you think you're going to get away with not explaining it?" She asks, overproducing every look on her face and every wild gesture.

Theo's behind me then, and he drops his hands onto my shoulders.

"I asked her to marry me," Theo answers her. "Four times now." He starts to laugh as he kneads my muscles.

"What. The. Fuck," Maicy yells.

Theo bends my head back until it's touching the top of the couch and I'm looking at him. Then he kisses my nose and walks back to the kitchen.

"You just had to tell her didn't you? Had to be the one to say it," I call to his back.

He lifts his arm up and rolls his wrist silently saying, *yeah, yeah, yeah.*

"And you didn't tell me before because...?" Maicy can't let it go. Though, I didn't expect she would. To be honest, I forgot the damn thing was sitting on the entertainment center, box open, diamond front and center, sparkling. If I'd remembered, I would have hidden it. She's so good at over-talking things out.

I look at it again, for about the billionth time.

Nope, still not ready.

Definitely not.

It is gorgeous, though. He picked one just right for me. And obviously he did it without Maicy's help. The band is platinum, I think. And the diamond is circular and gray. Not clear, not black, but perfect and in between. It's also fucking huge, and it stands alone.

"Spit it out, bitch." She's antsy.

I sigh.

"He started asking me about a month ago," I start.

"Six weeks," Theo corrects from the kitchen.

"Okay, what-the-fuck-ever. He started asking me *six weeks* ago. I told him it's too fast. I didn't say no, exactly. I said not now. Not yet."

"That's sure as hell not a yes," Maicy says.

"Thank you," Theo calls to her.

"So now he leaves it there, begging to be stolen, so I can look at it, knowing he's not going to stop asking," I say.

Maicy stares at me, open mouthed, nail polish threatening to drop from the brush and onto my leg or the couch.

"I didn't say not ever. I didn't say no," I shout. My hands in the air.

"She left out the best part," Theo interrupts again as he brings plates out for each of us. Maicy waits while he gets his own and comes back.

When he sits down to eat, she finally asks, "There's better?"

"When she said no the first time…" I cringe. I didn't say no. I do love him, and I can see him always making me better, happier. I said not yet. I'm not to that place yet. I hope I will be at some point, maybe soon. But not quite yet. "She also said *never* doesn't really exist, just like *always* doesn't either."

And I stand firm with that one.

Never and always are both bullshit. They're part of all the mess behind me.

Theo looks at me with something I can't name in his eyes. He does it so often, I should come up with a label for it. After squeezing my side, he continues. "She always used to say love didn't exist, but that changed when she fell in love with me." I look at him and beam, knowing the old me would have barfed; the smugness on his face is priceless. He says it so beautifully, I'm not so sure I said it quite that well to him.

But I'll take it, even if he gives me more credit than I deserve.

"She said since those two words are a fallacy, she has no idea if, or when, she'll ever say yes. But she hopes I never stop asking." He has Maicy choked up, and I'm already burying my head into his chest, feeling his words vibrate as he says the last bit.

Embarrassing.

He told me that night even if I said 'not yet' forever, he'd never stop asking—and I knew then it's not if, it's when. I know what I have with him.

"She told me the in-between of never and always, the gray parts, they make up most of life," he says, still balancing a bite on his fork.

Again, it's another point I was dead-on about.

Gray is everything.

Gray is what gets us through the horrible and the too-good-to-be-true. And for me, gray is perfect.

My head still under his arm, my ear to his stomach, Theo takes a breath to finish. It feels like he fills my lungs too. "And she said gray looks pretty good these days; worth the wait." I hear him smile. "I have to agree with her. I've found I kind of like gray too." Theo squeezes me against him and breathes into my hair. I hum one note, not sitting up. Maicy touches my back for a second, reminding me she's still in the room, before getting up to look at the perfect gray diamond.

Maybe soon.

"It's okay for now," Theo says with a smirk as I look to him.

For now.

"And okay is pretty alright with me," I add.

Dear Reader,

I hope you enjoyed reading *I Would Never…But If I Did*!

If you did, and you'd like more reader content from me, find the sign up for my newsletter, and all other links with my writerly content at: https://linktr.ee/mariainmadness.

Additionally, I'd love to hear from you or connect with you on my social media pages. You can write to me at maria.ann.green.author@gmail.com, connect with me on Instagram: https://www.instagram.com/mariainmadness/, on Facebook: https://bit.ly/2U7dY4a, on Twitter: https://twitter.com/missmariaann, on Goodreads: https://bit.ly/1pOpUU3, on Bookbub: https://www.bookbub.com/profile/maria-ann-green, and on Pinterest: https://www.pinterest.com/mariaannwriter/!

If you've enjoyed this book, keep your eyes peeled for the next published work, coming soon. And if you're so inclined, please feel free to leave a review as well; they are always appreciated and incredibly helpful for indie authors like me. Reviews and word of mouth can make all the difference!

Thank you so much for reading and spending your time in this little world I've put together.

Sincerely,
Maria Ann Green, Author

About the Author

Maria lives in Minnesota despite the frozen winters. Actually, she prefers snow drifts and icicles over summer and all that sweat running everywhere. She lives with her husband and little family, which includes a couple lazy cats who make great lap warmers. She absolutely believes in unicorns and ghosts, and hopes vampires are real too. She's a coffee in the morning and wine in the evening kind of person, preferably with a nap in between. She devours books, reading mostly in bed or listening to audio books in the car. She's a creative, mouthy, introverted, proud bisexual, highly-sensitive INFJ, Slytherpuff, dork with a lot of tattoos and a sweet-tooth.

Writing has been one of Maria's passions for pretty much her whole life. Creativity is a necessity for her, always. After working in the Mental Health field for almost a decade, she's now living her dream as a stay at home writer, kiddo wrangler, professional snuggler, and constantly-tired-person. When it comes to her writing, she specializes in dark and twisted thrillers or gritty, angsty contemporary romances. But no matter the genre, she always prefers writing deeply flawed characters with dysfunctional relationships. She's pretty sure the whole "unlikable character" thing is a conspiracy, because every character she loves have been labeled this way. Ridiculous. And because of this, she's pretty much found it impossible to write anything without at least a little mayhem.

Maria was once told she painted with her words, and that phrase stuck with her - because writing really is an art, and good stories are true masterpieces. She's always trying to grow and improve in her craft, shooting for a masterpiece of her own someday. And she plans to write forever, because writing gives Maria the ability to disappear into new worlds and create people within twisting plots, all from the comfort of her couch. She will always believe that though not every story is for her, and her stories aren't for everyone, every story has a reader.

Acknowledgements

First of all, thank you to all of my readers, from the occasional to the constant to the accidental. Thank you to *every* single person reading this book and any of my others. Thank you for giving your time to me and my words. Thank you from the bottom of my heart. I will always appreciate you for helping me continue doing what I love. And I hope you never stop reading.

I'd also like to thank all of my amazing friends and critique partners for every bit of help, every insightful comment and encouragement or criticism they've given me over the years, and will hopefully continue to give. I couldn't write without such phenomenal friends. I'm so incredibly lucky. The list isn't exhaustive, but these wonderful people include Kim Graff, Kathryn Trattner, Heather DiAngelis, Carly Green, Tory McNidder, Irina Hall, Scarlett Eichler, and Christina Robins. Thank you for always pushing me forward. I also want to thank Heather again, who doubles as my editor. Thank you for your attention to detail and your ability to help make this and all of my books strong enough to face the world.

Thank you to all of my supporters and friends that give me everything I need to paint stories with words. Thank you especially to Scarlett for dragging me to events that help me cultivate my creative side. I know you're always game for trying something new with me, for reading my pages, or for pushing me when needed. And to all of my family, who helps me be a better person and supports me even when I'm not always the best I can be, thank you.

Most importantly, I need to add a huge thank you to my amazing husband and our monster who support me *without fail* through every adventure and endeavor. Without you and your never-ending love, my creativity could never have the space to flourish, and projects like this book would never be finished. Thank you for helping me carve out the alone time I need to write, and to be a better me. For everything you do, thank you, and I love you both so much.

Made in the USA
Monee, IL
09 September 2020